The guards ce

Shots rang out as they fired blindly at Bolan's shadow, and he ducked back into the room. Dilvan and Faizal were still battling, and he was running out of options.

Dilvan stumbled backward, knocking a computer monitor to the floor, and Bolan took aim with his 9 mm pistol. Just as he fired, Faizal jumped forward, pushing the younger man out of the way.

"Why the hell did you do that?" the Executioner asked as his friend fell to the floor.

"He beat me at the keyboard. We need him."

Bolan looked up in time to see Dilvan through the door and rolled to his feet. But he was too slow. The bullet from the close range pistol tore through the air. He felt the impact, knew he was hit, and then the cold darkness took him.

Don Pendleton's Mack Bolan®

Decision Point

A GOLD EAGLE BOOK FROM

W⚡RLDWIDE®

TORONTO • NEW YORK • LONDON
AMSTERDAM • PARIS • SYDNEY • HAMBURG
STOCKHOLM • ATHENS • TOKYO • MILAN
MADRID • WARSAW • BUDAPEST • AUCKLAND

Recycling programs
for this product may
not exist in your area.

First edition March 2012

ISBN-13: 978-0-373-61551-3

Special thanks and acknowledgment to
Dylan Garrett for his contribution to this work.

DECISION POINT

Printed in U.S.A.

All forms of tampering with human beings, getting at them, shaping them against their will to your own pattern, all thought control and conditioning is, therefore, a denial of that in men which makes them men and their values ultimate.

—Isaiah Berlin
1909–1997

A person must accept responsibility for his or her own actions, no matter the cost. But when someone takes away your free will and your ability to act, others have to get involved.

—Mack Bolan

CHAPTER ONE

The waters of the Malacca Strait were gray and choppy, mirroring the low-slung clouds overhead. Heather Daniels stood at the rail of the supply ship *Favor's Pride* and watched Singapore slowly fade into the distance. For all her travels, she'd never been in a place quite like it. Singapore was a city of contradictions—beautiful, modern architecture, neon lights and all the technological conveniences of the United States crashed against old, run-down buildings, poor sanitation and desperate poverty. Like many of the other cities she passed through, Singapore wasn't a place she would miss, but then again, her purpose there had only been to secure supplies for the next stop on her voyage.

Once they'd cleared the Malacca Strait, the ship would bear northwest toward the Andaman Islands and Port Blair, right in the middle of the Bay of Bengal. The small city was serving as a staging area for tsunami relief efforts in Sri Lanka and other parts of Indonesia. It was also a holding area for the hundreds of displaced and lost children, whose parents had either disappeared or died in a disaster that had claimed thousands of lives.

Four years as a nurse practitioner had given Heather the skills she would need to help with the many medical needs of the children, but her true calling was her work as a missionary, trying to bring a little faith and light to those who desperately needed it. As far as Heather was concerned, spiritual needs were just as important as medical ones. Maybe more.

As the ship began tacking north, she turned away from the rail. The ship wasn't fancy, but she would be comfortable enough in her small cabin, though the heat would probably be stifling. The first mate, a man named Simmons, was making his way across the deck and paused, tipping his seaman's hat politely. He was tall and lanky, with several days' growth of beard on his face and scraggly black hair that looked to be in need of a good washing. He'd also been friendly and polite.

"You doing all right?" he asked, settling the hat back on top of his head. "Not the kind to get seasick, are you? If so, you'd best stay by the rail and watch the horizon. That'll help."

"I'm fine, thank you," she said. "And I don't get seasick. How long until we make Port Blair?"

"If the weather holds in the Strait, we should be there within a few days. This old tub isn't fast, but she's steady." He rubbed his stubbled jaw contemplatively.

"And if it doesn't?" she asked.

He shrugged. "Then we'll get there when God says we should."

She laughed lightly. "That will be true in any case, my friend."

He laughed and headed toward the bow, while she moved on toward her room. Once in her cabin, Daniels settled onto her bunk, opened her briefcase and pulled out the small laptop. The computer was a necessity for keeping track of the numerous organizational details, but it was also her one indulgence allowing her to journal and communicate with family and friends. A small guilty pleasure filled her as the computer whirred to life and pictures from home popped up on her screen. She kissed the tip of her finger and pressed it against the picture of her family clumped together on the porch.

Knowing that she wouldn't be able to send it until they reached Port Blair, Daniels began the draft of a letter to her father. They had a strange relationship that was complicated by the fact that just over eight years ago he'd been the President of the United States. Now he traveled all over the world giving lectures and playing the role of diplomat as much as a man who was known behind his back as President Iron Ass could do so. Jefferson Daniels didn't particularly approve of her chosen vocation. Mentally, she corrected herself. He approved of the vocation—missionary work was a wonderfully valuable thing in the world. He didn't approve of *her* being a missionary. The risks, he'd often told her, were far too great. She was his only child and he was overprotective, but she loved him dearly.

Daniels snuggled back into her bunk as the boat rocked its lullaby with the waves. *Favor's Pride* wasn't a particularly fancy ship, nor was she speedy. Most supply ships she'd been on weren't. With a cruising speed of about twelve knots, no journey was going to be fast, but the steady thrum of the engines was reassuring, and the crew seemed capable. She scrolled through her supply lists and noted what she would need from the next group of missionaries that would be out the following month.

This time on the ship, she knew, was only a brief lull before the hard work really began, and it was important to get her rest. She shut her laptop down for the night and decided to doze until it was time for the evening meal.

FORTY HOURS INTO THE journey, more than halfway there, the sound of booted feet running on the metal deck caught Daniels's attention. In her experience, sailors didn't run unless something fairly dire was happening, and unless the weather had suddenly changed, the skies had been clear that morning. She closed her laptop and set it aside before moving to the small porthole that served as a window in her tiny cabin. Three more people ran past, and she turned and moved to the door. Her instinct was to throw it open and rush out to see what was going on, but she had spent enough time in dangerous places to know that caution would serve her better in this situation.

She peered through the porthole in the door and felt her entire body tense as two men with guns ran through the short hallway toward the bow of the boat. Both of them were wearing all-weather coats with a large patch on the back, depicting a great white shark with an eye patch curled tightly around a half skull sitting atop a pile of gold. A shudder of panic ran through her body as she realized that these could only be pirates of some kind. The Bay of Bengal had been a haven for pirate activity for years, and the countries affected appeared unable to do anything serious to curtail it.

Shots rang out and Daniels involuntarily flattened herself against the bulkhead. She needed to hide, and fast, before she was found. Running to her bunk, she grabbed her medical bag and the precious laptop, stuffing it in on top. She quickly slung it over her head, then grabbed a rubber band off the tiny table next to her bunk and pulled her long, brown hair into a pony-tail, so it would be out of the way. Her mind raced as she considered ways that she might get off the boat and came up with only one idea. The pounding of footsteps on the metal plating of the deck outside, the shouting of orders and demands, made her heart race.

Daniels ducked low as she moved to the door. She heard more shouting as the pirates began rounding up the few passengers aboard, along with the still-struggling crew. Forcing herself to breathe, she waited for the sounds to move toward the bow, and when they did, she risked one peek through the porthole, then swung open the door. Her only chance was the stern, where an emergency launch boat was stored. She ran for it, trying to keep her steps as light as possible, but her feet contacting the metal rang out like a gong to her ears.

A shot tore through the air in reply to a sudden yell of anger, and Daniels felt her heart stutter in her chest. Risking a glance over her shoulder, she saw two men lifting a body over the railing. The first mate. She didn't stop moving, because there was no place to hide, anyway, but the emergency launch was in sight.

She could hear their boots connecting with the deck

and ignored the yelling once they spotted her. Daniels could see the boat, but knew she could never get it launched. She ran to the railing and looked down at the water being churned up from the propellers, just as the high-pitched whine of a bullet passed over her shoulders.

"That would not be a wise choice."

She froze, slowly raising her hands. The low, accented baritone sent a chill up her spine. She turned to see a tall man with a scar across his cheek staring at her. He took a long drag on the cigarette he held. If he wasn't trying to kill her, she might have thought he was handsome, but the gun pointed at her squashed that flickering thought.

Daniels took a deep breath and tried to remember her father's advice about panic. "Being scared to death is fine," he'd once said. "Just don't let your enemies see it."

She pushed her shoulders back and stared into the man's dark brown eyes. "I don't know, chopped up by a propeller seems a little more merciful than raped and tortured by thugs."

For almost a full minute he simply looked at her, then a smile touched his lips. "It appears that our catch today is more lucky than we could've known. Some days the sea favors the fisherman more than the fish." He offered an odd little half bow. "It is a pleasure to meet you, Miss Daniels."

"You know who I am," she said. It wasn't a question. "Then you know that harming me would be a disastrous choice on your part. The U.S. doesn't take kindly to its citizens being kidnapped, especially ones that belonged to the first family."

"We're not here to hurt anyone," he said. "It's not profitable."

"Tell that to the guy that was filled with holes and dumped over the rail."

"An unfortunate necessity. This is not the White House and you will not find anyone waiting for you in the West Wing. Here things are not so easy to discern," he said, shrugging. He pointed at her shoulder bag. "What are you carrying in your bag?"

"Medical supplies," she said. "I'm a nurse."

"Give it to me," he demanded. When she hesitated, he gestured impatiently with his gun. "Now."

She handed it over to him and he opened it and removed the laptop. "This is not a medical supply," he said. Without another word he flung it over the rail and Heather watched it disappear into the water. Part of her heart sank along with it. Two years of missionary work was detailed on that hard drive—her journal chronicling the highs and lows of the life she'd chosen, her joys and her failures, not to mention GPS tracking—all gone in a brief, floating moment.

He finished digging through the bag and then returned it to her. "Come with me," he said, gesturing with the gun once more. "My name is Daylan Rajan. I'm in charge of this group. I know you Americans like to cause trouble, but if you can manage to behave yourself you will be allowed to wait with the other passengers until we reach a safe harbor."

"And if I don't?"

"Then you will be bound and gagged and tied to the railing where I can keep an eye on you."

"I guess I'll go with option one. Where are we going, anyway?" she asked, heading toward the bow where the other missionaries and crew were being held.

"An island that does not welcome outsiders," he said. "Once we are there, the commander will decide what to do with you."

She stopped and looked back at him. "You speak fluent English," she said. "And you don't dress like a band of raggedy pirates. You're too organized. Who are you people?"

"We are people that you don't want to make angry," he said. "Now move to the front of the boat."

"You could stop this, you know," she suggested. "Take the boat and the supplies and just let us go."

"Supplies are helpful to our cause and we always need more vessels, but hostages are worth far more. And you are worth more than all the other hostages here combined. So you see, I cannot let you go."

"You can," she said shortly. "What you mean is that you won't."

"As you will," he said. "Enough talking. Do not make me regret my leniency, now get up front with the others."

Daniels nodded and kept moving, taking her place by the other hostages who huddled together for the illusion of safety. She watched carefully, trying to remember faces and names, and decided after a time that these were not pirates in any traditional sense. These were soldiers and while many of them were young—

some were teenagers—they acted more like military men than the grasping pirates that haunted the waters near Somalia.

The soldiers crewed the boat, while the craft they'd arrived on gave them an armed escort. The hostages were kept up front, under constant armed guard, and only allowed to move around in the small area of the bow. It took the better part of twelve hours for them to reach their destination, a small island with a well-sheltered cove.

Numerous boats were lined up at the docks. Not far inland, she could see several buildings, including what looked like a main house. Most of the buildings were typical for the region, old wood siding with thatched roofs on stilts, but the main house was more modern. Quite large, with sloping rooftops and a large deck on one side. It was on stilts, as well, and Daniels expected that floods were quite common on many of these islands.

Unfortunately she had no real idea where she was in relationship to anything else. She only knew that they'd been traveling southeast instead of northwest. But there were dozens, maybe even hundreds, of small islands along the coast of Malaysia and this could be any one of them. Lost in her thoughts, she didn't hear the man who was obviously the leader of this group until he cleared his throat.

"When we reach the dock in a few minutes, you will come with me," he said. "I will present you to the commander."

"What about them?" Daniels asked, pointing to the other hostages.

"Some will be ransomed, if there are those who can pay for them, or they will be ransomed as part of a larger arrangement. The others will find a different fate."

"You will kill them, then," she said, trying to contain her anger and despair. "How pointless."

"You have come to a very dangerous part of the world, Miss Daniels," he said. "Do not presume to know anything about us."

He stood next to her as the boat reached the dock, then he motioned for her to precede him down the gangplank. She stopped and looked out over the island once more. The pier where the boat was moored was not suited for the large vessel, which dwarfed the other boats that were in port. Trucks were lined up, waiting for the stolen cargo to be unloaded, as soldiers moved some of the passengers along the dock including the other missionaries.

"Let's go." He pulled her farther down the dock.

Worried for the fate of the other missionaries, she said, "Shouldn't I be near the other hostages?"

"You are different. They will be part of a larger negotiating package. You will be ransomed separately."

"I don't want to be treated any differently than anyone else," she snapped.

He stopped and spun. His eyes bored into her, dark and fierce.

"Sometimes, it is necessary to kill a hostage or even several to make a point. If you are with them and this happens, you would be just as likely to be chosen for death as the others, as no one but myself knows your true identity. If you want to live, you come with me.

If you want to take your chances…" He shrugged and released her hand. "Then go with them." He pointed to where the other hostages huddled in a small group.

One man was yanked to his feet in front of a video camera. He attempted to flee, but the pirate was quick and efficient, slitting his throat with a large blade, as the other hostages screamed in horror. The crimson spray splattered all of them, adding to the terror of the scene. The man's body dropped to the deck. Daniels looked at Rajan.

"This is not a game, Heather." He pointed at a dark sedan rolling to a stop on the edge of the pier. "The man who is about to get out of that car is Kabilan Vengai, the leader of the Ocean Tigers. He is not a patient or kind man, so keep your answers short and direct."

The combination of Rajan's warning and the arrogant stride of Vengai as he moved down the pier had Daniels cringing inside. His arrival brought the activity on the pier to a near standstill. Everyone watched as he approached. He was about her height, just under six feet, and reminded her of a tiger stalking its prey. The military-style clothing didn't hide the scars on his arms that looked as if someone had tried to fillet them and, failing that, had burned the skin.

Rajan didn't wait for him, but closed the distance and started his report. Daniels caught only every few words, but what she did understand was the look of disdain that Vengai was sending her way. They finished speaking and Vengai strolled in front of her, looking her up and down as though she were a particularly interesting painting rather than a person.

"I did not believe it when Rajan first told me, but he is right. You are the daughter of President Jefferson Daniels of the United States."

"He's not the President anymore," she said. "Just a man."

Vengai chuckled under his breath. "If you believe that, you must think quite poorly of him. No man is ever an ex-President of your country, for he is still addressed as Mr. President, is this not so?"

She bit her lip and nodded her agreement.

"You are truly a treasure fished from the sea and were you my daughter, I would never allow you to travel in such a dangerous place as the Bay of Bengal. What will he pay, I wonder, for your safe return?"

Remembering her father's time in office, Daniels shrugged. "I doubt he'll pay you anything," she said, trying to hold on to her courage. "President Jefferson Daniels does not negotiate with terrorists."

Vengai chuckled once more. "He will for you," he said. "You see, presidents and politicians like to say things like that, but they only mean that for other people. They never mean it when it will actually affect them. He will negotiate for you, of this I am very certain." He reached into his jacket pocket and pulled out a cell phone. From another pocket, he removed a small business-card-size piece of paper. He dialed a series of numbers, then handed the phone to her. "Call him. Now."

She took the phone and saw that all the prefix numbers were entered. She added the area code and phone number for her father's cell phone, then pressed Send.

After several long seconds and a handful of clicks and beeps, the call connected.

Her father answered on the second ring. "Who's this?" he said.

"Dad, thank God you answered, it's me," Daniels said. "Don't hang up."

"Heather, where are you calling from? I didn't recognize the number."

Before she could respond, Vengai snatched the phone from her hand, activating the speaker-phone function. "President Daniels, now you know that your daughter is alive, we can proceed with business. We are holding your daughter and if you want to see her alive again, you will follow my instructions exactly."

"Who the hell are you?" her father snarled. "Where is she?"

"This will be the only call, Mr. President, so I suggest you write down what I'm about to tell you. Within ten days, you will transfer…twenty-five million dollars in U.S. funds into the following account." He rattled off a string of numbers. "When the money is received, your daughter will be released. That is all."

"Dad!" Daniels said. "I'm on an island somewhere near—" The slap that interrupted her came out of nowhere and she couldn't stifle the yelp of pain as she went down. Rajan was standing over her.

"Ten days, Mr. President, or your daughter dies."

He clicked the end button on the sound of her father's nearly incoherent yelling.

"This is all so unnecessary," she said. "We have nothing to do with your war or your money. We're here trying to help the people of your country."

"Miss Daniels, what you arrogant Americans seem to misunderstand is that we want no help from you. We don't want your people in our country, but you refuse to go home and continue with these…useless efforts."

Daniels held her tongue. She knew better than to argue with an extremist. But with her father there were two things she knew for certain. She'd never heard him sound so angry.

And he would never pay money to a terrorist, not even for her.

CHAPTER TWO

As a soldier, Mack Bolan, aka the Executioner, fundamentally believed that there would never come a time in his life when training was unnecessary. On the other hand, even an experienced soldier could find that he'd bitten off a bit more than he wanted to chew. While that wasn't the case this time, Bolan felt that the Le Parkour training he'd been spending his time on was pushing him toward his limit.

The course he was facing today was the last challenge in this training run, and for all of his previous training—Special Forces, rappelling, high-altitude jumps and just about every kind of military work in the world—none of it could have prepared him for the intensity of Parkour. Bolan had become interested in the discipline that was sometimes called freerunning after watching some action film extras on a DVD. Realizing that not all of the stunts were special effects or done with wires, he'd listened to one of the film consultants talk about Parkour and the discipline of body manipulation, jumping, climbing and negotiating obstacles with the most speed and efficiency. As the stuntmen and -women were launching themselves up the sides of buildings, leaping over concrete barricades and moving with amazing swiftness, Bolan determined to explore Parkour for himself, adding it to his already formidable battlefield skills. For a man in his line of work, those kinds of skills might make the difference between life and death.

Standing at the base of the Eiffel Tower, Bolan waited with his instructor for the signal to begin. It had been a grueling five days of training, and he felt as though he'd mastered the basics, but there were maneuvers he still longed to perfect. They had received a special dispensation to use any means necessary to reach the top of the Eiffel Tower, rescue the mock hostages and disarm the terrorists. Nothing else compared to the challenge.

The monitor dropped the flag and Bolan raced up the stairs. The steep staircases surrounded by mesh fencing for protection worked as more of a launch pad than an obstacle. Bolan turned one corner and saw a shrapnel grenade. Using the momentum from running, Bolan launched to the top of the fence, anchoring with his hands but pulling his body up and over in one graceful movement. The small explosion behind him didn't diminish his movement, pushing off with his feet and jumping through the air to an adjacent set of stairs.

Bolan pushed off of the top of the fence with one foot, jumping in a zigzag motion down the mesh walls that enclosed the stairs and moving back after his prey. There were three opponents waiting for him at the next turn. He leaned back as the larger one in the middle swung a bat, then reached out as it went past him, grabbing the end. He swung his weight with the bat and knocked the other two down as the extra pressure brought with his speed made a complete circle.

Angry, the opponent dropped the bat and tried to grapple Bolan. The Executioner picked up the discarded bat, jabbed the last guard in the solar plexus and then rushed past him. The final turn was filled with small gadgets on the steps that were to mimic explosives that would detonate on impact. Bolan ran back three steps to pick up speed, launched over the first two and bounced off the side of the fencing like a trampoline without touching the step. Back and forth across until he was clear of the devices. His last jump he rolled on the landing where the hostages were being held. He pulled his pistol with paint rounds and fired off two quick shots, killing the villains.

Everyone in the tower clapped. Bolan smiled, out of breath but elated that he was able to clear the obstacles. He stood on the platform and talked to his hostages, members of the team that had been training with him. They congratulated him, impressed at how quickly he had learned the skills, and talked about springing from one set of stairs to another and the risks of jumps from a given height or a moving object. He enjoyed training with other like-minded military men, and while France wasn't known for its military prowess, the men he'd been training with were all part of a special antiterrorist unit and were as good as anyone he'd ever worked with.

Just as he'd caught his breath, Bolan's phone vibrated. He pulled it out and glanced down at the number, which he recognized at once as belonging to Hal Brognola, the director of the Sensitive Operations Group, based at Stony Man Farm. The most elite antiterrorism agency in the world that answered only to the President of the United States, Stony Man Farm, Virginia, had been his brainchild. Now he worked with them on select missions, keeping a good arm's length away from any kind of permanent arrangement. Still, when Brognola called, there was always a good reason.

He tapped the key that accepted the call. "Yeah."

"Striker." Brognola's voice came over the line. "I'm glad I could reach you. Are you still in Paris?"

"Still here," he said. "It's been good, but long. Today's the last day. What's going on?"

"There's a situation that I'd like to bring you in on. How soon can you be back in D.C.?"

Bolan could almost hear the sound of Hal chewing on one of his expensive cigars and realized that whatever was going on must be pretty serious. He almost never asked him to come in for a mission briefing. Remembering an invitation from a new friend about the chance to accompany him on a test flight of a new plane, he said, "If all goes well, I can be on the ground by eight tonight."

"From Paris?" Brognola asked, his voice a bit incredulous. "The Concorde isn't flying anymore, you know."

"It's a new plane of sorts. Where do you want me?"

"The White House," he replied. "I'll make sure you've got gate clearance as Colonel Stone. Stop off at the Farm and get a uniform from Stores, Striker."

"It must be my day to be surprised," Bolan said. "You've asked me to come in for a mission briefing *and* you want me at the White House in a military uniform."

"The situation is…delicate. Just get back here

ASAP and I'll have more details for you when you arrive."

"On my way," he said, ending the call. He quickly thanked his hosts and explained that a personal emergency had come up and he had to leave right away, rather than stay for the celebration planned for that evening. Everyone shook hands, and Bolan made his way back down the Eiffel Tower before he placed another call to arrange his transportation back to the U.S.

THE TEST FLIGHT TO D.C. went off without a hitch, and the plane had performed flawlessly.

A quick call to Stony Man Farm had resulted in an Army colonel's uniform and credentials being dropped off at a hotel Bolan occasionally used when he was in Washington.

The pilot of the experimental plane had decided to play tourist in D.C. for a few days, so the plane would remain in a private hangar that had been arranged before he'd left France.

The soldier showered, shaved and changed into his uniform, then arranged for a car service to take him to the White House. The process at the gate couldn't have been more simple. His uniform commanded automatic respect and when he gave his name—Colonel Brandon Stone—and provided his credentials, he was immediately given access and an escort inside the building.

Once inside, he was met by a man in a nondescript, dark blue suit that all but screamed Secret Service. "Colonel Stone, if you'd follow me, please?" he said.

"Of course," Bolan replied, not bothering to look

around too much. It wasn't his first time inside the White House and given his line of work, it likely wouldn't be the last time. Still, it was an impressive landmark and the source of many of the missions he'd undertaken over the years. He wasn't inside the building often, but he'd had more than the tourist tour. That said, he was a bit surprised when he was led down a short hallway to an elevator. He knew where they were headed, but asked anyway.

"Where are we going?" he asked the agent.

"To the bunker, sir," he said, punching a code into the panel next to the elevator. The doors opened and he stepped inside. Bolan followed him, and as the doors shut, he noted that there was no panel or buttons indicating different floors. Instead, there was a keypad and a small, rectangular scanner.

The agent punched in another code, then stepped forward. A brief flare of light passed over his eyes, conducting a retinal scan. Finally a tone sounded, then an unseen voice said, "Voice authentication protocol."

"Agent Reilly Summers," he said.

"Voice authentication accepted," the system responded. "Destination?"

"Bunker," he replied.

The elevator began moving quietly down. Impressed at the security, Bolan kept quiet. It took less than a minute for them to descend to their destination and then the elevator doors chimed once and opened. The agent stepped out and Bolan followed.

"This way, Colonel Stone," he said, turning left and going down the hallway. He stopped outside a closed door. "Please go right in, sir. They're expecting you."

"Thank you, Agent Summers," he said. He opened the door and stepped inside, then paused in genuine surprise. Seated at the conference table was Hal Brognola and past President of the United States Jefferson Daniels. Seated next to Daniels was a woman Bolan didn't recognize, but who he assumed was his personal secretary or, perhaps more likely, his Secret Service agent.

"Mr. President," he said, entering the room and offering a salute, which Daniels returned. "Hal, it's good to see you again."

"Thanks for coming," Brognola replied. "Mr. President, you know who this is. Colonel Brandon Stone."

"Colonel *Stone*," President Daniels said. "I appreciate you coming. I understand you were overseas when Hal got in touch."

"Yes, sir," Bolan said. "But that's hardly important. When Hal calls, I answer."

"Take a seat, Colonel," Daniels said. "And Hal can bring you up to speed on the situation."

Bolan sat and looked questioningly at Brognola. The very fact that they were meeting inside the White House—in the secure bunker, no less—meant that whatever was going on had already been sanctioned by the current President. Most likely, this was deemed the most secure location for President Daniels to have a meeting with someone like Brognola. Too many questions would have been asked if they'd tried to do it at the Pentagon.

Daniels didn't speak and didn't look at Bolan, his eyes focused on a problem that wasn't in that room. As President, he had been known to be principled and unwavering. There were many who liked him, but once his mind was made up there was little that could be done to change his position. His complete support of the military was widely known, but his tunnel vision had caused problems, as well. Whatever this problem was, weighed on him. He looked tired. The salt-and-pepper hair that he'd sported as President was now almost completely gray, and the lines in his face were that of a worn battle commander.

"Okay, Hal, let's have it," Bolan said.

"On the surface, the situation is fairly simple. President Daniels's daughter, Heather, has been kidnapped in the Bay of Bengal. They're demanding a twenty-five-million-dollar ransom within ten days, or they say they'll kill her," he said. "The problem is that it isn't that simple."

"Clarify, please," Bolan replied. "While I admit that's a large sum of money, they obviously know who she is."

"They do," the big Fed said. "When President Daniels got the call, he contacted me. Fortunately, he recorded the call. We've got some audio people working on breaking it down completely right now. But what tipped me off that something was different was how they wanted the money."

"My understanding is that most pirating operations work on a cash-and-carry basis," Bolan said. "Euros usually."

"They provided an account number and wanted the money to be wired," Daniels said.

"That is unusual," Bolan said. "I assume you looked into it?"

"We did," Brognola said. "That's when things began to get interesting. It's not just a dummy account. It's buried under five different holding corporations that we've found so far, not a one of them real."

Bolan considered this information for a moment. "These aren't pirates," he said. "They don't have the kind of money or structure to set up something like that."

"Exactly," Brognola said. "It's got to be a terrorist organization of some kind, but we don't know who yet."

It could be any one of a number of large organizations that operated in that part of the world, and—he couldn't rule it out completely—it was possible, however unlikely, that it was simply a very evolved pirate operation. "I don't mean to be disrespectful, Mr. President," he said, choosing his words carefully, "but is it possible that they'll release her if you do pay?"

"That's a fair question," Daniels replied. "The short answer is that I can't care about that."

"Sir?"

"I think Hal's right. This move smacks of a highly organized terrorist organization. I'm heartsick that they have Heather, and there's not much I wouldn't do to ensure her safe return. But this isn't just a question of negotiating with terrorists, Colonel. This would be funding them. And twenty-five million dollars in that part of the world might make them all but unstoppable. They could take over an entire region or buy arms and equipment that we don't want those kinds of people to have." His voice was hoarse and tired, and he shook his head. "I can't pay them, Colonel. That's where you come in."

"You want me to go and get her," Bolan said.

"That's part of the mission," Brognola said, "but, with all due respect to President Daniels, it's just as important that we figure out who these people are and put a stop to them. If we don't, the precedent could make every high-ranking politician's family in the world a potential target for this kind of activity. Right now, the illusion of security and the threat of extreme violence is a powerful shield. If we fail, that illusion goes away in a hurry."

"Understood," Bolan said. "I'll need all the intelligence you've gathered so far, and then I'll get started on finding a solid lead."

"When will you leave for the region?" Daniels asked.

"When I know where I'm going, sir," Bolan replied. "It doesn't do us any good to thrash about blindly over there. It's a highly corrupt area and we'd be spotted before we could do your daughter or the country any real good."

"I don't like it," he admitted, "but I don't have to." He turned his attention to the woman sitting next to him. "Colonel Stone, I'd like you to meet Michelle Peterson. She's part of my Secret Service detail these days, but she worked with both CIA and NSA before that. I'd like her to join in your investigation and your mission as my personal representative."

Bolan caught Brognola's warning look, though it had been unnecessary. His old friend knew that he far preferred to work alone. "Mr. President," he said, once more choosing his words with caution, "you know that I've been working in special operations for a long time, and I generally work alone. Many of the missions that you know we undertake are too dangerous for someone without the proper training and I'm not usually in a position, for lack of a better phrase, to play babysitter."

"I respect what you're saying, Colonel Stone, and your service," Daniels said. "I can even set aside my feelings enough to know that the mission priority has to be taking out these terrorists. But don't think for a minute that this isn't personal. I want my daughter back, alive, and I want the bastards who did this as dead as old dad's hatband. Agent Peterson will be going along with you, and she won't need any babysitting. I can assure you of that."

Until now, Bolan hadn't paid a great deal of attention to the woman seated on the other side of the table. Secret Service agents specialized in blending into the background, and until the President had brought her up, he'd assumed that her only purpose in being there was for him. Now he turned his blue-eyed gaze on her. While she was dressed in what he'd come to think of as the unofficial uniform of those who served in protection details—a black, button-down dress with a white blouse beneath that showed a hint of cleavage. She had dark brown hair that brushed the tops of her shoulders in waves and a very attractive face, with full, almost pouty lips.

"Did you want me to stand up, Colonel? Maybe take a turn about the room so you can get a complete examination?" she asked, cocking one eyebrow slightly. "Maybe you'd just like to see my résumé?"

"Agent Peterson," Brognola said, trying to ease the tension, "I'm sure you can understand why the colonel might wish to know more about your qualifications for a mission like this."

She got up out of her chair and walked around the conference table. At a guess, Bolan put her at not much over five feet tall when she wasn't wearing heels. She stopped when she was close enough to his chair that she could reach out and touch him. "Colonel Stone," she said, "I've done field operations in Africa, the Middle East and South America for both the CIA and the NSA. I'm more than capable of taking care of myself, and if the President had been willing to allow it, I would've taken this operation on my own. I've known Heather for most of her life, and I'd willingly take a bullet for her. Can you say the same?"

Bolan got to his feet and stared down at the woman in front of him. Without changing the direction of his gaze, he said, "That's the problem here, Mr. President. This is personal for her and on these kinds of missions, it can't ever be personal."

"She goes, Colonel," Daniels said. "I'm afraid I must insist."

"It's all right, Colonel," Brognola said. "Maybe an extra set of hands and eyes will be a good thing."

Bolan grudgingly nodded his acceptance, then held out a hand toward the woman, which she took, and they shook on it. Then he leaned down, casting his voice so that only she could hear him. "Agent Peterson, if you get killed, I won't shed a tear. I won't stop to bury your body and I won't ship you home with a nice flag-draped coffin. And if you get in my way or make it impossible for me to do my job, I'll take you out myself. Do we understand each other?"

Keeping her own voice at a whisper, she said, "We understand each other fine, Colonel. Just remember that it goes both ways."

Her tone was completely serious and in that moment, Bolan decided that he might like this woman. She had guts and was willing to stand up to him—so far, at least. He wondered if she'd live through what they were about to do, then shrugged off such considerations. For now, the mission was all that mattered.

"I think we're all set here, Hal," he said. "Unless there's anything else, Mr. President?"

"Not at the present, Colonel," he said. He, too, got to his feet, and they shook hands. "Bring her back for me, Colonel, and kill those bastards who did this."

"Yes, sir," Bolan said. He saluted once more, then turned to Brognola. "You'll send me everything you've got?"

"You'll have it first thing," the big Fed said. "Thanks for coming in, Colonel."

Bolan shrugged. "It's what I do." He turned to the woman. "I'm staying at the Premier Hotel. Meet me there at 0800 tomorrow morning and we'll get the ball rolling."

"I'll be there," she said, then turned her back on him.

Bolan let himself out of the room, knowing that the man in the hallway would escort him to the upper floors and ensure that he got out of the building. He'd head back to the hotel and grab a quick bite before hitting the rack and trying to catch a little sleep.

The next day promised to be a long one.

CHAPTER THREE

In spite of his first-class accommodations, the red-eye flight from Singapore to Washington, D.C., hadn't been very restful. But Kabilan Vengai was used to going without sleep. He'd been running nonstop for almost a year and rarely slept more than a few hours a day. Many men would be exhausted under such a strain, and it would show in everything about them: their appearance, mental state and the decisions they made would be compromised by the constant drain. Kabilan, however, thrived on his role, and if someone were to compare him to a vampire that feeds on power, he wouldn't have been deeply offended.

Standing in a small ballroom in the Ritz-Carlton, he looked up at the ornate ceilings and took a deep breath. Part of him wished that his army was nearby so that he could order the hotel ransacked, hostages taken for ransom, and then allow his men hot showers and a good night's sleep in a comfortable bed. The other part of him knew that such luxuries weakened men like those who served him—they were field men, one and all, and while they might enjoy the sleep, it would only distract them from their true purpose. He slugged down the last swallow of the watery cocktail he was holding and shook his head. This wasn't where he wanted to be at the moment.

But the ostentatious reception for the Tamil People's Action Committee meant to raise funds for his people was necessary. It was another tool—a sometimes laughable, often degrading one—but a tool nonetheless. Kabilan knew that perception mattered a great deal in the world, and if he was going to restore the rightful sovereignty of the Tamil people, he had to play on this stage equally as well as he did when he was leading his men to successful raids on the ocean. He put his empty glass on the bar and ordered another, then turned his attention to the room.

Most of the people here were displaced Tamils who had come to the United States and made enough money to support the cause of their people back in Sri Lanka, India and other parts of Indonesia. A handful were businessmen with interests in that part of the world—a couple of whom were more than willing to overlook the defeat of the Tamil Tigers and continue to use them to work around the Sri Lankan government whenever possible. He would walk through the room, shake hands, nod in understanding at their sincere concern at the plight of his people. He would watch as they opened their checkbooks and tried to solve problems with money. In turn, he would present those checks to the executive director of TPAC, then take the money for himself, buy the weapons and equipment he needed, and so, in a sense, solve problems with money. He hated the deception, and it was a far greater crime than any piracy he sanctioned. It was also necessary.

Still, the money raised here was simply a cover for his true purpose, and Kabilan scanned the room once more. While holding the hat here and conducting good raids on the seas had proven lucrative, neither was cost-effective or fast enough for his long-term goals. Though his recent capture of President Daniels's daughter had been unanticipated, and he held few doubts that the man would pay her ransom as soon as he realized that her death would be the only thing he could accomplish by not paying. If they didn't pay, her death would serve their cause just as well. Killing such a high-profile hostage would be a show of power unlike any other and show the world that they weren't to be trifled with. But money wasn't everything and while it could buy many things—weapons, especially—what he truly needed was something that would level the playing field.

This night he was going to take delivery of that weapon. The Ocean Tigers, who had once been known as the KP Branch of the Liberation Tigers of Tamil Eelam, were one of the few remaining hopes for the Tamil revolution. When Kumaran Pathmanathan had disappeared at the hands of the Sri Lankan Secret Police, it had been left to him to find a way to continue.

Vengai had immediately moved his forces into a new area and modified the immediate mission to piracy on the high seas. Much of the work his men had done was blamed on other groups, and the ransoms paid were an excellent way to raise funds. They simply weren't enough, the Daniels girl notwithstanding. Using contacts he developed in the technology field, he'd groomed a new contact over the past year and the moment of delivery had finally arrived.

Unfortunately his contact had yet to put in an appearance.

He moved away from the bar and began making his way across the room. He paused from time to time to talk with someone or to answer a question. About halfway, he felt a light touch on his arm and looked down to see the executive director of TPAC, a dark-haired woman in her early thirties, hired for her lobbying skills, staring at him. She was Tamil, but only in the most remote sense. Her grandparents had been from there, but she had no real idea what being from Tamil meant.

"Mr. Vengai?" she asked. "A moment of your time, please."

Seeing that she had someone in tow, he softened his gaze and allowed a faint smile to pass across his features. "Of course, Ms. Nilani. What can I help you with?"

"I'd like you to meet someone," she said. "This is Mr. Borelli. He's quite interested in our cause, and wanted to be introduced."

"Ah, Mr. Borelli," Vengai said, offering his hand. "A pleasure to meet you."

Borelli was a stout figure, almost portly, with thinning hair and an off-the-rack suit that fit improperly. His hands were soft. "The pleasure is mine, Mr. Vengai. I've been looking forward to this since USTPAC announced you'd be in attendance. How goes the battle?"

"Not as well as we would like," he said, "but it's not over—what is the saying?—until the fat lady sings."

"Well put," Borelli said. "Well put, indeed."

The man affected a near-British accent, but he obviously was American. "So, Ms. Nilani says you have an interest in our cause?"

"Oh, yes," he said. "I've read about the situation quite extensively as part of my job, and I must say, it seems that the Tamil people have been very shabbily treated."

"I see," Vengai said. "And what do you do, Mr. Borelli?"

Borelli smiled then, and for a split second, a very different person was standing in front of him. "I work as an analyst, Mr. Vengai. In Langley."

So, he was CIA. Interesting that he'd be so direct in his approach. "How goes the battle for *you,* then?" he asked.

The man laughed. "Don't misunderstand, sir. I'm not here in any official capacity! I'm just an analyst. I don't make all that much, but I'd like to contribute— provided that my contribution is completely anonymous."

"That can be easily arranged," he said. "Simply make your contribution with cash."

"And should that go to you or to Ms. Nilani?" he asked quickly.

Damn the man. He knew that TPAC was a front. If he told him to give the money directly to TPAC, she'd have to deposit the funds in the main account; if he said to give it to him, she'd have a lot of questions. "Ms. Nilani can handle that for you," he said with barely concealed ire. He wondered if Borelli were playing some kind of game, for his own amusement, or for more serious purposes.

"Very good, then," Borelli said. "I'll bring it by the office on Monday." He offered his hand once more. "I won't take up any more of your time, Mr. Vengai. Thank you."

Vengai nodded. "Thank you, Mr. Borelli. Drive safely tonight."

Recognizing the vague threat, Borelli grinned once more. "And when you return home, you do the same. Travel safely, that is." Then he turned and walked into the crowd.

Ms. Nilani, who'd been silent the entire time, shook her head. "That was strange," she said. "I'm not sure I understand what he was doing here."

"Neither do I, Ms. Nilani, but I expect that you could find out. Why don't you make a phone call and see what you can learn about Mr. Borelli?"

"Right now?" she asked. "In the middle of the fund-raiser?"

At that moment Vengai saw his contact come into the room and linger near the kitchen doors. "No, but make no mistake, people like him come to events like this for two reasons—one, he wants to upgrade his contacts and has something he wants to sell, or two, he's here to tell us that he's watching. I have a feeling that it was the latter," he said, waving her off. "But I want that information by Monday at the latest."

"Of course," she said, then turned and resumed her role in working the room. Briefly, he watched her go. She was good at her job, but not a very observant person. On the other hand, a person who did what he or she was told without asking too many questions was perfect for his uses.

Before he could be engaged again in a lengthy conversation, he moved quickly across the room to where his contact, a computer programmer named Tim Wright, was waiting for him. Wright's appearance matched his profession: dark hair, cut short in a functional style, a short-sleeved, polyester dress shirt, khaki pants and loafers. He stood almost six feet in height, but wasn't in great physical condition. The spare tire around his midsection suggested a life spent sitting, and not on the ab-cruncher machine at his local gym.

Vengai offered his hand in greeting when he got close enough. "Mr. Wright? It's good to meet you in person."

Nervous, Wright nodded. "Yes, I'm…it's good to meet you, too." He held up his attaché case. "Should we go somewhere to talk?"

"Yes, let's get out of sight before you disappear into a puddle of sweat."

The nervous man pulled out a handkerchief and mopped his brow as they ducked out of sight. Like most conference hotels there were any number of places that seemed to be in view of everything and yet completely secluded at the same time. Vengai led him to an unoccupied conference room that was set up for the next day. The dark room was illuminated only with light spilling in from a small break in the air wall that separated the one larger room into two.

"You are not used to this kind of…work, are you, Mr. Wright?"

"No, I'm usually as loyal and patriotic as they come, but I need the money."

"Your words do not reassure me. How do I know that we won't complete our business, and then I'll step outside to find myself surrounded by federal agents?"

"Mr. Vengai, they may set up elaborate schemes in movies, but if I were caught trying to steal this software from the office, I wouldn't be here. They don't set up stings, just deal with what's in front of them. I just want to get this done, get my money and get out of here."

Vengai watched as Wright shifted his weight back and forth, carefully holding the case in front of him as if it were an explosive. He grabbed the handkerchief and mopped his brow once more but then immediately readjusted the case so it was away from his body.

"Show me," Vengai said.

"There's nothing to show, really. Your guys know how to upload satellite data, I presume?"

"Yes, of course."

Wright popped open the case and pulled out a small box. He opened the box and displayed a portable hard drive.

"This contains the software to get me into military satellites?"

"Yes. This is a new program that I wrote. The software on here will give you access to virtually every military satellite in the world."

"How is this possible?"

"The hardware components for military satellites are the same in almost every industrialized nation. Private industry tries to keep things proprietary, but the militaries are so concerned about what one has and one doesn't that things are pretty similar. There are minor variations in the coding, but they are easily decoded by the algorithm included in the software. You must, however, be careful when you tap into an actively running program. The satellites can be fed and controlled with this software, but if there's an active command running, and you try to piggyback on top of it, the analysts will see the deviation."

Vengai grunted in disgust. "This seems worthless. How can I make use of satellites that aren't running?"

"No, Mr. Vengai. You don't understand. Unless there is current monitoring, you won't be detected, and even if you are you can override and take over completely, but then they will trace it out eventually. Most constant monitoring happens on satellites that are tasked for research from universities. Most military-use satellites are simply tasked with a single event. When the program provides it, they move on with their mission, ignoring the satellite until they need it again."

"Ah," he said. "I see, but looking at what others do is not all I wanted. You promised more."

"This software is not just passive observation of data," Wright continued, warming to his subject. "You can send commands to the satellite, giving it a specific task, such as scanning satellite phone signals, surveillance operations and even bouncing remote detonation signals for embedded weapons. So long as the satellite isn't being tasked with something else, your commands won't be detected at all! With this software in place, you could peek inside a bedroom of the White House and no one would even know. The military would see it as simply their satellite passing by.

If your guys are smart and things are well planned, you could use a Russian satellite to remote command a U.S. bomb and the Russians would be blamed, not you."

"Yes," Vengai said. "And if we simply want to watch what commands are being given to a satellite…?"

Wright nodded enthusiastically. "You can do that and be totally unobserved. It's everything you asked for."

"Good," he said.

"And now…what about what I asked for?" Wright said. "I'm not providing this to you for free. I told you the debts I have to pay. The guys who want their money are serious, but I have a feeling that my luck is about to change."

Vengai looked at the nervous programmer who talked so fast he had a hard time keeping up, but he'd heard the most important things he needed to know. He could spy on anyone and his satellite expert would have no problems using the device. "I have your payment," he said, pulling an envelope from inside his suit and placing it on the table.

Wright barely hesitated before shoving the hard drive at him and grabbing the envelope. Vengai smiled as Wright flipped it open and, leaning over the table, laid out the bills. His hands trembled as he began to count the money, but the profuse sweating subsided as his thrill replaced his fear.

"It's all there, per our arrangement," he said. "Ten thousand in cash and the account number for a fund in the Cayman's containing another ninety thousand.

Unless, of course, you've changed your mind and decided that you want to be a part of our team."

"No. I'm an American. I wouldn't be helping you guys if I had any other way out my current predicament. I wouldn't do well in the back jungles of some third-world country."

Wright continued to count, Vengai rolled his eyes. Without hesitation he reached out, grabbing the back of Wright's head, and slammed it into the table. Vengai took advantage of Wright's dazed state—keeping one hand on the back of his head, he used the other to provide the counterpressure he needed and twisted until he heard the satisfying crunch of the vertebrae popping out of place, cracking, then severing the spinal cord.

Wright crumpled on top of the table. Vengai replaced the money in his coat and grabbed the limp form under his arms, then dragged him into the nearby audiovisual room. He pushed the rolling carts with projectors and microphones out of the way, and shoved the body inside and out of sight. Then he calmly closed the door, grabbed the briefcase and returned to the fundraiser.

He should have taken my offer, Vengai mused.

VENGAI SMILED WHEN HE opened the door to the luxury hotel room. He held the smile through the initial software boot up and even when they hit their first wall, but his smile turned into a smoldering glare when his technician told him that the code was incomplete.

He roared with fury and threw the glass in his hand into the wall. He paced around the room, ranting about

Wright and the expense of setting him up. He should have known the sweaty technician was up to something when he handed over the hard drive so easily. The situation had nagged at him, but he knew Wright would never have kept the secret for long and so killing him had been the only solution, but it was too soon.

"Sir, I think I have something," one of the technicians said.

Vengai stopped his ranting and stood in front of the computer. The young computer technician trembled as his fingers moved over the keyboard. He was new to the Ocean Tigers and very willing, but Vengai hated his timidity. The youth was a prodigy, and he recognized that while he could train the village idiot to fight there were few in their ranks that possessed the same kind of technical skills. Once he had gotten past his initial fear he reprogrammed all of their computers and helped to reroute the bank funds so nothing could be traced back to the Ocean Tigers. With his help they had stayed hidden and would remain so until he wanted the world to know the power they had.

"What is it, Dilvan?" he asked, trying not to snap. "What have you found?"

"He left the information for the pieces of the code. They're attached to the bank account he set up. Once the money is verified in his account, then the code will be released."

"Well, since he won't be getting the money, how do we get the code?"

"I might be able to hack his bank account, but this guy was careful. The code for this will only recognize his computer. I need access to that if you want me to get the code."

"Can't you fill in the missing code?"

"No, sir. Computer codes are like a math problem. Sometimes if you have enough variables you can piece together what is missing by creating a formula, but he was clever and left an unsolvable puzzle without his personal code."

"Damn! Fine, we'll get you his computer. Maybe we'll get lucky and there will be even more that we can gain from his system."

"I would say that is certain, sir."

"Why is that?"

"If I'm reading the code right, this program isn't just a satellite program."

"What do you mean?"

"I mean that this software is built to hack almost any form of military programming out there. If we can get the rest of the code, it's possible that we could hack into almost any military or intelligence database in the world, completely undetected."

Kabilan felt the smile return to his face. Wright's deception was a minor setback, but it appeared that he was going to get even more than he'd paid for, if he was just a little patient. "We'll get the code," he promised. "One way or another."

CHAPTER FOUR

Bolan sat on the bed, looking through the intelligence that Brognola had sent to his handheld computer. What they had so far was pretty minimal. Heather Daniels had been en route to Port Blair on a supply ship with a bunch of other missionaries, and they'd left out of Singapore. But there was a lot of water between those two points and hundreds of places to hide. He replayed the audio from the call.

Daniels's voice didn't waver as she spoke, but the tension in her tone spoke volumes as the fear behind the words resonated from the recording. The man who made the ransom demand, on the other hand, didn't sound rattled or tense at all. He was direct and matter-of-fact and the forceful slap had likely come from someone else, not the man speaking. He also wondered what the audio techs might be able to pick up from the background once they'd had time to dissect the whole recording. Bolan checked the time and decided that Brognola was likely still at his office.

He picked up his phone and dialed the number from memory.

"It's me," he said when the big Fed answered.

"Let me turn on the scrambler. Done. Have you had a chance to review everything we've got so far?"

"I have," Bolan said. "It's not much to go on. Once

we have everything that we need, Heather Daniels is likely to be dead if she isn't already."

"Agreed, but we're working on it. We have come up with a theory that might fit."

"Let's hear it," Bolan said.

"We've got an intelligence report on the region that mentions rumors that the KP Branch of the Liberation Tigers of Tamil have reformed in that part of the world."

"The LTTE?" he mused. KP Branch was the group's nickname, taken from the initials of its top operative, Kumaran Pathmanathan. "I thought the Sri Lankan government had finally put an end to those guys."

"That's the common belief," he said. "But this group, calling themselves the Ocean Tigers, is operating a lot more like a military than a bunch of pirates. They're organized, efficient and deadly. Their tactics are way too familiar."

Bolan considered the information briefly. "It fits," he agreed. "Do you have anything else on them?"

"Nothing concrete, but if this is the LTTE back in action, then you're heading into a hell of a hot zone. They've always been the real deal, and if this is a reformation of the KP Branch, there's even more going on beneath the surface than just piracy."

"Interesting," Bolan said. "What do we know about this KP Branch?"

"They were pretty secretive and mostly dealt with weapons smuggling, explosives and dual-use technology. They wreaked havoc in that part of the world for a long time, and destabilizing the government was their specialty. Supposedly they went out of business when their leader was arrested. It's the dual-use tech that worries me."

"What do you think they might be after? Civilian stuff with military applications?"

"That's the most likely scenario," Brognola said. "So maybe someone stepped into the role of leader and is taking them in this new direction. We just don't know precisely what that direction is or who the man running the organization might be, but I do know that they can be formidable and if they are setting their sights on political captives their appetite has gotten a little bigger."

"At least it's a place to start," Bolan said. "Do you have anything else for me?"

"One thing," he said. "But I'm reluctant to mention it, since I know you're already reluctant. It's about the woman, Agent Michelle Peterson."

"What about her?"

"She wasn't lying when she said she did field ops for the CIA and the NSA, but she ended up getting pulled from the field toward the end of President Daniels's last term. It was only his intervention that got her a spot on his personal detail."

"Why was she pulled?" Bolan asked.

"She had a mission go bad. Really bad. She was working a case in Libya and was taken. They held her and tortured her for two months. When she finally got out of there, it was six months before she could walk again. They wanted to retire her, but the President intervened and she ended up assigned to him. According to her file, she was diagnosed with severe PTSD."

"That's not all that surprising, considering what

happened to her," Bolan said. "Not many people can live through a situation like that without problems."

"That's true," Brognola said. "But I wanted you to know. Despite the fact that he's no longer in office, President Daniels has an enormous amount of influence with the current administration, and he and this woman are obviously close. And she might be unstable. If something goes wrong, it could come back and bite us right on the ass. I tried to talk him into letting you go this alone, but he wants someone who is interested in his daughter's safety and will make it a priority. He knows that any other operative will put the mission first and he wants to make certain that his daughter isn't collateral damage. He can talk a big game about her not being the objective, but I guarantee that she is Agent Peterson's objective."

Bolan sighed. "We'll just have to hope she's tough enough to handle it," he said. "I prefer to work alone, but the President insisted, so I'll just have to make the best of it. I can always find a convenient place to stick her if she becomes too big of a problem and then deal with Daniels later."

"It's your mission, Striker, but taking her into the field might be a good way to get yourself—or her—killed. I've never been willing to lose an operative to satisfy the politicians, even the President."

"I appreciate the heads-up and I'll let you know if things are becoming problematic. You'll get back to me with any additional intelligence? We need to get moving on this quickly if Heather has any chance of coming out of this at all."

"I should have more for you in a few hours," he said.

"Thanks, Hal. We'll talk soon."

Bolan clicked End on his cell phone and flipped back through the file one more time. There were things he would need in country and even more than usual if he couldn't convince Peterson to stay in the States and provide support. He knew she wouldn't, just as she likely knew he'd try anyway.

Bolan wasn't a sexist. He'd met any number of women capable of doing good work in the field. It was never a question in his mind of capability, except on an individual level, and it had nothing to do with gender. But in his experience, a woman in the field could be distracting, and in a situation that was personal—as it was in this case—a person was less likely to make objective decisions and that almost always ended badly. Bolan knew that he personally operated most effectively when he worked solo, pulling support from individuals in the area who could serve as resources to the needs of the mission at that particular moment, rather than dealing with the complexities of a partner or a full team.

He pulled out his laptop and booted the system. After going through the installed security protocols, including thumbprint and retinal scans, he opened his contacts folder and began to search through them. One name came to the top of the list, but Bolan almost groaned aloud at the thought of dealing with this man. Still, Bashir Faizal, for all his flaws, was as good as money could buy and in this case, it might not cost him anything.

Bolan picked up his phone and began to dial. Bashir's resource phone, as he called it, required a password. When Bolan heard the tones he dialed the password and waited as the call rerouted. He got an answer after two rings.

"This is Bashir."

"Hello, Bashir. Matt Cooper."

"Ah…my old friend! Long time. Who can I help you blow up today?"

"Well, I hadn't planned on blowing up that drug boat, but who would have thought they booby-trapped their own stash?"

Faizal laughed. "I told you they would," he said. "Remember?"

"I remember," he said dryly. "Are you ever going to let it go?"

"Same old Cooper, no sense of humor for these things," he said. "All right, I'll let it go for now. How can I help you? I still owe you for saving my life."

"You owe me twice, as I recall," Bolan said.

"You only risked yourself one time for me, my friend. The other time you were saving your own skin and I got to tag along."

"Fair enough. I'm putting together an op in that part of the world, somewhere in the Bay of Bengal, if my intelligence holds up. Hostage rescue."

"The Bay is bad news, Cooper. The word is that the Ocean Tigers are prowling those waters these days and they aren't like normal pirates."

"Who are the Ocean Tigers?"

"I don't really know who they are—no one does—

but I do know that they are a patch of bad that you don't want to get pricked by."

"Are they the kidnapping kind?"

"They have ransomed some. But if it's them, then you may just as well save yourself the trouble of coming. Decent pirates treat their prisoners like they would treasure, because this is how they make their money. The Tigers, they only ransom a handful of their prisoners, and then they still play games, making people pay and pay. The rest they toy with, making demands no one can meet, then executing them as some kind of political statement. Military and law enforcement ignore them because they're too dangerous to tangle with and have too much money. Not like the Somali pirates at all."

"Hence the need for an operation, Bashir. I'm going in before they have an opportunity to execute this particular hostage."

"Does this one hold state secrets or something? Diplomat's daughter?"

"Bashir, I'm about to change the operation target to you."

"Fine, fine, what do you need?" he asked. "If it's not too outrageous, you'll get it."

"I'll get everything I need because your life— twice—has to be worth at least that," he growled.

Faizal laughed again, and agreed to get him whatever he needed.

Bolan ran through his list and hung up the phone with Faizal before he could ask him more questions. He picked up Daniels's picture and ran his finger along the side of it again. He couldn't put his finger on why this mission was nagging at him until he thought about how much Peterson cared about the young woman. He sighed as he put the picture down.

Emotions got a person killed; he'd seen it time and again. He pulled his Desert Eagle out of its holster, popped out the clip and worked the slide, ejecting the bullet from the chamber. As the bullet popped into the air, he reached out and snatched it, smiling.

Maybe he was just fast enough to save them all.

THE POUNDING ON THE DOOR came earlier than Bolan had expected. He glanced at the glowing lights of the clock brightly telling him that it was a mere 4:30 a.m. He rolled off the bed and didn't bother putting on a shirt to go with blue Navy SEAL sweatpants. He glanced through the peephole, but knew before he looked that it would be Peterson. She was motivated, he'd give her that, and he wondered if she'd slept at all.

He pulled open the door, the bright light from the hallway spilling into his dark hotel room.

"It's about time, Colonel Stone," she said as she marched past him and into his room. "Though I expected a military man like yourself to be dressed and ready to roll by this hour."

He smiled at the Secret Service light outfit. Black slacks, black dress boots with a two-inch heel and a dark blue long sleeved shirt. He had yet to meet a Secret Service agent who didn't look proper all of the time, and he couldn't help but notice that she filled out her clothes in all the right places.

Bolan ran a hand through his hair and walked over to the coffeemaker in his room. He could hear her pacing behind him and smiled to himself as he filled the reservoir and pressed the start button.

"We don't really have time to mess around," Peterson said.

"Are there armed gunmen coming down the hall?" he asked quietly.

"No."

"Bomb in the building and it's about to go off?"

"No, don't be ridiculous," she said.

"Then we have time for coffee," he said.

He watched as she sat primly on the edge of the small love seat. He sat in the high-backed chair next to her and propped a foot up on the coffee table, rocked his head back and closed his eyes. He smiled again when she let out a long sigh.

"Listen, I hate to wake you, but I've got the information that we really need, and I can get us on a flight out of the country in an hour. I already have my cover documents and alternate identification. I just need to know if I'm getting cover documents for you, as well. And I have the latest intelligence from the State Department. But we have to hurry to make the flight."

"No, you don't," he said, not bothering to open his eyes just yet.

"Yes, we do. I talked to the pilot on my way over. He wasn't happy about being woken at this hour, but he owes me a favor."

"I wasn't talking about the flight. I have no doubt that you could have Marine One on top of this hotel in thirty minutes if you put your mind to it. I meant that you don't hate waking me or you would have waited for the sun to rise before trying to save the world."

She stared at him in disbelief. Her face flushed and she pulled together her purse and the stack of documents that she'd sat on the table.

"I told the President that I should go this mission alone. I should have just left without you last night..." she muttered.

Bolan reached out his hand, catching her by surprise, and pulled her back down to the love seat. Her eyes narrowed as she pulled her hand away.

"Hold on, Michelle, and take a deep breath. *I* haven't seen your intel and whether you like it or not, I'm not going to go charging off into Malaysia until I'm certain of my target. That's not the part of the world where going in unprepared will serve you. Why don't we start with what you've got so far?"

She relaxed slightly and opened one of the file folders. "The local government there is still trying to get their legs after putting down the LTTE. With such a diverse population and the influences from India and the other Asian nations, they fight to hold on to what they have, so we don't believe that there is any official government agency involved. They'd like that influx of cash, but aren't prepared to have the Western world descend on their doorstep with this kind of action. The best lead we've got is a new pirating operation going by the name of the Ocean Tigers," she began, but he cut her off.

"That's our best lead, too, at the moment, but it's not enough."

"Why?" she asked.

"I spoke with some of my contacts. This Ocean Tigers group is hard-core and what I'm hearing is that if they are the ones that have Heather, it's possible they'll collect the ransom and kill her anyway. Worse, no one knows where their base of operations is located. The best resources in the area are hard-pressed to keep track of anything with the ever-changing political climate. For all we know it's a dissenting faction of the government trying to wrest control and install a new leader. If we charge in there without knowing everything we can then we're likely to get a lot of people killed, including us."

She nodded, but didn't show any other reaction to that news. Bolan was pleased that she didn't respond and appeared to be taking the information in and processing it. Too much emotion in a situation like this would be deadly to them both and probably Daniels, too. If she couldn't keep it together he would have to find a way to ditch her and go in alone. It was really his preferred method, anyway. It was tough enough to watch his own six without needing to watch someone else's.

"You seem pretty gung ho to leave here, so where is it you intend to go?"

"Same as you do with any missing persons case—where she was last seen. Singapore. You're shaking your head, you disagree? I don't want the trail to get cold."

"The trail is already cold. If that's all we can come up with, then we could start out that broadly, but that's like looking for a needle in a stack of needles. And Singapore is a cesspit. We're doing some additional digging, and I want to see what that intelligence tells us. If it really is a branch of the LTTE, we'll have a better chance of finding them if we can follow the money than we will just wandering around the Bay of Bengal and hoping we find the right island."

"But you don't *know* that the LTTE has anything to do with the Ocean Tigers," she objected.

"I don't *know* enough to think it is or isn't anyone. I don't have enough information to make a conclusion, but I've been doing this a lot of years and know to trust my gut. If their financials are barely there, then we know they don't have the money for this kind of operation that the Ocean Tigers are running, and we're dealing with another group. On the other hand, if their previous supporters are starting to shell out serious dough, we can look deeper."

"According to the State Department, there are dozens of piracy operations running in that part of the world," she admitted. "You're right. We don't want to end up in the wrong snake pit. Heather doesn't have that kind of time and neither do we if these guys are planning more serious action."

"Exactly," he said. "We've got to be methodical about this or the whole mission will come crashing down around us. I know that time is critical for Heather, but the reality is we need to be more concerned about squashing any terror plots that they might be hatching."

"Still, given how many groups there are, why are you focusing on this group?"

"This feels too well organized and finessed," he said. "We already know that the Cayman account they want the money sent to is totally blind. A cover company for a cover for another cover, at least. Most of the groups working over there just aren't set up that well and it doesn't fit the typical pattern."

"Agreed," she finally said. "I just hate feeling this helpless. Heather is a...she's a fine young woman. The thought of what might be happening to her turns my stomach. I know that the mission is more, but I want to get her back."

"We'll have to hope she's got some of her father's fight in her," he said. "So, if you don't mind, I'll get dressed and we'll go have some breakfast. We can review everything you've got and maybe by then I'll have heard some more from Hal. Between us, maybe we can narrow things down a little."

Bolan watched as skepticism, reluctance and finally acceptance crossed over her face.

"Okay, but I'm driving."

CHAPTER FIVE

Heather Daniels opened the car door to a wave of despair from the camp. A group of children were sitting in front of a small metal building with a soldier pacing in front of them. The dirty faces were streaked with tears, and one little girl was sporting a bruise that took up almost half of her face. The children weren't looking at the soldier that was set as their guard. Daniels followed their gaze across the compound to two more of the Ocean Tigers dragging the bodies of two men from the side of the building. Fresh blood still oozed from their wounds, and they tossed them onto the bed of a truck without a word.

Daniels stumbled and dropped to her knees, feeling a wave of nausea roll through her stomach. She had seen death before, but this was different. She had spent the entire car ride with Rajan telling her that she would be safe and his kindness had disarmed her. She'd not expected to open the door to such horrible visions. The air itself reeked of violence. She looked back at the children with tattered clothes and broken spirits. The girl with the bruise dropped her head into her arms and tried to muffle her sobs. Her heart ached for the horror that they'd been put through and knew that it was a long way from being over.

Taking several deep breaths, Daniels waited for the

nausea to pass and when it did, she wasn't so much afraid as she was angry. Trying to contain her rage behind gritted teeth, she rose to her feet and turned to face Rajan, her arm swinging before she even realized it. He caught her hand in midair and pulled her tightly into his body. She thrashed around and tried to pound on him, but his grip was too tight—tears filled her eyes. He grabbed the back of her hair and whispered in her ear.

"I know," he snapped, his voice urgent in her ear. "But don't do this here. I can't protect you if you make a scene."

She leaned back, stunned, and then pulled away. Something told her that Rajan wasn't like the other pirates, but now wasn't the time to deal with it. She turned and walked over to the group of children. The sentry that had been diligently pacing in front of them blocked her path. Daniels turned to glare at Rajan. He nodded and she turned and pushed past the sentry.

The children didn't hesitate, instinct telling them that they had a champion. They clamored around her, their voices rising in several different languages. She reached down and lifted a little boy that couldn't have been more than two, settling him on her hip. With her other hand, she pulled the bruised and battered little girl to her feet and brought her in close. The child clung to her leg ferociously. Daniels ran her thumb along her cheek and gave her an encouraging smile.

"Where do we stay?" she asked Rajan. The challenge was there in her tone and she wondered if Rajan would let it stand. She had no real idea how long her captivity would last and if there was any chance that she was making it out of there alive, but she would do everything in her power to make the situation better for the children while she could. She watched Rajan move closer with one raised eyebrow. She hugged the children in closer and the girl shivering into her side strengthened her resolve.

"Come with me," he said, his face betraying no emotion. Daniels nodded and motioned to the children to follow her, doing her best to reassure their uncertain expressions as they walked through the main camp. The camp consisted of a larger main house that looked like an old island villa. Set up on a small set of stilts instead of a traditional foundation, it had a wraparound porch that might have looked inviting if it weren't for the armed soldiers at the entrance. There were at least six other buildings, three that were metal and three that were wooden huts of more recent construction. A group of women stood to the side washing laundry, and several teenagers were being drilled in a courtyard to one side of the buildings. She watched the women attempt to focus on their chores, but glance up with worried looks. Daniels wondered how many of the children on the island belonged to them and how many had already had their children killed in the conflict.

She paused briefly to focus on the teenagers, really little more than children themselves, being trained to be soldiers and her heart ached for them. She had spent most of her time trying to help those who had escaped the fate of being a child soldier and teaching them how to find their heart and soul again. So much of the training that they endured was about ripping away their innocence and destroying their ability to have compassion for themselves or anyone else. Perhaps even worse than the loss of innocence and compassion was the loss of faith, belief and wonder in the world itself. Their worlds had been stripped of hopes and dreams and replaced with death.

She stopped as they were walking and waited for Rajan to turn. He paused but didn't turn initially. She stayed rooted in place and waited. Finally she said, "I want them, too."

"Those you cannot have," he said, turning to face her.

"Why not?"

"We need them to fight," he replied, shrugging. "They are not children. We need soldiers."

"You mean, you need killers," she snapped. "They aren't men yet, either."

"They are trained to fight, for their homes and their families. Sometimes that means killing, yes."

"I've seen this kind of recruiting before," she said. "I'm betting that you already destroyed their families."

"Those men who did not come voluntarily were killed," he said. "That is the way of things."

"You're a monster."

"It was not I who killed them," he said.

"What does it matter if you killed them or had someone else do it? They're still dead, and when your little faction here is destroyed these children will have no one to take care of them. I've been taking care of children just like them for years now and trying to help them rebuild. Trying to give them hope."

"You do this by giving them another God to pray

to. That does not help. We become their family. If they have a need we fill it. We do not offer empty promises."

"And neither do I. Yes, we teach them prayer, but we also teach them to read and write. We teach them to think for themselves and how to find their hearts again after people like you have ripped them out!"

He reached out and slapped her.

Daniels stepped back, stunned. He hadn't been violent with her, but as she looked around she realized she was causing a scene. Two other soldiers ran up with guns pointed and the children began to cry.

"Get them inside," Rajan said.

Daniels stared at Rajan as he walked away and turned to face the soldier that was pointing a rifle at her. He wore three red hash marks on the sleeve of his jacket. She had a sneaky suspicion they symbolized kills. She reached out for the little girl's hand and they walked ahead of the soldier into the house. She was surprised to see that the house was fairly modern. Sofas in the front room, wood floors and wood paneling. The heat and humidity were broken with fans placed strategically throughout the residence. The soldier behind her didn't give her time to reflect on the surroundings, but shoved her forward. He was taller than the soldier with the red and looked a little more raw around the edges. His emblem was different than Red's, the emblem of the shark around the skull set onto a black X. There was a sense of completion about the design, as if he had surpassed the red hash marks and had completed his head count.

The two soldiers moved them into the center of the

room. One waved the children down to the floor, but stopped her from following. She looked at the two soldiers as they ushered her away from her little band. A slow smile crept across Red's face and he motioned with his gun for her to move. When she didn't move quickly enough, the larger soldier grabbed her arm and pulled her into the adjacent room.

Daniels heard the children begin to cry. She tried to quell her own rampant fear. She moved away and tried to position herself near the window. She dashed around the small desk and chair, but Red cut her off. Her heart was racing and she tried to think of a good prayer, but the only thing she could think of was, "God, please get me through this."

She gasped when the second soldier grabbed her hair from behind and used it as a means to propel her around the room. He shoved her forward onto the desk, slamming her head into the wood. She struggled against him, but as she started to escape Red was on the other side of the desk, pushing his weight down onto her shoulders.

She could barely breathe with all of the weight and tried to cry out as the soldier fumbled around trying to rip away her clothes. Red laughed as her arms flailed. Her fingers made contact with a pencil and she wrapped her hand around it and managed to swing her arm forward and jab it into Red's side.

His shriek was short-lived and had him slamming his elbow down on her back. She felt the fabric of her clothes begin to tear as the onslaught continued. Her ears were ringing from the pain and lack of air as her chest was compressed by their weight.

Red released her, and she glanced upward in time to see the bullet blast through his skull. The brute behind her was ripped away, and she turned to see Rajan land a punch to his midsection and then an uppercut connected with his jaw. Fury marred his normally serene expression. With Red dead, the brute began to explain his position so rapidly that Daniels didn't understand. Her breath came in gulps as she tried to readjust her clothing.

Rajan reached out and grabbed the soldier by his hair and dragged him outside. Daniels staggered out of the room in his wake. She collapsed in the doorway and watched Rajan in the middle of the courtyard with the soldier on his knees. He was yelling, but she could only make out a few words as the others gathered to watch the spectacle. He pulled a pistol from his holster and didn't hesitate dropping the soldier in front of the group. He began to yell again as he marched over to the house. He stood on the porch and pointed at Daniels clutching the doorframe.

Still shaky on the language and reeling from the events she made out one word. "Mine."

Rajan reholstered his pistol and helped Daniels to her feet. He walked her past the children and into a small bedroom. Fear pulled at her, but she tried to relax. He sat her on the bed and went into the adjoining bathroom, returning with a cool, damp rag. She pulled her knees into her chest and pressed up against the headboard.

He started to run the cloth along her forehead, but she took it from him and used it to wipe down her tear-streaked face. It felt wonderful on her skin and she took several deep breaths, to bring herself back under control. Daniels knew that without Rajan those men would have raped her without a second thought.

Taking a seat in a chair next to the bed, Rajan said, "I'm sorry I had to strike you. I can't have anyone challenging my authority here. Any weakness might provoke a challenge. I'm also sorry I left you alone before I established that you were not to be touched."

She didn't speak, but sat with the cool rag against her skin. She had never had her world so completely turned upside down. She tried to swallow, but her mouth was dry. "May I have some water, please?" she asked.

He nodded and left the room quickly, returning a few moments later with a bottle of water from the kitchen. "Drink this," he said. "You will feel better."

"I'm not sure I'm ever going to feel better," she said. "I feel filthy and I don't even know why."

"Because even though those men did not rape you, you know what they planned. They treated you like… like you had no value. That is why you feel dirty."

Catching her breath, Daniels said, "You're a psychologist, too?"

He laughed softly. "No, but I am not unfamiliar with such traumas."

"That's not very reassuring," she whispered.

He shrugged. "You will stay here until the ransom is paid. If you behave, the smaller children may stay here with you and you can school them, but you may not approach those in training."

She looked around the room and reflected on what she understood from the courtyard. Pirates always extracted a price and she began to ponder the reality that he may be showing her kindness because he expected her to share his bed.

"And where will you sleep?"

"I will sleep with the soldiers in the bunkhouse. This room will be yours alone. I will send two other women for you to have as servants, but you must not task them with anything that is forbidden. They are not worth what you are, and you would be risking their lives for the trespass."

"I don't understand you."

"Ransom and piracy are part of the way of life here," he said.

"No, that I get, but I don't get you. What is it you want from me?"

"You'll understand everything in due course. This will be the only time I ask, you must trust me and you must do what I tell you. This is not all what you think."

MICHELLE PETERSON STARED at the man across the table from her flipping through the State Department reports that she acquired. He had everything that a special ops military man was supposed to: muscular physique, mysterious good looks and enough training and skill to render a small country's entire military inoperative in under an hour. This morning, however, he was dressed in civilian clothing, and something about him nagged at her perceptions. He didn't act like a military man, strictly speaking, and he sure didn't seem like a traditionalist when it came to operations. She trusted President Daniels completely, so when he'd said that a man named Hal Brognola was the person to turn to when Heather was taken, she believed him.

What she didn't believe was that the man sitting across from her was in the Army. The fit didn't feel quite right to her. She needed to know more about him before they went into the field. This wasn't the kind of mission she wanted to tackle with someone she couldn't trust.

"May I ask you a question, Colonel?" she asked.

He took another sip of coffee and nodded. "Go ahead."

"You aren't really active military, are you?"

He cocked an eyebrow at her. "What makes you say that?"

"Men with the rank of colonel wear their uniform—understandably—with a great deal of pride. You aren't wearing yours today."

"Uniforms attract notice," he said. "We don't need that right now."

"Also," she added, "military men don't work alone. Even special ops guys have field teams. You don't. Not to mention your file is sealed. The only military personnel files that are completely sealed are files of people that don't really exist. So who are you really?"

He sighed, obviously thinking about her words and what his response would be. "All right, Agent Peterson. Here's what I can tell you. My name is Matt Cooper, and yes, I am also known as Colonel Brandon Stone."

"So who is Hal Brognola, really?"

"He's real," he said. "We work together sometimes, doing missions that have a vital interest to national security. That's all you really need to know for our purposes and all you're going to know, period. Anything else is above your clearance."

She thought he was probably lying. This man might have dozens of identities. But the President trusted Brognola, and this was the man Brognola said could get the job done. "Fair enough—for now," she said. "But if you aren't as capable as Hal Brognola convinced the President you are, I'll figure that out. I won't have anyone risking Heather."

He shook his head slightly. "Agent Peterson, you've just summed up the problem with your involvement rather nicely. This mission isn't about Heather. She's secondary, and even President Daniels knows that. If you can't get your head around that idea, hit the road right now."

"Heather may be secondary to you, Matt Cooper or Colonel Stone or whoever the hell you really are, but she's primary to me!" Peterson's voice started rising slightly toward the end of her rant, but she noticed it and toned herself down. "I don't care about the LTTE or pirates. I care about her. This family means a lot to me, and I will not fail them."

"Take a deep breath, Agent Peterson," he said mildly. "One step at a time, okay? I plan to save Heather, but we can't do anything until we understand what we're walking into. I don't mind going into the den, but I'd like to know how big the lions are before we jump into the black."

She pushed the eggs around on her plate as she contemplated the mess she was in. There were few situations in life she couldn't handle, but Heather being held captive seemed to be putting her over the edge. She'd known the Daniels family for years—before he became President—and had been around the family so long that they were *her* family. She'd been there when Heather graduated. And she knew what captivity meant.

She also knew that Cooper was right, she needed to slow down and take one step at a time or she would spend the entire mission running in circles.

The slow, gnawing anxiety of prefield work that once made her adrenaline pump was now almost paralyzing. She was determined not to allow it to control her or the outcome of this mission, but she wasn't so prideful to only rely on herself. She needed Cooper, or whatever his real name was, and needing anyone was really against her nature. If he really was as good as Brognola had told President Daniels—"He's the best special operations man I've got and if he can't get it done, no one can."—then he'd be invaluable.

Cooper's phone rang and Peterson rolled the fork along the edge of her plate anticipating that this would be the call that would get them moving in the right direction. She was determined to control herself, but inside she could feel the clock ticking and her imagination had no trouble whatsoever filling in the details of what might be happening to a young woman she cared about deeply.

CHAPTER SIX

Finishing his conversation with Brognola, Bolan glanced at his handheld computer and saw that the data had arrived, then said, "Yeah, I got it," and hung up.

"What is it?" Peterson asked.

"It's better if I show you."

Bolan pulled out a small device about the length of a ruler, but circular. He tugged the small cord from the end and plugged it into his handheld computer. He pulled a transparent sheet that had been spiraled inside and spread it out on the table until it formed a legal-size sheet. Bolan punched keys on the handheld computer and the transparent paper came to life. He reached forward and touched the glowing icons, dragging them with his finger and tucking them away.

"What is that?" Michelle asked.

"It's a fairly new piece of tech I've got access to for the purposes of field testing. My phone has enough processing power to work as a PC and this allows me computer access anywhere I go. It automatically links up with a satellite and gets me resources that I might not have otherwise. Some things I can even work on as a 3D hologram, like building schematics, but its interactive capabilities in hologram form are limited and not very responsive to touch."

Peterson reached out and touched the images on

the table. The sheet itself reminded her of an over-head projector transparency. The icons moved when she slid her fingers across the page. The icons were so sensitive that she was able to spin one, blow it up and shrink it with just a flick of her finger.

Amused at her response, Bolan asked, "Would you like to play some more or would you like me to show you what we found?" Without waiting for her response, he moved two picture icons up on the screen.

"You're going to love this," he continued. "All of our data is starting to come together. This is Kabilan Vengai. We think he's the current leader of the Ocean Tigers. As we suspected, the Ocean Tigers are a newly formed branch of the LTTE, likely taking the place of the old KP Branch. After the former leader was deposed, there was some dissension in what was left of the ranks. Vengai solved this problem by having his chief opponent strung up by his entrails."

"It's not all that uncommon to display the body of an enemy," Peterson said.

"He wasn't a body when they put him on display," Bolan said shortly. "Rumor has it that Vengai made sure they were extra careful when they pulled him apart and kept him squirming for a good long while."

Peterson swallowed and nodded for Bolan to continue.

"This guy," he said, enlarging the second image, "we're not so sure about."

"Who is he?" she asked. "Do you have an identity?"

"Maybe," he said. "We ran his image through some facial recognition software against a few of our databases. He's one of Vengai's favorites right now, but we don't know where he came from or really anything else. The only name we've got for him is Rajan. He's in charge of most of the hostage negotiation, but…"

"But what?"

"He seems to show up at critical times and defuse tense situations. He's not what I would expect from this kind of organization. The LTTE is hard-core and wouldn't play well with someone who tried to keep the peace. We've got some people looking for more information on him, and when we find out more, I'll let you know. What little we have on him was buried in a highly classified email within the Sri Lankan government server. That suggests that this guy isn't what he appears to be on the surface."

"Maybe a plant or a spy of some kind? That might give us an advantage, right?" she asked, trying to ignore the feeling of hope blooming in her stomach. If he was there, maybe he'd try to keep Heather safe.

"Maybe," Bolan admitted. "He might be someone we can negotiate with or he might simply be another very dangerous obstacle. We can't take anything for granted right now."

Obviously trying to shrug off her feelings, she said, "I guess he goes into the bad guy column for now. We have so little that I'm willing to hold out a little hope."

"We just don't know," Bolan said. "He's an anomaly and anomalies bother me. Organizations like the LTTE don't survive for very long with dissension in the ranks. You know as well as I do that it's about making believers out of their troops." He shrugged. "I imagine we'll know soon enough."

Bolan slid several scenes across the device until he

came to a financial report. Peterson traced her finger along the columns as he spoke.

"Hal pulled up this data, but with your intelligence background he figured you'd probably spot something faster than one of his analysts."

Peterson scanned the document once more, then highlighted several transactions. "Can you run a search and correlate on these?" she asked.

He nodded and entered the command for the search function to cross-reference against known terrorist organizations and matching institutions.

"There it is," she said.

The small screen displayed the information for a political action committee located in the Washington, D.C., area called TPAC. Bolan traced his finger and spun the image back his way and sent out an immediate search for known contributors to TPAC and any connections to known members of the LTTE. While the search was running, a secondary search recorded a media alert. Bolan tapped the icon and an article appeared on the screen, with a man's name and picture. Tim Wright.

"Oh, that's right," Peterson said. "I saw that come across the wire this morning. This guy was supposed to be an amazing programmer and he was murdered last night. Everyone was talking about it because they say he was the best."

"People always say that when someone dies," Bolan replied. "It's human nature to be complimentary to people once they're dead."

"In this case, I guess the praise is deserved. There are some people at pretty high levels of defense trying to figure out how his work is going to be completed, let alone continued. He's one of those Rain Man types that can look at a piece of code and tell you how to get the recipe for grandma's cookies or in this case crack just about any computer in the world."

"What kind of programming did he do?" Bolan asked.

"He worked for a government contractor that developed software and programming for our satellites. The problem with satellite technology, much like a lot of military technology, is that it's created by one person and then pirated out to other agencies by spies, trades, et cetera. It's not my area, but what I hear is that they were working on creating proprietary programming that will make it more difficult to hack into our systems. My guess is that he was also trying to keep some back doors open into other systems that are trying to upgrade, as well."

Bolan detached the cord and rolled up his display.

"Michelle, do you believe in coincidence?"

"You mean, like, a guy that designs sensitive software is killed at a fundraiser known to be sympathetic to a reemerging terrorist organization?" she asked.

"Yeah," Bolan said, "I don't, either."

THE OFFICES OF THE Tamil People's Action Committee were in a small, nondescript office building on the outskirts of Washington, D.C. The building had a street number on the outside, but no signage indicating who held the various office spaces. After parking, Bolan held the door for Peterson as they entered the building. Inside the small lobby, they stopped at the occupant register and noted that the TPAC offices were on the third floor. None of the other office suites was occupied.

"Is it just me or is it strange that this building has only one occupant?" Bolan asked.

"It's strange," Peterson agreed. "Maybe it's the economy. And this isn't exactly a prime location."

"True," he admitted. "I guess we'll see."

They took the elevator up, and it opened onto a short hallway that led to the reception area of TPAC. The outer room was dominated by a large reception desk and a floral-print couch for those who had to wait. A rack of brochures about the Tamil people and posters depicting scenes from the war in Sri Lanka were the only other decorations. The receptionist was a gray-haired woman of about sixty, with a severe frown and nails painted a shade of pink that could best be described as flesh-toned. Her desk was neat and orderly with her name plaque—Myra Pepper—polished and shiny. "Can I help you?" she asked.

"Yes," Peterson said. "We're here to see Chellam Nilani?"

"Do you have an appointment?" she asked, with one eyebrow already arched skeptically.

"They do," an accented voice said before a dark-haired woman came around the corner to interrupt. "I'm Chellam Nilani," she added. "The executive director for TPAC. You must be Ms. Peterson and Mr. Cooper, yes?"

"Yes," Peterson said, extending a hand, which the woman shook briefly. She was tiny, but exuded self-confidence.

"Nice to meet you," Bolan said.

After telling the guard-dog receptionist to hold her calls, Nilani said, "Please, come with me." She led them along a short hallway and into a sparsely decorated office.

Her desk was cluttered with pamphlets, books and enough paperwork to sink a barge. "I apologize for the apparent mess," she said, gesturing toward the stacks with one hand. "I can never keep up with the paperwork."

"Who can?" Peterson asked.

"Please," she said, indicating two chairs as she took her own. "Sit down."

They both sat and Nilani said, "Now then, how can I help you? I wasn't quite clear on your needs after your call earlier."

As they'd discussed, Peterson took the lead. "We'd like to speak with you about the man who was killed at your fundraiser the other night," she said.

Nilani nodded. "Oh, yes, it was tragic. Such a talented programmer and a very sad way to die. We were so sorry at his loss." She paused, then added, "I'm not sure I understand your interest…."

Bolan removed an identification-card holder from his coat and flashed it in front of her. "Homeland Security, Ms. Nilani. Our interest is classified and your cooperation is expected."

Picking up on his lead, Peterson said, "So he worked for you?"

"No, no," Nilani said. "He wasn't regular staff, but he did volunteer for us from time to time over the past six months or so. We aren't a very large organization, so volunteers are invaluable. He was very dedicated."

"What did he help you do?" Bolan asked.

Nilani shrugged. "Nothing out of the ordinary. Just getting our computers set up and making sure our network ran properly. Technology support is expensive, and I was happy to have his expertise."

"Look," Peterson said, "we know that your organization raises funds to help with the Tamil struggle in Sri Lanka—"

"No, you misunderstand our purpose," Nilani said. "We are a political action council. All the money we raise is used here. We are lobbyists, of course, but our influence is very limited."

"Ms. Nilani," Bolan said, "we can prove that TPAC money is being funneled out of the country. We can have a court order to confiscate everything in this office and freeze your bank accounts in less than five minutes."

Apparently outraged, Nilani shot to her feet. "How dare you—"

Peterson held up her hand. "We aren't interested in that particular aspect of your operation. And if you don't know where the money is really going, that speaks more to your lack of effectiveness as an executive director than it does anything else. If you do know, then spare us the dramatics. All we really care about is if Tim Wright's death was part of something much bigger."

Nilani's shoulders slumped. "I…I just do what I'm told," she said. "I'm an American citizen, but my grandparents were Tamil and they raised me. I always wanted to help our people."

"So you've suspected something wasn't right?" Bolan asked.

She nodded. "Of course, Mr. Cooper," she admitted. "But I know nothing of Mr. Wright's death. I don't make a habit of killing my best volunteers." She glared across the desk. "In any event, you're not getting any of our data. I have lawyers that will keep you tied up in federal court for years before you could even get a look at what you confiscated."

Reaching into her briefcase, Peterson pulled out a file and dropped it onto the table. Nilani flipped it open and thumbed through the papers. Bolan raised an eyebrow and Peterson tilted her head, smiling.

"As you can see, these are your most recent bank records. We know about the contributions that you sent back to Sri Lanka when the LTTE was in full swing. We also know TPAC money can be directly traced to the presence of at least two LTTE fighters that have been in the United States."

"I…" she said, still looking through the pages. "I was not aware of any of these transactions." She gestured to her computer. "I can even show you our account records. They don't match!"

"Then help us," Peterson said. "As a sworn law-enforcement officer I could arrest you with what I have right now and take you in, but I'm not really interested in you unless you present a problem."

"What will happen to the people involved?" she asked quietly. "I do not know they are guilty of anything. I don't want to see innocent men caught up in some government conspiracy."

"They're soldiers with the LTTE," Bolan said, "and they'll be dealt with by the State Department. You should worry about your own hide right now. Ow—"

Peterson continued to rock the foot of her crossed leg back and forth. Bolan brushed the shin she had just kicked and shook his head. He might be willing to let Nilani go, she was already on the watch list, but the ex-soldiers roaming free were outside the line.

"What do you need to know?" she asked.

"What was he working on for you?" Bolan asked.

"Really he just did what needed doing. He worked on our website and our donors and retailers databases, anything to keep us up and running."

"Tell me more about your databases," Peterson said.

"He helped us set up a way to track retailers—large ones—that took advantage of impoverished people like the Tamil. Then we could use that information to hit them hard with boycotts and protests."

"So everything you did was really in the name of all that is good and decent?" Peterson said. "I'm sorry, Ms. Nilani, but I'm not buying that you were completely clueless this whole time. What were you doing that was a little more active for the cause?"

Nilani began to squirm in her chair. There were few things Bolan liked more than having a criminal on the ropes, and the idea of getting rid of an organization that was part of getting people killed made it all the more sweeter. And seeing Peterson push the woman just right was a bonus he hadn't expected. She was better than he would have believed.

"I had him get some information for me," she said. Her voice was now a bare whisper.

"What kind of information?" Bolan asked.

"About the military in Sri Lanka. I have friends that said they needed it."

"You mean, you have friends in the LTTE that were trying to evade capture when the Sri Lankan government was closing in on them," Bolan said.

"You don't understand!" Nilani cried. "I…they were friends and needed my help! It didn't matter, anyway. The secret police closed in too fast. The information didn't do them any good."

"So how did he get the information?" Michelle asked.

"I don't really know. I'm not really into the tech stuff. I can make a brochure, help organize our political meetings here and follow the leads, but most of this stuff is over my head. I just do what I'm told. He just made sure it all happened when it needed to."

"But he didn't have the contacts. You did," Bolan said.

"So who was your contact?" Peterson asked.

"My contact is dead, killed fighting for the cause."

"I think that we need to take a look at your computer."

"Be my guest, but if you're looking for anything that Wright left behind you'll be wasting your time. I gave him access to all of our computers, but unless he needed to fix something on that computer itself he always used his laptop. He said our systems weren't equipped with the right software."

"I think that I'll take a look anyway," Peterson said.

"This is my computer and I don't think that I'll allow that. The cause is more important than my personal well-being," Nilani protested.

"From what I understand, without TPAC, the cause doesn't exist," Peterson said.

She reopened the file on Nilani and thumbed through the pages. "Your only full-time staff is your secretary. Because of all the violence, you no longer get the celebrities to flock to your banner, and once it was announced that anyone associated with your organization could go on a terror-watch list, they all but abandoned you. So TPAC goes and the cause dies," Peterson said.

Nilani hesitated for a moment and then pulled up her contact screen. Bolan skirted around the desk and hovered over her until she relinquished her chair. Gesturing for her to move to the other side of the room, he pulled a thumb drive out of his pocket and plugged it into a USB port. The software from the drive immediately launched a screen.

"What's that?" Nilani asked suspiciously.

"A handy hacking program I've used in the past," he replied, keeping his own voice quiet. "It can hack most computer setups and all I have to do is type in the search parameters and it will do a smart search for those files first."

"Your search won't find anything," Nilani scoffed. "There are thousands of files on my computer that have information on Sri Lanka and our cause and some not in English."

"Thank you for reminding me to add the language

parameter," Bolan said. "I think that should about do it."

The progress wheel for the program spun for another minute and *Complete* flashed across the screen. Bolan ejected the drive, tucked it into his pocket and smiled at Peterson.

"I think that we have all we need."

Peterson and Bolan walked out of the office with a blustering, complaining Nilani stalking them to the door. They rode the elevator down and returned quickly to the parking lot. Bolan got behind the wheel of the car and Peterson slid in next to him.

"What the hell was that all about?" Peterson asked.

Bolan grinned. "First, what I told her about the software is true. This drive pulled any and all information that she had about the region. I'll send the data off to Hal and let his people start sifting through it."

"And second?"

"The drive also implants a program and a live feed from her computer to mine. Anything she accesses we can see, including live chats. In an hour, we'll have a data stream set up by our tech people so they can track everything she's saying and doing on that computer."

"We don't know that she's really a part of this," Peterson objected. "She seemed sincerely upset."

"No, but what we do know is, bad things keep coming from her and the people that she associates with. All we have to do is catch them in the act. We'll keep the data off site and if it looks like she is going to be doing something illegal then someone can send an anonymous tip. Regular law enforcement will be able to stay out of the mess and their case will be strong because there is no trail that leads to them."

"So, now what, Cooper?" Peterson asked.

Bolan pulled out his handheld computer and typed in Wright's name. His address flashed across the screen. "Now we go and see what we can find at Mr. Wizard's apartment."

CHAPTER SEVEN

After leaving the TPAC offices, Bolan and Peterson headed for a restaurant in nearby Arlington, Virginia, to plan their next steps. The Eventide Restaurant was a three-story building that sported a bar, restaurant and rooftop patio. Memorabilia lined the walls, and its claim to fame—aside from the good food—was that the secret meetings of the Odd Fellows Society had been held there. The irony didn't appear to be lost on his companion, but the place was busy and anonymous.

They found an open booth in the bar and took a seat. The blue-velvet seats looked warm and inviting. The leftover chill in the air from the afternoon spring showers was eradicated by a warm crackling fire. They settled into the booth and politely listened to the specials before they told the waiter they would need a couple of minutes before they could decide.

"So, we're going to Wright's apartment next?" Peterson asked, setting her menu aside. "What do you hope to find there?"

Bolan shrugged. "I'm not certain. But his death is no coincidence and he was obviously working for the LTTE in some fashion. My hope is that we'll find out where this Ocean Tigers group is operating from, but any information would be helpful at this point."

"I suppose that's true enough," she said, her voice sounding discouraged.

"Things aren't moving fast enough for you, are they?" he asked.

"Not really," she said. "There's a part of me that just wants to get on a flight to Singapore and start trying to track her down. We're on a clock and I can feel it ticking in the back of my head."

"I understand the impulse," Bolan said. "But in the case of this mission, information really is power. We could wander around Singapore and the Bay of Bengal for weeks and not find her. If we make too much noise looking for them, they'll just kill her and move their location to a different place. No one wins."

The waiter came back, and Peterson ordered a lobster bisque and a sandwich, while Bolan decided to take a chance on the Charcuterie Plate, which was a selection of cured meats, grilled bread and spicy mustard.

After he left, Bolan continued. "The simple fact of Wright's death makes me believe he knew something that they didn't want him to reveal. We'll have to hope we get lucky and find something helpful."

"Seriously, Cooper? You're counting on getting lucky?"

"I never count on it, Michelle, but I don't object to it when it happens, either," he said, ignoring the opportunity to use a play on the words.

"I hate counting on luck during a mission," she said. "It's…it's bad luck."

Curious, he said, "Is that what happened to you in Libya? Bad luck?"

She did a double take, then slowly set her glass of soda on the table. "I don't know," she replied. "Maybe it was bad luck. I don't think so, though."

"So what happened, then?" he asked. "Did you make a mistake?"

"Everyone makes mistakes, Cooper, but to answer your question, no, I didn't. I think Libyan Intelligence probably got a tip, maybe even from someone on our side, and they acted on it." Her eyes were far away for a long minute, then she added, "It doesn't matter, really. It happened so long ago that it feels like it was a different person."

He nodded. "I understand, but I've known plenty of people who never really get over something like what you went through."

Her eyes flashed once, and behind them he saw true anger. "I'm not some exhibit, Cooper, to be used to scare trainees. I don't know how you know what happened to me—those files were supposed to be sealed—but what I went through over there is no one's business. Especially not yours!"

Bolan leaned forward, pinning her with his eyes. "If it impacts your performance on this mission, I'll make it my business, Michelle. Do you understand? I need you to be focused and ready, and I need to know if you'll do what I tell you, when I tell you."

"I'll do my job, Cooper, probably better than you do yours. Let's just drop it, all right? We'll eat and then we'll hit Wright's apartment and see what we can find."

"All right," he said, somewhat regretting bringing it up. So far, other than being a bit more impulsive than he'd like, she'd done her part. "I apologize if I offended you."

She took a deep breath, then offered a half smile. "Your apology is accepted. It's just not something that I like talking about. I talked it to death with the shrink they assigned me, and when I didn't want to dwell on it anymore he gave me a bad evaluation. Shrinks are all the same, they haven't any clue what it's like to be on the front line and when you don't want to talk to them about something they couldn't possibly under-stand they use a bunch of terms like PTSD. You aren't very good with people, are you, Cooper?"

He considered it for a moment, then said, "I'm fine with those I trust, and I do my job well. I'm not so great with those who might be mission liabilities."

The waiter brought their food to the table, of-fered them refills on their drinks, then disappeared once more. After he was gone she said, "I've got to trust you, Cooper, because President Daniels and Hal Brognola say you're the man for the job. But they also said I get to come along, so that means you're going to have to trust me—at least a little bit—to do my part. I won't be a liability."

He looked at her for a long moment, then smiled. "Eat your lunch," he said. "The wizard's lair awaits."

THE APARTMENT COMPLEX where Tim Wright lived was less than a mile from Dulles International Airport. Tucked between several hotels and strip malls, it was a small, brick building that had obviously seen better days. A sign in front of the complex advertised that all apartments were furnished and rentals were available by the day, week or month. Long-term tenants were probably rare, and Bolan guessed that most people who stayed in them were in the capital for a brief period of time that was too long to stay in a hotel and too short to rent anything nicer.

He would have guessed that Wright's place would have been in a nicer area. Programmers at his level typically made very good money. They parked in an empty space and took the stairs that ran on the outside of the building to the second floor. A long, concrete-floored hallway led to Wright's apartment, which was on the right.

Walking down the hallway, Bolan pulled out a small strip of metal with an electronic device attached to one end.

"What is that?" Peterson asked.

"It's my all-access pass."

"How does it work?"

"The metal is a reactive alloy. When I insert it into the lock, the device reads the tumblers and produces a short electromagnetic surge that unlocks them. When the light turns green, I open the door, take out the file and the alloy returns to its natural state," he explained.

"It sounds like a high-tech skeleton key to me," she said. "Is there anything that you can't get into?"

"It only works on traditional locking mechanisms," he said. "So its use is fairly limited."

"I had you pegged for a kick-the-door-down kind of guy," she replied.

"I do that when it's necessary, but when subtlety will suffice, force can wait." They'd just reached

Wright's door when the sound of something crashing to the floor came from inside the apartment.

Bolan reached out and pushed Peterson against the wall, and both of them paused to listen. When she started to reach for the gun beneath her jacket, he shook his head. "No guns," he said. "You can't question dead people."

She let the gun slip back into the holster and watched as he quietly slipped the smart key into the lock. A few seconds passed and the light turned a bright green.

"You don't have to do this, you know," he said, knowing that it would annoy her a bit and somehow finding a little humor in her facial reaction.

"Are you ready or do you just want to hang out here and chat?"

"I'm always ready," he said, turning the doorknob silently and slipping the smart key back into his coat. "Go!"

He shoved the door the rest of the way open and saw that the apartment had already been ransacked. Two men were standing in the living room and they spun to meet his assault, reaching for weapons.

They weren't going to get to them fast enough, so Bolan went into a slide, doing a leg sweep to take out the closer one, then completing the spin and coming to his feet in time to throw a solid uppercut to the second man's jaw. He joined his partner on the floor, trying to roll away from the sudden attack.

Bolan followed, seeing Peterson closing on the first man out of the corner of his eye. His opponent gained his feet, backpedaling in the small space to try to gain some room. Suddenly his stance shifted and Bolan recognized the opening movement from Silat, a Malaysian martial art.

He closed the distance between them, preferring to get in close enough to avoid some of the more dangerous body locks or ground attacks that a skilled practitioner of the form could use. He also suspected that the man might go for a weapon, in which case, closer was definitely better in this small apartment. The man met him partway and tried to get a lock on his arm, but Bolan reversed the movement and drove an elbow into his face. Blood spurted as it broke and the man stifled a scream.

He finished the movement, driving a hard right into the man's solar plexus and turned in time to see a third man coming out of the bedroom. He pointed a .45 at Peterson and barked, "That's enough!"

She stopped and turned, even as Bolan stepped away from his own opponent. He was happy to see that the man Peterson had been fighting was already on the ground, looking as though he'd been hit by a small tornado. She raised her hands slowly.

"Gnani, Pegan, get up!" he said. "We've got what we came for." He shoved a hard drive into his coat.

The two men got to their feet. Bolan didn't want to let them go, but the fact of the matter was that even if he could get out the Desert Eagle in time, he'd be hard-pressed to take them all without either himself or Peterson getting hit. This wasn't the time.

"Cooper…" Peterson said. "Are you just going to stand there?"

The men were backing out of Wright's apartment,

and he nodded. "Even I'm not faster than a speeding bullet," he said. "I'm sure we'll be seeing these men again soon enough."

The gun-toting man grinned widely. "I doubt that very much," he said, then ducked out of the door. The sound of their feet running down the hallway sent echoes back through the thin walls of the apartment.

"Do we follow them?" she asked.

"No," he said. "Let's take a look around here first. We surprised them, and it's possible they overlooked something."

Peterson peered around the small apartment. It was covered in computer equipment and empty pizza boxes. The lack of natural light, daunted by the heavy curtains, gave the room more of a gloomy basement feel than that of a productive supergenius. Peterson strolled around the room and wondered about Wright. She knew tech guys were usually into their computers at home, but why was this kid hiding out in a dank apartment by the airport?

"You all right?" Bolan asked. "You seem to be off in your head somewhere."

"Yeah, I'm fine. I was just thinking about Wright. If he's a computer geek, he should be making plenty of money. This whole place has a sense of desperation, and I'm just wondering why."

"Well, it fits. I don't know why he would be desperate, but being willing to deal with the LTTE would be a move of either greed or desperation. This place certainly doesn't look like he was motivated by greed. Most of the uber-tech guys aren't. As long as they have a live screen and internet, they rarely come up for air."

Peterson went to the main desk and sat in the chair. The guts of the computer were lying in pieces, the hard drive taken by the Tamil men. She filtered through the debris on the desk to look for any evidence of what he had been working on. She opened the drawers and hit pay dirt. Taped to the bottom of the last drawer was a DVD.

"Hey, Cooper, check this out."

Bolan looked at the DVD.

"Where was that?"

"Taped to the bottom of the drawer," Peterson said.

"My guess is that the only other thing of value is the hard drive. I don't want to chance running that on an unsecure system. Let's get back to my hotel room and we'll boot it up and see what's there. Let me make a quick call, and I'll have this apartment secured."

Bolan quickly punched the numbers into the cell phone and waited for Brognola to answer.

"Striker, what do you have going on?"

"Getting shot at," Bolan said.

"You must be on the right trail, then."

"That's my thought. We were following up on a lead at the apartment of a computer genius who turned up dead. Other people got here first and we were attacked. I think they got what they came for, but we found something else."

"What?"

"A DVD that was hidden. We'll check what's on it and I'll let you know, but I don't have time to go over this place with a fine-tooth comb."

"Give me the address and I'll send a team right away to secure everything. I'll dig deeper on this

LTTE thing, since all signs are pointing down that road. Do you need anything else right now?"

"No, but I'll get back to you."

THE DRIVE TO THE HOTEL was quiet. Bolan and Peterson walked into his hotel room. He watched her as she crossed the room and slipped off her jacket and folded it on top of the nearest chair. She sat in the chair, crossing one leg over the other, and unzipped her boot. Bolan watched, mesmerized at the small feminine gesture. She'd done well back at Wright's apartment and before at the TPAC office. He was starting to feel impressed with her. On top of that, she was damned attractive. She looked up into his gaze.

"Do you mind? I just wanted to get a little more comfortable."

"Not at all," Bolan said. "Take off anything you like."

She grinned. "I think the boots will be sufficient."

Bolan turned away from the woman and booted up his computer. The screen came to life, and he launched the protection software. He felt her hand on his shoulder and tried to ignore the fact that her breasts were brushing up against him as she watched him work.

"That's the new CIA antivirus software package, right?"

"Yes," he said. "It scans the data on the disk before the files are opened, so it can keep out immediate threats."

"Yeah, I know. Did you launch the ghost, as well?"

"The what?" Bolan asked.

"They didn't tell you the best part of the package. Let me in there and I'll show you."

Bolan moved out of the chair and watched her fingers enthusiastically run across the keys. He leaned in and watched as she modified the program.

"Most antivirus software can scan files prior to launch, but the biggest threats are those that attack either the software running on a system or the infrastructure of the computer—or even the network—itself. Before, when we'd run into things like this, about the best we could do was nuke the virus. It was like taking a cannon to a duck."

"So what does this ghost thing do?" he asked.

"It does two things. First, it allows us to copy the virus itself, removing it from wherever it's buried in the files, and lock it away, so it can be analyzed and tracked back to its creator. Like doing an autopsy on a serial killer. The second thing it does is isolate all the data on the disk *before* the virus can do any damage. The threat is gone, but the hard data is still in place for us to analyze."

She looked through the files.

"All I see is the video file," Bolan said.

"Me, too. I'm almost afraid to watch it."

She clicked on the video link and Tim Wright's face filled the screen.

Hello. If you are looking at this video something didn't go as planned and I'm guessing that I'm dead or in prison, but probably dead. First, I'm sorry that this all happened. I didn't really plan on it, but I got in too deep and I didn't have another way out. Once

I stole money from the corporate accounts, I knew I was past the point of no return.

I want to make it right, if I can. I can't undo what I did, but I can tell you how to get rid of it. The code to launch the kill program is embedded in the end of this video, but it will only work if the code is entered into the system that is running the software I've created. It can't be done remotely, and even working backward through a compromised satellite won't work.

The software I created...it's a monster. I have included the specs for how it functions in this video file, as well. This software will wreak havoc all over the control protocols that are already in place. I'm really sorry. I hope no one gets hurt because of my mistakes.

Bolan and Peterson glanced at each other as the code for the kill program began to roll across the screen. Bolan tried to decipher the code, but programming language always looked like an alien cipher.

"Satellite program?" Bolan asked.

"Controlling satellites is what concerned me more," Peterson said. "I'm pretty good with code, but it would take me a while to filter through this."

"Michelle, I'm going to send this to my tech guys. This is suddenly a lot bigger than Heather being kidnapped or even the LTTE reforming. I have a feeling we're going to need that kill program. And we've got to get to whoever is in charge here in the States before he leaves the country."

"What makes you think he's still in the country?"

"Because you don't send thugs to search an apartment and steal hard drives if you already have everything you need. But I'd bet that they are close to having everything now and if this gets out of the country, we're going to have a hell of a time stopping it."

"How fast can your people analyze all of this?" she asked.

"Faster than yours," he replied. "We'll just have to hope it's fast enough."

CHAPTER EIGHT

Vengai paced the floor of the small hotel room, moving as restlessly as a tiger in a cage. Everything from the green stripes of the wallpaper to the ridiculous floral print of the couch seemed to annoy him more with each minute that he was stuck waiting for his men to return. Coming to the United States was always a risk, but feeling as though he couldn't leave was such an oppressive sensation that he could hardly stand it.

Right now, Rajan and his men were no doubt conducting more raids—fighting for the cause in a direct way—while he sat and waited. And waited. The hotel-room door handle turned and Vengai spun, his 9 mm pistol half drawn and ready—almost hoping—for a showdown. Instead, the men he'd sent to Wright's apartment stepped through the doors.

"Finally!" he snapped. "What did you find?"

His eyes took in the tattered appearance of two of the men, one of whom had a fresh bloodstain on his shirt, a nose that had been crushed and a set of bruises coming up beneath his eyes. Something had gone wrong.

"What happened?" he asked when they'd shut the door.

"We went to Wright's apartment as you instructed

us, and we began a search, but we were interrupted by two people, a man and a woman. Both fought well, and the man was an expert fighter. We weren't prepared to take on a mercenary."

"That's what you're supposed to be!" Vengai snapped.

"Sir, you've trained us well, but we were ambushed and unprepared. The fault is ours, though we were able to recover the hard drive from his computer before we left."

Grabbing the soldier, Vengai slammed him against the wall and took the hard drive from him. "I don't want excuses. I want results. You'll go back again tonight, and I'll send someone who has the kind of expertise that we're looking for and you will get me everything that he had in that apartment. Everything." He released the man and took a deep breath. "I presume they are dead?"

"Sir?"

"The man and the woman, you killed them, yes?"

The man shook his head, fear showing around his eyes. "No...no, sir. You said to be discreet."

"I am surrounded by incompetent fools," Vengai snarled. "Get out of my sight for the time being!"

The men left the room without another word.

"Utter idiots," he muttered under his breath. If this man and woman were law enforcement, there was no telling how close they were to discovering Wright's involvement with the Ocean Tigers. He needed to conclude his business here in the United States and get out of the country quickly.

The software was the key to the future success of

the Ocean Tigers. With the information it would provide, he wouldn't be forced into the same mistakes
previous leaders of the LTTE had made. They were
shooting in the darkness, unable to compete with the
intelligence capabilities of the government suppress-
ing them. The software Wright had developed would
bring the LTTE operation into the light.

"Dilvan!" he snapped, waking the young man from
his nap on the couch. "Wake up!"

Dilvan sat up, rubbing his eyes. "Sir?"

Vengai handed him the hard drive. "See what's on
this immediately. It's from Wright's computer. And do
it quickly!"

Dilvan took the drive and headed for his own
system, leaving Vengai to start pacing the room once
more. The only thing that connected him to Wright
was TPAC. Stealth was the key to his success. His
forces weren't as strong as they had once been, and
there were many in his country who were supportive
of the new government. People were tired of the fighting. This was their last chance to snatch victory from
the jaws of defeat.

Vengai pulled out his cell phone and dialed. Three
rings before he heard the female voice on the other
side. He liked Nilani. It was too bad that she would
have to die, but not until she served her final purpose.

"Miss Nilani, I'm so glad you answered. I just
wanted to thank you for your hospitality again."

There was a long pause before Nilani answered
him. "Mr. Vengai, I'm happy we were able to help,
but we've had a tragedy and I'm afraid I have things
to handle."

"I heard about the unfortunate loss of your volunteer. Allow me to express my condolences," he said.

"Yes, well, he will be most difficult to replace."

"Perhaps I can take you to dinner and thank you in person. Surely, you could use a break from the stress of your job. Your work is much appreciated by our people and a reward is in order, I think."

"I don't know...."

"Oh, you must come. I insist. You know I must return to Tamil soon and I would like to express my appreciation in person. My days are so limited and I enjoy the company of those who understand the difficulty of the fight that we are in."

"Yes...yes, of course. I'll meet you at your hotel at seven."

"Perfect. I'll see you then."

THE KNOCK SOUNDED AT the door and Vengai opened it to a nervously smiling Chellam Nilani. He returned her smile and opened the door further. "Come in, please," he said.

She stepped past the threshold and came to a dead stop, her eyes widening in shock and fear. Vengai shut the door and locked it behind her. He came up behind her and placed his hands on her shoulders.

"I'm glad that you've come, Miss Nilani. I need your help."

The two technicians sitting at the table weren't enough to make the woman know his level of seriousness, but for her to see her receptionist, Myra, strapped to a chair, bloody and beaten, was enough to get anyone's attention.

"Oh, my God! I don't understand," she said. "What have you done to Myra?"

Nilani tried to go to her assistant, but Vengai's fingers bit into her shoulders, holding her in place. When he released her, she ran to join the woman.

Vengai laughed. "Of course you understand. The LTTE and, more specifically, the Ocean Tigers need money and information to operate effectively. TPAC has been a perfect fit for those needs, as you know. You understand the fight that we're in, and you also know that in order for us to achieve victory, there is no sacrifice we must be unwilling to make."

Nilani tried to back to the door, but Vengai grabbed her arm and pulled her forward. He wanted her to see, but not to give comfort. The isolation was important. He wondered about the fear and the helplessness that had to be running through her, and it spurred him on. She was an American and worse, she was a politico and knew all of the word games, but words were empty and hollow when faced with the realities of war.

"But, but…Myra has been helping us," she said, stammering. "She's done nothing wrong!"

"Of course not," Vengai soothed. "But she is an American and appears to be quite loyal to you. It took some…convincing to get her to talk to us about the two Homeland Security agents who spoke to you today. Isn't that right, Myra?"

The beaten, bloodied form cried and gurgled blood in response. Vengai smiled in response. He had been tense, feeling uncertain of how to proceed, but finding a traitor made him feel most at home. Traitors he knew how to deal with. He knew the rules and steps to take for vengeance, but the political landscape and technology were much more complicated.

"She didn't know anything!" Nilani cried, turning on him. "Why didn't you just ask me?"

"Sit down, Miss Nilani," Vengai said. "I am going to ask you. Sadly, Myra didn't know very much." Stunned, she stumbled toward the chair he indicated.

Taking a seat next to her, he continued. "Now, I need to know more about who you talked to, and I need to know what you told them. My men ran into a man and a woman when we searched Wright's apartment, and I suspect it was the same two people you spoke to."

"They asked a lot of questions about Tim Wright, and I told them that he volunteered for us. They said they could prove that the TPAC money was being funneled out of the country. I didn't tell them anything, really, and I didn't cooperate." Her voice trailed off, then she looked at him. "Did you kill Mr. Wright?"

"I do what must be done. What else did you tell these people? Did they ask about me?"

"No, they didn't even mention your name. They just wanted to talk about Mr. Wright and who he was connected with. They asked about the LTTE, but I told them that we don't support them."

"What else happened?" he asked, getting to his feet. "Did they take anything?"

Slowly she nodded. "Y-yes. I think so. They copied files from my computer."

"I see," he said, stepping behind Myra. His hands moved like a flash as he reached out and broke her neck, killing her instantly.

Nilani cried out and staggered to her feet, her eyes wide and horrified. "Oh, my God, you killed her. You killed her." She repeated the words over and over as she backed into a corner and cowered there, sobbing.

"Shh…" he whispered, crossing the room and kneeling next to her. "I know you did the best you could, Miss Nilani. And you've been very helpful. My men will take you back to your apartment. You won't have to worry about this anymore."

Nilani leaned into the soldiers that were escorting her out the door. Vengai watched as they walked outside and then waved a third over to his side.

"Get rid of them both. We don't need more problems before we leave the country."

THE STILLNESS OF THE island at night was an illusion. Heather Daniels lay in her bed listening to the guards pace by outside the house. The breeze from the bay washed over the small piece of land, slipping through the thick trees caressing the house, making its way back out to sea. Watching the fan slowly spin to circulate the air in the room, she contemplated the surreal experience of being held captive, threatened and watching people die. The helplessness of her own captivity remained dwarfed by the thought of her co-workers and friends being mistreated where they were being held. The pent-up fear and frustration filled her eyes with tears. She took a deep breath and wiped them away. She couldn't allow herself to indulge in the overwhelming feelings.

She rose and paced the room. Her friend Michelle had been held once, but she refused to talk about it.

She said that getting on with life was like surviving being held captive, you focus on the moment and the next step forward. If you think about more than one step, it could overwhelm and consume you. She couldn't be consumed. Not now. She needed to get help.

The creaking shutters took her to the window. The large wooden frame and small perch beckoned to her. She sat on the ledge and closed her eyes against the battered emotions and bruised soul. The camp sentries were the only moving creatures. She opened her eyes and stared out into the expansive grounds. Small ashcan fires were burning around the perimeter, casting light and shadow on the surrounding building. She watched the guard for the house nuzzle a woman on the porch. The woman in his arms nodded toward Daniels and then pulled him by the hand around the side and into the shadow.

She couldn't believe he was leaving the house unprotected. With no time to waste she ran to the bed, grabbed her shoes and then slipped out of her window onto the wraparound porch. Careful not to go the same direction as the amorous couple, Daniels darted across the small courtyard, sidling up to a small garden shack.

Staying to the backs of the buildings, she made her way to the beach. Crouching behind a bush, she waited at the edge of the tree line and listened to the water lapping the edge of the shore. Taking a deep breath, she bolted from her hiding place and sprinted to the dock. Her feet grazed the wooden dock, her heart leaping for joy.

The blood pounding in her ears as she wrestled with the moorings of a small boat and the tight ropes bit at her fingers. Chips of wood sprayed up around her as the shot pierced the wooden pier, knocking her backward.

She didn't bother to look up or try to run, she knew she was caught.

"Get up!" the soldier yelled.

Daniels had never been one to accept the status quo and there was nothing about the current situation that was helping to change that pattern. She glanced up at the soldier pointing a rifle at her and laughed. She had to wonder if the stress was making her insane or if it was because she felt protected by Rajan, which was stupid because he was the one who had kidnapped her in the first place.

"Why?" she asked.

The soldier started toward her, and Daniels put her hand up as he jerked her upright. He shoved the rifle in her back and marched her back to camp. The camp was more active when she returned, more guards patrolling and glaring at her as she was escorted into Rajan's office and shoved into a chair. The soldier was muttering under his breath, but Daniels managed to hear the last part. "The general will finish you, and Rajan, as well."

Slamming the door, the soldier left the room and Daniels jumped up and began to pace. The silence was killing her and she jumped when the door swung open and Rajan stepped inside. He paused and stared at her for a moment before leaning on the edge of the desk.

"Look, I know you're treating me well and I should

be a quiet little captive, but I…" She dropped her hands and sank into the chair in front of him. "I'm not very good at following the rules, and being cooped up like a caged tiger got the better of me."

He continued to stay silent and watch her. She squirmed under the pressure of his gaze and started to stand again. Rajan reached out his hand and slipped it behind her neck, pulling her into his arms. His lips met hers and Daniels was stunned by the advance. She sunk into his kiss and his embrace for a moment and then shoved backward and away.

Rajan ran a hand through his hair. "My apologies, I should not have done that. I guess I'm not very good about following the rules, either."

Daniels stared at him, stunned and confused.

"Go on, Heather. Go back to the house and care for the children, but don't make my soldiers come for you again. I'm not always here to guarantee a happy ending."

THE MORNING SUN BROUGHT confused thoughts and little sleep. Daniels washed and dressed in a daze, running the night's activities over and over in her mind. She resolved to push it away and continue her routine with the children. They headed for the beach and she lost herself in the beauty of the island. The sleek blue water washed along the sand and Daniels sat watching the little ones playing at the water's edge. Shielding her eyes from the sun with her hand she tried to spot the two oldest girls trying to dunk each other in the deeper water. Spotting them, she smiled and scanned the closer area again, counting little ones as she went.

It all seemed normal and calm, with the exception of two soldiers with machine guns ready to mow them down if given the order. The children were why she was in this part of the world in the first place. Two of the five-year-old boys dug in the sand and filled the pots and pans that she'd retrieved from the main house. If history held true, they would begin their training when they were ten and by twelve they'd be seasoned killers. She couldn't let that happen; she needed to talk to Rajan.

Daniels took the kids back to the house, fed them lunch and tucked them in for a nap before heading back out to confront Rajan and plead for his help. She knew that there had to be a way to get to him without him getting the better of her.

The guard from the night before was on her watch again. She had tried to talk to him earlier, but he was the most inflexible of all her watchers. She waited for him to make a round toward the back of the main house and headed off to see Rajan.

The sentry for his office glared at her as she walked into the building. The offices were in a smaller house, but just as modern. The air circulated and whisked away most of the water that was beginning to pool on her skin. She walked down the hall and paused outside his door. She could hear him speaking on the phone and the conversation stilled her waiting hand.

"No, I can't clear the camp yet. Vengai will know soon enough. We have to wait to see if he has the device. The young soldiers are training well, but they will be completely Ocean Tigers if we don't move soon," Rajan said.

Her watcher showed up outside and began yelling at the office sentry. If someone else heard what Rajan was saying, they'd kill him. She tried to push it all out of her head.

She stepped inside to Rajan's stunned look and flattened herself against the door, pointing to the other side.

"I want to finish what we started last night," she said.

Rajan hung up the phone and glanced over her shoulder. Daniels's heart raced as Rajan stood. She kept gesturing to the door as she moved to stand in front of Rajan. She could hear movement in the hallway and knew they were going to try to cause problems again. She slid onto the desk in front of him and pulled him into her arms. Rajan needed no further prompting, pressing her back on the desk and sliding his hand up her thigh.

The door crashed open and her watcher barreled in with two other guards.

"The prisoner...oh, I'm sorry sir."

"Get out, you idiot."

"You said to watch her, sir, but she left the bungalow without permission."

"She has my permission to come to me any time she pleases, now get out!"

Daniels buried her head into Rajan's chest, trying to hide her smile. The door closed and she looked up at Rajan.

Rajan sighed and stepped away from her. "What is it you're doing here, my temptress?"

"Rajan, tell me what is going on. If I hadn't snuck

in here then someone might have heard you talking on that call."

"I don't know what you're talking about."

"Look, I'm not dumb and I need your help. I've got to get these kids out of here, all of them. They aren't ready to fight and die for a cause. They should be in school, learning and growing."

"Heather, you don't know what's going on here and no one goes anywhere. I have a job to do, and I'll send every one of those 'children' into battle if I have to. Now get out of here and don't think to say any of this to anyone. Do you understand?"

"No, I don't understand. I know that you're not the evil person that you want me to think you are, but I will go and play my part."

"Don't underestimate me, Heather. I'll do what I have to do to complete my mission."

CHAPTER NINE

Michelle Peterson was pulling on her coat to leave when the knock came on her door. Glancing at her watch, she swore under her breath. She'd promised Cooper that she'd pick him up at eight and they'd begin the process of tracking down Kabilan Vengai. Picking up her laptop case, she crossed the sparsely furnished hotel room and went to the door. She took a quick look through the peephole and didn't recognize the person standing on the other side, but his appearance screamed cop.

"Who is it?" she said, raising her voice loud enough to be heard.

"Detective Bryant, Capitol Police," he said.

"Show your identification, please," she said.

He held it up so that she could see it and she unlocked the door, but stayed put so he couldn't enter. He wore a rumpled suit and a tan trench coat that had seen better days about a decade earlier. His brown hair was in need of being cut. "How can I help you, Detective?" she asked. "I'm running late for an appointment."

"You're…" He paused to consult his notebook. "Michelle Peterson, Secret Service?"

She nodded. "I am. What do you need?"

"I need you to come with me, ma'am. We have some questions we'd like to ask you."

"About?" she prompted.

"Yesterday, you met with a woman named Chellam Nilani?" he asked, though it wasn't much of a question. "She had you in her appointment calendar."

"Yes, myself and a friend had a short meeting with her. What's going on?" she asked, wondering where this was going with a sinking feeling in the pit of her stomach.

"Well, Ms. Nilani was found this morning, along with her secretary, Myra Pepper, floating in the Potomac. Homicide." He flipped his notebook shut. "So you can see why we might want to talk with you...and your friend."

Thinking quickly, she said, "I'm happy to answer your questions, Detective Bryant, though I'm surprised the Capitol Police caught the case. Aren't you primary enforcement for Congress?"

He nodded. "As you know, Ms. Nilani was the executive director for a registered political action committee. It was decided that our involvement might be beneficial."

"I see," she said. "I was just on my way out to pick up my friend. Should we meet you at the D Street office?"

He appeared to be considering the idea of asking her to ride with him, but finally he nodded. "That would be fine, ma'am. What time can I expect you and...?"

"Matt Cooper," she stated, deciding that if that was the name he'd used with her, it was probably the name he'd use with any local police. "We should be there within an hour."

"Fine," he said. "I'll see you soon, then." He turned and went back down the hallway toward the elevator, while she shut and relocked the door. She immediately pulled out her cell phone to call Cooper, who answered on the first ring.

"Everything all right, Michelle?" he asked, not bothering with a greeting. She tried not to feel annoyed with him.

"Chellam Nilani and her secretary were found dead this morning," she said. "A detective with the Capitol Police was just here—I've got no idea how he found me—and wants us both to come in for questioning."

"That's not good news," Bolan said. "It's too close to when we talked to her to be coincidental. She was killed for talking to us or because someone believed she talked to us."

"But she didn't tell us much of anything," she said. "What's the point in killing her?"

"I don't know," he said. "But it's all connected to Wright's death, I'd bet on it."

"Let's not make waves with the Capitol Police," she said. "I know the chief detective over there, so let's go in and talk to him right away."

"Fine," he said. "Come pick me up and we'll go straight over."

"I'll be there shortly," she said, hanging up.

THE CAPITOL POLICE STATION lobby was filled with people when they arrived. Bolan found the dichotomy of clean officelike exterior compared to the cold matter-of-fact interior interesting. The reception area was sectioned off from the rest of the building by a large pane of bulletproof glass. A metal speaker allowed two-way conversation. They walked to the window and Peterson stepped forward.

"I need to see Detective Moriarty, please," she said.

The woman in reception looked down her glasses and then pointed at the number wheel on the wall. "You'll have to draw a number and then an officer will be with you as soon as we can."

Peterson pulled out her badge and showed it to her. "I think I'll jump to the front of the line. I need to see Moriarty *now*."

With a vague harrumphing sound, the woman said, "Why didn't you say you were law enforcement to begin with?"

"Because people asking for help from law enforcement shouldn't have to take a number," she snapped.

The receptionist glared at her as she buzzed the door open and Bolan and Peterson walked in. He was beginning to like her more and more, in spite of her somewhat cold exterior. She was passionate in her beliefs and, so far, had been willing to follow his lead. Now it was his turn to take the backseat while she took point. It would be interesting to see how she handled it.

On the other side of the glass, the Capitol Police station wasn't unlike many other police departments. Desks were stacked with reports long overdue and files in need of organizing. Suspects and witnesses were being questioned or led away in handcuffs. From the break room, the sound of loud, boisterous laughter from overstressed officers could be heard. They were only a handful of steps inside when a man he assumed was Moriarty met them.

"Thank you for coming so quickly, Michelle," he said, shaking her hand. "I'm sorry to bring you in on this."

"Detective Moriarty, this is my friend, Matt Cooper," she said.

The Executioner shook his hand and sized up the man standing in front of him. Moriarty was in his late forties, with silver streaks running through his dark hair and a solemn expression that turned to joy when Peterson walked in. He gave Bolan only a momentary glance before returning his full attention to Peterson.

"Let's go into my office," he said, turning and leading them through the maze of desks and cubicles to a glass-walled private office. Unlike most of his cohorts his desk was neat and clean, and there were no personal mementos that Bolan could see. He was either single and lived for the job, or he really separated his work and home life.

Moriarty opened a file folder that was sitting on his desk and fanned out the pictures from the crime scene. It was obvious that both women had been beaten and tortured before they were killed.

"I take it we're not suspects," Bolan said.

"Not at the present time, Mr. Cooper," he said. "While I don't know you, I do know Michelle and this isn't... She's not capable of this kind of atrocity."

"So, why am I here, Moriarty?" Peterson asked. "I'm sort of busy right now." She paused, then added, "And I'm not on duty, so how'd you find me?"

"It took some doing," he admitted. "After we real-

ized that you'd met with Chellam Nilani, I called over
to your boss, who told me you were on temporary
leave from your duties with President Daniels, but last
he'd heard, you were still in Washington. From there,
it was just a matter of tracing your credit card."

"I see," she said.

"Anyway," he continued, "you're here because she's
dead and I wanted to know about your meeting with
her."

Peterson considered her friend for a moment, then
said, "I hate to tell you this, but I'm afraid that's above
your pay grade."

His eyes narrowed sharply. "This is a homicide investigation, Michelle. Nothing is above my pay grade.
I'm the lead detective on this case, and I need to find
out if this was a random thing or if something else is
going on."

Bolan started to say something, but Peterson put a
hand on his arm, interrupting him.

"We'll tell you what we can, but some of what we're
working on involves national security and we won't be
able to reveal that right now."

"Fair enough—for the moment," he said, looking
as though an entirely different set of words were in his
mind before he shifted gears. "What's your involvement in this, Mr. Cooper?"

Thinking quickly he said, "I'm working as a special consultant with Michelle. Technical issues and
that kind of thing."

"You don't look like a tech geek," he replied.

Before that aspect of the conversation could go any

further, Peterson cleared her throat loudly. "What is it you want to know?" she asked.

"What was your meeting with Nilani about?"

"A person of interest to our…project…was killed at a fundraiser for TPAC. One of their volunteers."

"What was his name?"

"You must be busy this week," Bolan said. "How many other people were killed at fundraisers?"

"Wright. His name was Tim Wright," a voice said from the doorway.

They all turned to see a man standing in the doorway and holding up his CIA credentials. His short stature and well-rounded belly did nothing to lessen his air of authority. Bolan sighed and sat back in his chair and wondered what new twist was about to come their way.

"I don't recall inviting you into our conversation, let alone my office," Moriarty said.

"No one invites spooks, they just show up," Bolan said.

"My name is Borelli, and I invited myself, since I need to know why Ms. Peterson and Mr. Cooper are interfering in my investigation and getting my key suspect killed in the process," he said, moving farther into the room and leaning comfortably against the wall.

"Why were you investigating her?" Moriarty asked.

"Above your pay grade," Borelli said.

Moriarty's face turned from his practiced civility to red ire in a matter of moments. Cops hated it when the Feds butted in and hated Feds talking around them even more. Peterson tried to rescue the situation.

"Maybe if all of you could stop trying to protect

your egos, we could answer the questions that need answering and move on with our day? I have a feeling based on Mr. Borelli's sudden presence that things just got more complicated."

Borelli moved to shut the door, then turned and stared at Moriarty. Bolan waited to see who would win the silent game and was a little surprised that Peterson cracked first.

"I really don't have all day for this, gentlemen," she said. "We know that Nilani's political action group was funneling money overseas to terrorists that might or might not be connected to the LTTE. We know that Wright was a computer expert and we know that he's dead, as well. We also know that none of this is random."

"So the question is, who's behind it?" Moriarty asked.

"Kabilan Vengai," Borelli supplied.

"Who's he?"

"He's very bad news, connected, and not someone your guys are equipped to handle," Bolan said.

"My guys are the best, Cooper—" Moriarty began.

"At what they do," Peterson interrupted. "Look, we all know you have a job to do and that you guys are great at it. But we have a job to do, too, and frankly, we're better at it than you. We don't need anyone else hurt or killed, and the more regular law enforcement people get involved in this, the worse it will be. So for now, do what you normally do, turn up the heat on your sources and see if you can get us some information that will help, but let us take him down."

Moriarty thought about it for a minute and then

slowly nodded. "All right, Michelle. I'll give you forty-eight hours to get this Kabilan Vengai. If you don't, then I'm turning this town upside down. Three deaths in under a week makes us look bad and the media will be breathing down my neck once they realize all of this is connected."

"Glad we got that settled," Borelli said. "Now, if you don't mind, I'd like to borrow your office for a moment."

"You've gotta be kidding me," Moriarty said, getting to his feet. "It's my damn office."

"For a moment, if you please," the CIA agent repeated, holding the door open for him and making little "hurry along" gestures when he didn't move right away.

Moriarty slapped the file on his desk closed and stomped out of his office. He'd wanted a seat at the table, Bolan knew, and didn't like being cut out of the investigation. He leaned back in his chair and folded his arms, waiting for Borelli to talk.

"So," he said once they were alone, "tell me about the President's daughter."

"Now who's asking about things above his pay grade?" Peterson said.

"And here I thought you were in a cooperative mood. You do know what Wright had been working on, don't you?"

"Why don't you tell us?" Bolan said.

"Some kind of software programming for satellites," Peterson said.

"Ha! More like the keys to the kingdom. I won't bore you with the details that I'm sure you'll be hearing about very soon anyway, but if Wright's software works, what Vengai can do with that technology could cause a global disaster. This isn't a Sri Lanka problem or even a regional problem for Malaysia. This is a full-on disaster if he realizes what he has and figures out how to utilize it."

"Explain," Bolan said.

"We recovered some of Wright's work from his office. His software is a kind of hacking program that adjusts to security protocols on the fly. Very advanced. With it, Vengai could hack into any satellite in the world, including ours, and use them for his own purposes."

Bolan let that sink in for a minute, then nodded. "So he could conceivably launch weapons or get personnel files or anything connected to those satellites."

"Exactly," Borelli said. "This is far bigger than the kidnapping of Heather Daniels."

"We're not going to give up on Heather," Peterson said. "And we don't even know if he's the one who's got her." She didn't ask how the CIA knew about the kidnapping.

"Look, I don't care about the Daniels girl," Borelli said. "My job is to get this damn technology back at all costs. And I don't need you two cluttering up the playing field or scaring Vengai back into hiding. We don't know where he's operating out of for certain and if he disappears now, finding him in time is going to be impossible."

"He's right," Bolan said. "Getting this technology back is more important."

Peterson turned her gaze on him, and Bolan knew

in that moment that this mission was personal for her. If her eyes could shoot lasers, he'd already be on fire. As it was, she kept her voice low and even as she said, "I understand your point, Borelli. You've got your mission and I've got mine."

"Just stay away from Vengai and his people," he said. "You've already gotten my best lead killed."

Before she could speak again, Bolan shot her a warning glance. "Of course," he said. "We'll stay completely out of your way. We're running into dead ends, anyway."

Peterson looked as though she wanted to talk, but he gave her a faint negative head shake, and Borelli turned to the door. "Good, that's all settled then. Have a nice day." Then he stepped out and left them.

Before she could start shouting, Bolan said, "Not here and not now, Michelle. Let's go somewhere private to talk."

She wasn't happy, staring daggers into his back the whole way, but she followed him out of the building.

SOMEHOW, HE MANAGED TO put her off until they got back to his hotel room. By then, she'd worked up a pretty good head of steam, so once he'd shut the door, he just let her talk for a while, and while her voice rose to the occasional near shout, she kept the volume manageable. She covered a wide array of subjects, including the duplicity of CIA agents, the foibles of male law-enforcement officers, and wound back around to her general frustration with their lack of progress and the fact that the clock was ticking on Heather Daniels's life. All in all, it was a first-class rant, and when she finally finished, he told her so.

At first he thought she'd start up again, but then she caught herself, took a deep breath and then laughed. And laughed some more.

When it was over, he said, "Feel better?"

"I do," she admitted. "Thank you."

"You're welcome."

"So where do we stand?" she asked. "If we're not going after Vengai…"

"Oh, I never said that," he replied. "I said we'd stay out of his way. In truth, Borelli helped us immensely." He pulled out his handheld computer and began to set it up with the transparent screen.

"How?" she asked.

"Because if he's convinced that Vengai is responsible for Heather's kidnapping, then that's more evidence that we're on the right path. Now the question is finding him or someone who knows where he is."

"That makes sense," she said. "But how do we find him?"

Bolan launched his system and activated the program he'd left on Nilani's computer. "I hope we'll be able to do it with this," he said, tapping keys to allow him access to her desktop. An icon appeared on the transparent sheet and he selected it with one finger, then expanded it. "This is her computer. So let's see what she did last night."

He selected the icon for her calendar and brought up the date of their meeting.

"That's our appointment," Peterson said, pointing to the entry.

"And the only other thing is that one," he said. "The Capitol Hill Suites, 7:00 p.m."

"There's no name, Cooper," she said. "For all we know, it's where she was meeting her boyfriend for dinner."

"Sometimes, you've just got to follow the trail," Bolan replied. "It's the only lead we've got right now." He shut down the handheld computer and rolled the screen back up.

"Here's a question," Peterson said, her voice thoughtful. "What does Borelli know that he's not telling us?"

"What do you mean?" he asked.

"He's on the same trail we're on, everything seems to lead to Vengai, but how'd he get there?"

Bolan paused to consider it, then shook his head. "I'm not sure. All that really matters is that we find him."

"You mean 'her,' don't you?" Peterson asked. "The mission is still to rescue Heather Daniels."

"*Him* leads to her," Bolan reassured her softly. "Though Borelli is right. If Wright's software works, Vengai could cause global carnage. He must be stopped, too."

"There's a lot of ifs in all that," Peterson said. "*If* Vengai has the software, and *if* it actually works, and *if* he knows how to get it running... Cooper, there's no 'ifs' where Heather is concerned. She's real, and she's out there. It's my job to find her and bring her home."

"Then let's get to it," he said, heading for the door. He could appreciate Peterson's focus on Heather, but the truth of the matter was simple. Forced to choose between Heather's life and stopping Vengai from launching that hacking software on American satellites, he'd stop Vengai. No one's life, not even the daughter of a President, was worth more than the whole country, let alone the world.

Not, he thought, shutting the door behind them, that he had any intention of trying to explain that to Peterson.

CHAPTER TEN

The Capitol Hill Suites was only a few blocks from the Capitol Building. It was a ten-story building made of slate-gray stone that advertised for people planning to stay in the area for a long period of time—each room was a suite with a kitchenette and a combined office-living room space. A halfhearted attempt at updating the lobby had been made, with tropical plants, waterfalls and dim colored lights providing an ambience that seemed horribly out of place with the exterior.

Bolan and Peterson had parked on the street and gone inside, but before they could even question the clerk at the front desk, he grabbed her arm and yanked her behind a potted plant that was tall enough to shield them from sight.

"What?" she whispered.

"Look there," he said, pointing as two men crossed the lobby and entered the washroom on the far side.

"The same men who were in Wright's apartment," she said. "How do you want to play this?"

Bolan scanned the lobby, which was empty except for the desk clerk. "I'm going to head to the washroom. I want you to go over to the clerk, show him your credentials, and tell him that no matter what he hears from the washroom, he's not to call the police. Catch up with me as soon as you've convinced him."

She started to say something else, but Bolan ignored her and headed for the washroom, leaving her no choice but to back his play. There were times for talking and times for taking action, and this was a case of the latter. He couldn't let them get out of the washroom and back into the lobby. Out of the corner of his eye, he saw Peterson head for the front desk.

The washroom was on the far side of the lobby, on the back side of a screening wall. He slipped through the door and saw that the two men were standing at the sinks, washing their hands and talking in what sounded like their native Tamil. Bolan knew that in this scenario, his best ally was speed and surprise.

He stepped quickly and quietly behind the closer man. For a split second their eyes met in the mirror, and Bolan saw that he remembered him. By then it was too late. The soldier wrapped his left arm around his target's throat and grabbed his head with his right. He twisted violently, snapping the man's neck with a loud popping sound, even as the second man spun and closed in, shouting.

A straight-on snap kick to the chest pushed the second man back several feet. He slipped on the tile and staggered backward into a stall. Bolan stepped over the dead man on the floor, closing the distance fast. He tried a strike to the face, but the man dodged sideways then stepped around him, grappling him from behind and trying to choke the life out of him.

The Executioner spun and shoved his feet against the wall of the stall, feeling the opposite one give way behind them. They smashed into the next stall, and

Bolan slammed an elbow backward, once, twice, and on the third time, felt the man let go of him.

Bolan twisted, got inside and drove a solid right to his opponent's solar plexus, then grabbed him by the shoulders and shoved him through the stall door and back out onto the floor. The slick tile surface allowed him to slide and scramble to his feet, but not before Bolan could kick him several times. The man somehow got to his feet, but didn't see that behind him, Peterson had entered the washroom.

Using the grip of her handgun, she hit him once, hard, at the base of the skull and he went down in a heap. "Well-timed," Bolan said, catching his breath.

"You were making enough noise in here to wake the dead," she said, looking at the carnage in the washroom. "Is that one...?"

"Dead?" he asked. "Yeah. We only need one."

"Let's hope you picked the one who knows something," she said.

"I picked the one who wasn't close enough to kill," he replied. "Let's get him tied up. Go find something that will work for that."

Obviously disturbed, Peterson nodded brusquely and stepped out of the washroom. Bolan pushed the dead man's body out of the way, then moved the unconscious man closer to the urinals.

Peterson returned a moment later with a large roll of duct tape. "I found this in the utility closet," she said, tossing it his way.

"That'll do," he said. "Take his other arm."

Peterson held one arm, while he held the other, taping them both around the cold metal flushing mechanism of the urinal. His head leaned against the bowl, and he was still out cold. Bolan shrugged and flushed the toilet. The cold spray hit his face and he started to come around.

"Why don't you go out and keep the clerk busy," Bolan suggested, "while I talk with our new friend?"

She shook her head. "No way, Cooper," she said. "I'm staying. Besides, the clerk is an illegal. I told him if he called anyone, I'd have him on the next plane back to his home country. He'll stay quiet."

"Let's hope you're right," Bolan said. He knelt and slapped the man's cheeks, bringing him the rest of the way out of his slumber. When his eyes focused and he tried in vain to move his arms, Bolan knew that he had his attention.

"I've got questions," he said. "You have answers. You'll give them to me or this is going to turn unpleasant."

The man spit in his face, then muttered what Bolan assumed was a swearword.

Wiping the spittle off his cheek, the soldier nodded. "Unpleasant it is," he said, rising to his feet. His foot lashed out, smashing into the man's balls. He screamed, the sound echoing in the small, tiled space, while he tried to curl into the fetal position.

"One last chance," Bolan said. "Answer my questions and that will be it."

The man stared up at him with pain-filled eyes, then said, "Fuck you," in a low, choked voice.

"In a way, I sort of hoped you'd say that," he replied. He took the roll of tape and placed a strip over the man's mouth.

"Cooper, what are you doing?" Peterson asked, her eyes wide.

Bolan turned a hard gaze on her. "You were a spook once," he said. "You know how this works."

"That's true," she said. "And I believed in it, right up until it was done to me."

"If you don't want to watch, then don't. Go out to the lobby and wait," he snapped. "This is our one lead and I'm not going to play nice in the hope he'll change his ways in time to save Heather's life or stop Vengai."

"He'll talk," she said, "which he can't do with tape over his mouth. Just calm down."

She crossed the small room and shoved past Bolan, kneeling next to the man. It took her only a second to capture his eyes, then she began to talk in a very soft voice. "I was captured in Libya once. They held me for a long time. They did things to me, very bad things. I was tortured and raped in ways that you cannot imagine. You understand?"

He nodded.

"Good," she said. "Now you must understand this. If you do not answer our questions, I'll walk out that door and leave you to my friend. He's going to do things to you, very bad things. He will hurt you in ways that you cannot imagine. You understand this?"

His eyes were a little bit wider and he nodded once more.

"That's very good," she said. "Now, I'm going to take the tape off, and you will answer our questions... and live." She reached out and pulled the tape off the man's mouth.

"Better?" she asked.

"Yes," he said. "I... Thank you."

"You're crazy," Bolan said. "He isn't going to talk and you're just making this take longer."

"Just ask him your questions, you maniac," she muttered, getting to her feet. "You always go too hard on them and then they can't talk." Her back was to the man on the floor and she winked at him, offering a short smile.

Good, he thought. She knew the game they were playing. Sometimes, the clichés of law enforcement worked best, and "bad cop, good cop," often worked better than most. He turned his gaze to the man on the floor.

"Don't make her regret this," he warned.

"Just ask your questions," he said.

Noting the trickle of sweat on the man's brow, Bolan said, "Tell me where your boss is."

"You killed him," the man lied. "That's him, there on the floor."

"Don't lie, sweetie," Peterson said. "If he'd been your boss, you would've been talking already."

Bolan paced forward, faking his readiness to plant another kick in the man's crotch when he said, "No!"

"Tell me where your boss is," Bolan repeated. "And stop wasting my time."

"He already left the country," the man said. "Late last night."

"He was *here?*" Peterson stressed, unable to believe it. "In the city?"

Ignoring her for the moment, the soldier said, "Then why were you left behind?"

His eyes closed, and Bolan looked up at Peterson

who shook her head slightly. He returned the motion with a negative head shake of his own, before he reached down and grabbed the man's ear and started to twist it, hard. "I'll tear it right off your head," he stormed. "So tell me why you're still here if your boss is already gone."

Bolan noted that Peterson cringed and turned away from the scene. The soldier didn't like torture, and would go only so far. He twisted harder and the man let out a little half scream, then said, "I was to search Wright's apartment again!"

"For what?" he pressed. "You already got the hard drive."

"We...we might have missed something," he hedged.

"Sorry, I don't buy it," he said. "You already had the main component from his computer. What were you going back to look for?"

When he didn't answer, Bolan yanked him to his feet, knowing that the man's arm sockets would be strained to their limits. He slammed him into the wall, then shoved a forearm forward into his throat.

"Don't!" Peterson yelled. She started to move forward, and Bolan pulled his Desert Eagle with his free hand.

"Back off!" he snarled, cocking the hammer and putting the gun to the man's temple. "I'm done playing games with this guy."

Peterson stepped back, her eyes boring into the man's as she said, "Talk to him, for God's sake. Do you want to die?"

The man was now drenched with sweat, and Bolan leaned in close. "Last chance," he whispered.

"We knew that people were investigating us," he said, his words almost tumbling over themselves. "We were to make sure that there was no evidence left behind in either Wright's apartment or the office of Chellam Nilani!"

"Now we're making progress," Bolan said. "Where did Vengai go?"

"He has returned to our base of operations," the man said. "In the Bay of Bengal. With the software and the money from the girl's ransom, he will be unstoppable!"

"Where?" Peterson snapped.

A shot reverberated through the washroom, killing the man instantly. Bolan released the man and hit the ground rolling, even as the second shot rang out and ricocheted around the washroom. "Move!" he yelled, bringing the Desert Eagle up into position.

Somehow, the man in the doorway had been focused on him and not Peterson, who leaped sideways, trying to get out of the line of fire. The shooter adjusted, trying to take her out as the closer threat, and bullets shattered the tiles as she moved. Bolan knew he had only a microsecond before she'd be dead.

He fired the .44-caliber Desert Eagle twice from his prone position. In the small washroom, the sound was like a bomb going off. The first round shattered the gun in the man's hand, and the second took him center mass. He fell back through the doorway, dead before he hit the floor.

Bolan got to his feet, then walked over and helped

Peterson up. "We don't have time to get caught up in this," he said quickly. "We've got enough to go on for the moment, so let's get out of here. You can call Moriarty and have him come clean the scene."

Shaken, she nodded and kept her silence until they reached the lobby. The desk clerk was peering up from behind the front counter. "What do I do?" he asked them. "What happened?"

"The Capitol Police will be here shortly," she said. "Until then, do nothing."

He nodded his agreement so fast that Bolan wondered if his head was attached by springs. Together, they left the hotel and headed for the car. On the way back to his hotel, Peterson called the detective, leaving it on speaker.

She quickly filled him in on the situation and he said he'd head for the hotel immediately, but that he had a lot of questions.

"Save them," she replied. "Or call Borelli over at Langley and let him deal with it. That asshole didn't bother to share information with us, so I don't feel all that concerned about sharing with him."

"What didn't he tell you?" Moriarty asked.

"Vengai was here," she said, her voice clipped and short. "Right here in the city and we missed him."

"You know how the spooks work, Michelle," he said, "better than most."

"Yeah, I do," she admitted. "That's why I'm done talking now. If you want to run all this up the flagpole, go right ahead, but I'm operating under direct orders from President Daniels, who got mission authorization from the White House."

He sighed heavily. "Just try not to leave me any more bodies to clean up," he said. "It makes our statistics look like shit."

"I'll do everything I can," she said, then hung up, turning her attention to Bolan. She stared at him for a long couple of minutes.

"What is it?" he asked, vaguely annoyed at her gaze.

"That whole situation back there," she said. "How far would you have taken it?"

Pulling to a stop at a light, he shrugged. "What are you getting at?"

"Would you have tortured that man—really tortured him—for information?"

"Does it matter?" he asked. "We got what we needed. We know Vengai has Heather and the software. Now we just have to get over there and find him."

"It matters to me, Cooper," she said. "You're a ghost, and I want to know what kind of man I'm working with."

Bolan thought about her question for a moment, then said, "I'm the man they call who gets the job done." The light changed and he pulled through the intersection, keeping his eyes on the road. And left her to ponder what that meant.

CHAPTER ELEVEN

As Bolan packed his duffel bag, he watched Peterson pace the floor of his hotel room. Her frustration was almost palpable. "At least now we know who has Heather for sure," she said. "I can call my friend and get us a flight to Singapore right away."

Bolan shook his head. "I don't think that's our best approach."

"What? Why?" she asked. "We know who we're looking for and we know where. There's no point in delaying any longer."

"I agree," he said. "But these Ocean Tigers aren't just some little piracy operation. They're organized, funded and have enough men that Vengai was willing to leave two behind just to try and clean up the mess, knowing that it was possible that they'd be arrested."

He tossed his shaving kit into the duffel, then zipped it closed. "We're going to need some help, I think, if we're going to pull this off."

"What kind of help are you talking about?" she asked.

"Well, for starters, we need someone who's not officially connected. Once Borelli catches up—if he hasn't already—he'll be working on putting an operation together to go after Vengai, too. Most likely a SEAL team, once they've pinpointed his location. So, if we do anything through official channels, he's going to hear about it, and our mission will be over before it starts."

"Don't we have the same objectives?" she asked.

"We do, but not in the same priority order. Borelli would happily let Heather die, if it meant getting the software back and putting Vengai out of business."

"So would you," she accused.

"Maybe, but I actually care whether Heather lives, so my approach will be to do both objectives at once. He won't take her into account at all."

"Why not? If he saved her, he'd be a hero."

"I'm guessing, of course, but Borelli doesn't strike me as the kind of spook who wants to be a hero. His target is Vengai."

"Then what's our next move?" she asked. "Who do we go to for help?"

Bolan pulled out his handheld computer, dialed a number from memory and held it up to his ear. The familiar voice answered almost immediately, and he wished he could spend time with his younger brother—without endangering his life. "Johnny? Matt Cooper," he said, knowing that his brother would recognize the alias right away.

"Are you on a secure line?" Johnny asked.

"I'm not alone," he replied. "I'm heading that way, from D.C. en route to Singapore, and could use a hand with an operation. Are you up for it?"

"Sure," he said. "When will you be here?"

"I'll be wheels up within an hour, maybe two, and there within a couple of hours or so." He looked at his watch, then Peterson. "Hold on a minute, Johnny."

"How fast can you be ready to leave?" he asked her.

"Where are we going?"

"Never mind," he said. "Now, how long?"

"I just have to stop by my hotel and pick up my things. I can be ready to leave right after."

Turning his attention back to his phone, he said, "Meet me at the Lindbergh International Airport by five."

There was a long moment of silence on the other end, then Johnny said, "How the hell are you getting here that fast?"

"I have access to a new toy," Bolan replied shortly. "Just meet me there."

"I'll be there," Johnny said, then hung up.

Peterson was staring at him. "Who's Johnny?" she asked. "And how are we going to get from here to the West Coast in a little over two hours?"

"Johnny's a friend," he replied. "I've worked with him before. He'll have equipment and contacts where we're going that will be helpful." He slung his duffel over his shoulder. "And we'll get there on a special plane. I have a pilot friend."

"You aren't really quite what you seem, are you?" she asked. "Is the real you somewhere behind all the aliases and equipment?"

Bolan shrugged. "The real me wants to get going. Are you ready?"

She turned and headed for the door. "Always," she said. "Aren't you?"

AFTER STOPPING BY HER HOTEL long enough to pick up Peterson's things and check her out, they went to

Dulles International Airport and then to a private hangar. Along the way, her companion had placed a call to someone who obviously wasn't thrilled about his using the plane, but ultimately had to have relented when Cooper said, "Think of it as a couple of additional test flights. When it's over, your pilot will bring it back to Paris, and you can have all kinds of helpful data."

There was a brief pause, then he added, "Yeah, I know. I break it, I buy it. It'll come back without a scratch. Have Jean-Marc meet us there." Then he hung up and continued driving.

When he'd led her to the plane itself, she'd been almost slack-jawed with amazement. It was some kind of executive prototype jet. "Who do you know that has one of these?" she'd asked, as the plane didn't have any specific corporate markings.

"It's a prototype," he'd said, opening the door to the cabin and leading her inside. He introduced her in French to the pilot, Jean-Marc LaLonde, then offered for her to sit up front in the cockpit with them. A short time later, they'd received fuel and clearance for take-off.

She sat in the navigator's seat and stared out the window, trying to ignore the blinking instrument panel and the fact that they were traveling at a speed of over a thousand miles per hour. She was a rated pilot, but the petty distraction of a new aircraft—no matter how cool it was—wasn't something she needed right now.

She didn't like to admit it, not even to herself, that back in that hotel washroom, he'd saved her life. A part of her felt annoyed. She'd spent years working on not feeling helpless again, and yet her savior made her feel more helpless than ever and somehow safe at the same time. It wasn't like her to be so… She wasn't even sure what the word she was looking for was. This whole mission she'd felt out of kilter and in some ways, out of her depth. She tried to focus on the problem, figure it out, but instead found herself studying his profile.

When he turned to look at her, she smiled.

"What?" Bolan asked.

"It's nothing," she said. "Just…this will sound ridiculous, but you seem to be able to do anything. I'm serious. Who could come up with a plane like this at a moment's notice?"

"Well, I suck at synchronized swimming," he said, grinning. "I never got around to mastering it."

"I'm serious." She laughed. "I've never met anyone who made me feel so…incompetent."

"You're not incompetent," Bolan said. "This kind of situation is never easy. When it's personal, it's hard to think things through. And there are lots of things I can't do, but I'm good at the things I do well. Does that bother you?"

"No. Well, maybe. Yes," Peterson said, stuttering to a halt. "I don't know. I guess I just don't understand. I've seen you operate and I've never seen anything like it. You always seem to stay calm, you're never rattled, and you always know what to do next."

"I thought you didn't approve of my methods," he said.

"It's not that," she said. "I mean…maybe I'm a hypocrite. I've seen your methods used before. I've used

those methods before myself. But that was before…"
Her voice trailed off.

"Before Libya?" he asked.

She felt herself nodding. "Nothing's been the same since."

"Did you expect it to be?" he asked.

"I thought…I thought I'd heal," she said. "Be who I was before."

"No one who goes through something like that comes out the other side unchanged," Bolan said. Then he chuckled as a thought crossed his mind. "You sound a bit like Congress."

"I sound like Congress?" she asked. "I don't get it."

"Congress likes to delay funding needed military actions or sanctioning an operation until the problem comes home to roost. By then, it's more complicated and a lot harder and more expensive to fix. Then they throw money at a problem and hope it will magically go away, but once you're dealing with the problem, it changes you. You've been in the field, you've seen what it is and how it works, yet now you quibble about things that a fresh recruit out of Quantico wouldn't blink at. Why?"

Peterson thought about it. "I guess because I've been on the receiving end of it and I'm not as desensitized to it anymore. Maybe that shrink was right when he told me I should stay out of the field forever. That I just couldn't do it anymore." She caught herself then and added, "Not that I'm saying I want to back off this assignment."

The pilot, who couldn't speak English, tapped a

key on the console, apparently logging some data for whomever owned the plane.

"No, I don't suppose you would," Bolan said, "but maybe you should."

"I made a promise to President Daniels," she said, feeling a little threatened. "And to myself."

"It's your call," Cooper replied. "Just remember, Congress doesn't try to fix a problem until it has to. And based on what you've told me, you never really fixed yours."

"Yeah? You want to play shrink now, too? So what's my problem?"

"Whatever happened to you in Libya," he said, looking at her seriously. "You took it personal. It wasn't personal. It was just how the game is played."

"They tortured me, Cooper. They raped me. How couldn't it be personal?"

"Because it wasn't you," he said quietly. "It was your job. They catch one of ours, that's what happens. We catch one of theirs, and maybe we don't rape them, but torture happens all the same. It's not about the person, it's about what the person represents. It's not personal. Once you get that right in your head, the rest will fall into place."

She wanted to rant at him; a part of her wanted to scream. But another part of her, maybe the part that had started to heal, heard his words and wondered if they were true. At least, if they were true for someone like him. The man they call to get the job done, he'd said, that no one else could do. That's who he was, and in spite of everything, he was getting the job done. He was implacable.

Still, she felt a little resentment burning in her chest. "You sound heartless when you talk like that. No feelings, no remorse."

She could hear the bitterness in his voice when he replied. "I have feelings," he said. "But I save them for those that are worthy of them. You don't, and that's why you're struggling."

His point hit home hard enough that she spent the rest of the flight in silence, staring out the window and thinking about what he'd said. It was damn uncomfortable that someone she didn't really know could slice her feelings open that way. No matter who or what else Matt Cooper was—and it was hard to deny that a part of her felt strongly attracted to him—he wasn't gentle.

Just before they landed, she wondered if that lack of gentleness in him toward her was part of the problem, too. He didn't treat her with kid gloves, like a baby bird or a broken glass. He treated her like a woman and an operative. She hadn't felt that in a long, long time.

THE FLIGHT TOOK HALF the time that was normally needed to make it across the country, and they landed without incident and parked the plane and pilot in a private hangar. Grabbing her bag, Peterson waited until her companion opened the cabin door and lowered the steps to the ground. Crossing the hangar toward them was a man who looked like a slightly younger, cockier version of Cooper—over six feet tall, with dark hair and blue eyes that looked out from beneath a strong brow, and a square jaw. He was a bit more lean than Cooper, but the defined muscles beneath his shirt were still in evidence.

Bolan came down the steps with his duffel over one shoulder. "Johnny," he said.

The two men shook hands and then embraced for a momentary hug.

"Glad to see you're alive, old man," Johnny said. "I was beginning to wonder."

"No need to ever wonder, and I'm not old." He turned and motioned her forward. "Johnny, I want you to meet Michelle Peterson. Michelle, this is Johnny Gray."

"Ah, yes," he said, offering his hand. "Our friendly neighborhood Secret Service agent. Hal told me she was part of the operation you're doing."

"It's a pleasure to meet you, Johnny," she said, feeling no surprise at all that he knew Hal, too.

"Ha, you hear that, Matt? She says it's a *pleasure* to meet me," Johnny said.

"That's because she doesn't know you," Bolan said with a grin. "Now, where's your vehicle?"

Johnny led them to a nearby parking lot where he'd parked his SUV. He took her bag and his brother's, tossing them into the back, then tried to hold the door open for her. Bolan shoved him out of the way. "You drive," he said. "I'll handle the doors."

Laughing, the younger man moved around to the driver's side and climbed in. Bolan waited until she was seated in the back, then shut her door and climbed into the front passenger seat. "Let's go," he said.

Johnny drove with the confidence of someone who knew his vehicle and the road intimately, and seemed to time the few lights perfectly. Other than briefly asking about the flight—he had all sorts of questions about the plane—the ride was quiet and gave her time to think some more. One thing that crossed her mind was that Johnny and Cooper weren't just friends. They looked too much alike, for one thing. Forced to guess, she would say that Johnny was Cooper's younger brother. But if they didn't want to reveal that relationship for whatever reason, she didn't see a need to force the issue. It wasn't any of her business.

The drive to their destination didn't take very long, and before she knew it they were pulling to a stop in front of a gate. Johnny rolled down the window and punched in a code on the keypad, and the gate opened. He drove up a fairly lengthy drive that Peterson could see was designed for security. Hidden cameras that only a trained individual would spot were hidden behind rocks and plants. The house itself remained hidden from view until the driveway curved past a line of heavy trees, revealing a white, tiered structure positioned on a cliff overlooking the ocean. It was quite beautiful, and to her trained eyes, a fortress.

She smiled as she got out of the truck, taking her bag from Johnny. "You're expecting an alien invasion?" she asked.

"What?" he said.

She pointed at the house. "I *am* trained to notice things like the cameras on the way in or the fact that all that privacy glass up there is also bulletproof."

"You got me," he said. "The aliens are coming any day now, but we're ready for them."

She laughed at his pretended innocence. "I like him, Cooper," she said. "He has a sense of humor."

"Try not to get infected with it, yourself," Bolan replied, pulling his own duffel out of the back. "In time, you'll learn to ignore it."

Johnny chuckled. "Same old Matt," he said. "He's got a sense of humor. He just doesn't like to show it." He turned and headed toward the door. "Let's get inside and I'll show you a little bit of Strongbase One."

"Strongbase One?" she asked.

"It's just a name," Bolan said, coming up behind them. "Let's get inside."

Taking his cue, Johnny keyed the code into the door, opened it and gestured for her to go inside. The main foyer was small, but on her left was a living room that looked as though no one really lived there. Black leather furnishings and glass tables with chrome accents, along with neutral pictures of the nearby cliffs and beaches were the only decorations.

"Let's get you two settled in and you can tell me how I can help," he said, shutting the door. "Michelle, go up the stairs and down the hall. Your room is at the end on the right."

"Is this your house?" she asked before going up the stairs.

Johnny laughed.

"No, it's just a place that's out of the way and gives us a chance to regroup when we need to," Bolan said. "Why don't you take a few minutes to get cleaned up, then we can all sit down and chat?"

Peterson found her room easily enough, and set her bag on the bed. She stepped into the bathroom, noting the perfectly folded towels and unused soaps. Splashing cold water on her face, she stopped and stared into the mirror, wondering about the strangeness of the mission and the two men downstairs. Johnny seemed closer to Cooper than anyone she could've imagined, though Cooper had struck her as a loner. Seeing him with Johnny made her rethink that opinion. She closed her eyes and tried to push the thoughts of being in his arms out of her head, but they kept resurfacing. She didn't want to feel anything toward the man, but his directness in dealing with her and how he handled himself were undeniably attractive. Shaking her head she went back downstairs, and found both men sitting in the living room.

"Did you find everything okay?" Johnny asked, getting to his feet.

"Yes, fine," she said, noticing that both men held a beverage. "What are we drinking?"

"Scotch neat," Bolan said.

Pleased, Peterson said, "Make mine a double," then took a seat on the couch.

Johnny crossed to the small bar that backed to the windows and poured. "Matt was just explaining the situation, but I'd like your take on it, too."

He returned from the bar and handed her the crystal glass. Inside, she could see the fine copper color of the Scotch whisky and smell it rising from within. It had been a while since she'd relaxed, and she took the opportunity to settle in a bit more, feeling warm and secure for the first time since the entire situation had started.

"I don't think I'll have much to add to what Cooper

has told you," she said, sipping on her drink and offering a nod of appreciation to Johnny. "What we know at this point is that President Daniels's daughter, Heather, who was doing missionary work in the Bay of Bengal, has been capture by a branch of the LTTE that are calling themselves the Ocean Tigers. At the same time, it appears they worked to acquire some kind of satellite-hacking software that is making everyone nervous, including the CIA. As you know, they have a real knack for taking the long view of things and not really caring who gets killed in the process so long as their mission priority is achieved."

"Matt says you want to go into Singapore, then look for her from there?" Johnny asked.

"That's the plan as I understand it," she said.

"Have you ever conducted an operation in that region?" he asked. "I hear that you used to be a field operative?"

"I didn't do much work in that area. I was mostly northern Africa and the Middle East."

"Singapore, really all of Malaysia, is a different deal," Bolan said. "It's a cesspit, and we're not going to be able to use official channels because the CIA is almost sure to hear about it and make the situation more complicated."

"So you've got to be sneaky," Johnny said. "I can help with that, but first there's something else we have to handle."

"What's that?" Peterson asked, curious.

"Dinner," he said just as the doorbell rang. "I hope you like pizza?"

CHAPTER TWELVE

After they ate, Johnny disappeared into the downstairs office to make some calls, while Bolan and Peterson shared a cup of coffee on the patio that overlooked the ocean. The sun had just disappeared, leaving trails of red and orange and violet behind in the sky. Gulls darted into the shallows, crying as they scooped up the little fish that swam, unsuspecting, in the water. The beach below was private and empty and for a long time, neither of them spoke.

Finally she said, "It's beautiful here."

"It is," he said, sipping on his coffee. "I don't get to come here often, but when I do, I try to take the time to enjoy this view at least once."

"Do you have a home, Cooper?" she asked. "A real one?"

"I have a place where I can unwind," he said. "I'm just not there very often."

"And your family?" she asked.

"I have a family of sorts," he told her, "but that hardly matters. I'm on the road a lot."

"It must be lonely," she said.

"It can be. Sometimes. But I've seen nearly everything the world has in it, the best and the worst of it, and I can say that I'm content."

She put her coffee mug on the table, reaching some

sort of internal decision. "I'd like you to come upstairs with me," she said, looking into his eyes. "Will you?"

Bolan looked at her for several long moments, gathering her visual beauty in with his eyes, knowing that she was broken in some ways and desperate to heal, to connect and feel again. He nodded, once. "Yes, but I—"

"Won't make any promises," she finished for him. "I know. Just take me upstairs, Cooper."

He set down his coffee, got to his feet and took her hand, leading her across the living room and up the stairs. He decided on her room, and once she was inside, he shut the door and locked it quietly behind them, then pulled her into his arms.

BOLAN DRIFTED OFF for a while, waiting for her to be deeply under. He came out of his light doze, smelling the fragrant scent of her hair and their togetherness, and ran a finger down her arm.

He sighed and rolled away, slipping quietly off the bed and pulling on his clothes. Then he slipped out of the room, shutting the door behind himself, and went downstairs. He found Johnny in the kitchen, brewing a fresh pot of coffee.

"I thought you were resting, Mack?" Johnny said.

"I was," Bolan said.

"Is that what you're calling it now?" he retorted.

"You rest in your way, I rest in mine, little brother," Bolan replied.

"She likes you, Mack, and she doesn't put up with your crap, either. I like her, but more importantly, I think you like her," Johnny said.

"That's the problem, isn't it?" Bolan replied. "It doesn't matter who likes whom. I've got a job to do and that sort of stuff just complicates things."

"Liking the woman you're sleeping with isn't supposed to be a problem."

"In this line of work it is and you know it. I can't be distracted thinking about her while I'm trying to do my job. Or worse, not thinking about her and letting her walk into a bad situation because I'm focused on my damn job. What I do and real relationships don't work, Johnny."

"So, what are you going to do?" he asked.

"What I came here to do. I'm going to leave Michelle here with you, where she's safe and out of the way, while I go and take care of this Vengai character and get back President Daniels's daughter, with any luck at all."

Johnny raised his hands in a gesture of surrender and shook his head. "Oh, no, Mack. You are *not* leaving me here to babysit her. You get to deal with the temper tantrum she's going to throw when you tell her that she's not going with you the rest of the way."

"I need you to do this for me, Johnny. She's stubborn, and she won't listen to me. Maybe she'll listen to you. Even if she doesn't, it's your job to keep her here and safe until I get back. More than anything, she needs to be off duty for a while."

"Didn't President Daniels order her to come with you?" he asked. "How are you going to explain it to him?"

"I'll have Hal handle it. At one time, she might have been a good operative, but she's lost her edge now.

She's slow to react and she won't make the hard calls when the time comes. If it comes down to a choice between Vengai and Heather, she'll choose the girl. She's better off here, mad, than over there and dead." He shrugged and gave his younger brother a grin. "Besides, you've got a way with women, right?"

"Yeah, well, I have a way with dogs, too, but you don't see me pissing one off and then expecting not to get bit."

"I need you to keep her here and out of harm's way, Johnny. I'll go in alone and get this done. It's better all the way around."

"Okay, Mack, but don't say I didn't warn you," he said. "When you come back, she's liable to claw your eyes out."

"That's just a chance I'll have to take. Just keep her here and safe."

"I'll do my best," he said. "You're heading out?"

"As soon as I can get to the airport," he said. "I never even unpacked my duffel."

"Take the truck," Johnny said. "It's got the gear you asked for in the back. I'll get a cab to take me out later to pick it up."

"Thanks," Bolan said. He shook Johnny's hand, then headed out to the driveway and the waiting SUV. The drive back to the hangar was quiet. He'd had a private word with the pilot, telling him to sit tight for a few hours until he returned. Wondering if he was doing the right thing by leaving Peterson behind, he considered the situation once more, then nodded to himself. The very fact that he was thinking about her and her feelings instead of what had to be done here told him that he was making the right call.

The pilot fired up the engines, checked his gauges, and Bolan saw that the plane had already been refueled. A call to Brognola had taken care of that, and the flight plan had been filed. The flight to Singapore, even with a jet that could travel as fast as this one, wouldn't be short, and the sooner he got there, the sooner he could find Vengai and take care of him, permanently.

And for missions like that, the Executioner was better off alone.

A LIGHT BREEZE FROM THE open window tickled Peterson's face. She stretched, but didn't bother to reach for Cooper. She'd felt him leave hours earlier. Part of her mind wanted to focus on what she'd experienced with him, if it had any deeper meanings for either of them, but another part of her knew that he'd been clear and, by leaving her to wake alone, he'd said everything without saying a word. It stung, a little, but she was also okay with it. For the first night since she'd left Libya, she'd slept without having a single nightmare. No matter what happened with Cooper eventually, right now, it was time for her to get back to work.

She climbed out of bed, took a quick shower and changed into clean clothes. Then she wandered downstairs and into the kitchen, where she found Johnny seated on a stool, sipping coffee and flipping through some kind of paperwork.

"Good morning," he said, rising to his feet. "Coffee?"

"Please," she said. "I didn't mean to sleep so late."

"That's one of the reasons this place exists," he replied, pouring her a cup and handing it to her. "To rest."

She saw that there was cream and sugar on the counter, and she helped herself. "Where's Cooper?"

"He left earlier to pick up some equipment. Weapons, I think," he said.

"Do you know when he'll be back?" she asked, taking that first heavenly sip. "This is good."

"Thanks," Johnny said. "He didn't give me a time, but I'm sure he'll call when he's on his way. How about if I make you some breakfast?"

"That's probably a good idea," she said. "Once we leave, who knows how long it will be before I get a normal meal again?"

"Good thinking," Johnny replied. He moved to the refrigerator and began to fill the counter with ingredients, whistling to himself. She picked up her coffee and stared out the windows. The view here really was incredible.

Johnny started whisking eggs in a metal bowl, and she glanced at her watch. She really had slept far too long. She wanted to get going. By her estimate, if she and Cooper could be in the air within the next couple of hours, they could be hunting Vengai by late that night. She strolled back to the counter and sat on one of the stools.

"So, tell me about Cooper," she said, noting his easy manner in the kitchen. A lot of men weren't comfortable in that space, but he seemed to know his way around better than most.

"You mean, tell you if he's a good catch," Johnny replied.

"No, I already know the answer to that," she said, laughing lightly.

"What's the answer?" he asked.

"That's easy, he's not. No one in covert ops is ever a good candidate for a relationship. Really, no one in law enforcement is good in a relationship. The kind of work we do creates a lot of trust and intimacy issues."

"So we should all give up and go home?" he asked. "My girlfriends will be heartbroken."

"Girlfriends?" she asked.

"I think of it as keeping my options open," he said. "But you didn't answer me. Are we doomed to a life of short relationships and one-night stands with people we can't bring ourselves to care about?"

She thought about it, then shook her head. "I don't think so. Our best options would be to save the real relationships for when we're done doing field work."

"And you're done, right, except for this mission?"

"Probably," she said, admitting it to herself for the first time. "I've got a permanent assignment with President Daniels, and it's a better life than what I had before."

"I imagine so," he said. "But just so you know, Cooper won't ever leave the field work behind."

"Ever?" she asked. "Why do you say that?"

"I know him pretty well," Johnny said, adding the mixture from the bowl into the pan. "Some people just… I think he's at his best when he's doing what he does."

"We all get older," she said. "He'll have to retire someday."

Johnny chuckled and shook his head. "Not Cooper. I hate to even think about it, but one day, he'll just disappear and all of us will know he's gone and cashed in his ticket somewhere. He'll die a warrior's death."

Peterson shuddered, trying to imagine viewing life through that kind of lens. "And you think he feels that way?"

"Yeah. I do."

"This is really good," she said, sampling the omelet.

"Thanks. Actually, I don't get to have a lot of company here, but when Cooper called and said you were coming, I stopped at the store."

"I know what you mean. Even when I get the chance to eat at home I'd rather order takeout and curl up and watch television, but that isn't a luxury that I get very often."

They finished their meals and Peterson helped him with the dishes. He made light, inane chatter, and she looked at her watch again, realizing that the window of time she wanted to leave in was long gone. She looked up and saw that Johnny was watching her carefully. And then she knew.

"That son of a bitch left me here!"

"Now, Michelle..." Johnny began, backing away from her and holding his hands up. "It's not what it looks like."

"You ass!" she snarled. "It's exactly what it looks like and you *helped* him. Did he even have things that he needed to pick up from you or was that just another lie?"

"He had things…" Johnny hedged, then tried again. "It was important to him to come here."

"He needed to get rid of me," she said, understanding suddenly.

She stomped out of the kitchen and back to her room, where she grabbed her ready bag off the bed. Johnny met her at the bottom of the stairs.

"Michelle, it's not like that. He's trying to keep you safe."

"Doesn't think a woman can do the job? We're good enough to bed, but not good enough to fight?"

"Hey!" Johnny shouted. "He likes the women he cares for alive, and if you knew him better, you'd never say those things about him. If he didn't care about you, he'd have let you come along and die all on your own out there."

"Well, I guess he'll just have to be disappointed," she said, heading for the door.

"There's no point in going out to the airfield," Johnny said. "He took off hours ago."

"I already guessed that!"

"Then, where are you going?" he asked. "Look, Cooper knows his business. He'll get the mission done. Why not stay here for a few days, catch some rest and let him do his job?"

"His job?" she asked, seething. "What about my job, asshole? Did you ever think about that? Did he?" She stepped closer. "Now give me your car keys."

"What?" he asked. "Where do you think you're going?"

"If Cooper went to Singapore, then I'll go to Port

Blair. That's closer to where Heather disappeared, anyway."

"It's a damn suicide mission for one person," he said. "Especially someone who hasn't been in the field. You're not mission-ready for an operation like this!"

Peterson dropped her bag, spun and caught him off guard with a back spin kick to his chest. The force was enough to knock him backward right onto his butt. Johnny started to get up, but she was on top of him before he had a chance to get very far, and she landed a solid punch to his jaw, knocking him unconscious.

"I'll show you ready, you jerk," she muttered. She didn't find any keys in his pocket and when she looked out front, she saw that his SUV was gone. Running through the kitchen and into the garage, she found another vehicle parked inside, a nice sporty sedan. The keys were hanging on the wallboard next to the door.

She grabbed them, hit the button to open the garage and climbed in. With or without Cooper, she was going to rescue Heather Daniels.

CHAPTER THIRTEEN

Peterson had an initial plan in mind when she pulled onto the highway, but to pull it off, she was going to need some help. It would take her at least a half hour to an hour to get where she was going, depending on traffic. She hit a speed-dial button on her cell phone, leaving it on speaker.

Two rings in, and President Daniels answered. "Michelle, tell me you have good news," he said.

"I'm making progress, sir, but I've run into a snag," she said.

"What's the problem?" he asked.

"The operative provided by Hal Brognola ditched me in California."

"California," he replied. "What are you doing there?"

"It's a long story, sir," she said.

"I'm hearing out of Langley that you and Cooper left some bodies behind in D.C., and one incredibly angry CIA agent," he said. "There's some pushback, so give me the short version."

She filled him in as quickly as she could on how she was following the trail of Vengai and that Borelli had left out the information that the man they wanted was actually in the city.

"At this point, sir, I need your authorization to

finish this mission alone and a path to requisition resources as I need them."

"I can arrange that, Michelle. You'll get what you need. Run it through Bill Philips at the White House, under the name Operation Hatchling," President Daniels said. "They're covering for this and helping me deal with Langley."

"Thank you, sir," she said, speeding up to make it through a yellow light. "I'll call with an update as soon as I have more."

"Where are you headed next?" he asked.

"I'm going after Heather, sir," she said. "So somewhere in the Bay of Bengal. I'll arrange transport once I'm in the region."

"Very well," he said. "I'll get ahold of Hal and let him have it. I gave specific orders, and I expected them to be followed."

"There's no need for that, sir. I'll take care of him personally."

"If that's how you want to play it," he said. "Still, I'll inform Hal that his man has gone off plan. Usually the man is rock solid. Keep me updated, Michelle."

"I will, sir, and thank you," she said, disconnecting. She had to stop at the next light and used the delay to scroll through her contacts. She found the listing she wanted and hit the send key to make the call.

"Coronado, flight ops," a male voice said.

"Michelle Peterson, Secret Service, for Commander Connelly," she said.

"One moment, ma'am," he replied. She waited on hold, then heard the beep of the call being transferred.

"Michelle!" Connelly's familiar voice said when he answered. "This is a surprise."

"I know, Pat, sorry to interrupt your day," she said.

"Not at all, it's good to hear from you. How's—"

"I don't have time for chitchat, Pat," she interrupted. "I need you to get me on a transport."

"Where to?" he asked.

She thought quickly. "Port Blair."

"Veer Savarkar? That's a tall order, Michelle," he said. "You know I can't get you out of the country without orders."

"Will White House authorization do it?"

"Of course," he said. "Do you have a point of contact?"

She gave him the information on who to contact and the name of the operation.

"I'll get on it right now," he said. "How soon can you be here?"

"I'm on my way now, Pat. Maybe thirty minutes out."

"All right. Let me make some calls. I'll authorize your entrance at the gate."

"Thanks, Pat," she said. "I owe you one."

"Only if I can pull this off," he replied, then hung up.

She drove in silence for ten minutes, still seething that Cooper had played her in that way. She'd thought he was treating her as an equal, but now she realized that he'd been humoring her until he could find a convenient way to ditch her. When she saw him again— and she would—she planned on doing her level best to kick his arrogant ass. Just imagining it gave her a sense of satisfaction, but the images also reminded her of being with him the night before. She shook her head, not allowing herself to fall into the trap of thinking that what happened between them made any difference at all.

She took the exit to the Coronado Naval Amphibious Base just as her phone rang.

"Peterson," she said, not recognizing the number.

"They don't teach you to kick and punch like that in Secret Service," Johnny complained.

"No, but they do in the CIA," she snapped. "You're lucky that's all I did."

"Damn it, Michelle," he said. "Come on back to the house. I need my car and we need to talk. I promised Cooper I'd keep you safe."

"I'm done talking, Johnny. I'm going to find Heather Daniels and bring her back home. I'm the only one that seems to care whether or not this girl lives or dies."

"We all care, Michelle," he objected, "but there are other things going on here, and you know that."

"Great, so Cooper can handle those other things and I'll get the girl. Sounds like a plan to me."

"You know I can't let you go," Johnny replied. "Don't make this harder than it has to be."

"I'd say that ship has already sailed, and Cooper was the captain. You're not on the hook for this, I escaped, remember. And Cooper is the one that took a detour on the plan. I'm operating directly under the authority of President Daniels. So, stay out of it. Good luck, Johnny." Peterson hung up the phone and pounded on the steering wheel.

"Of all the low-down, dirty…"

Everything about coming to San Diego had been about getting rid of her so he could focus on Vengai instead of Heather. Cooper was no different than Borelli. And somehow, no matter what he'd said, she'd allowed herself to think maybe she meant something to him. Instead she was just a bit of fun before he headed out into the field. A quick bounce on the mattress was all Cooper saw her as, the arrogant bastard.

Johnny had been spot-on. Relationships with field agents never worked. They were expert liars. Trying to put both Johnny and Cooper out of her mind, she checked in at the front gate of the naval base and was told to make her way to the airstrip and the parking area for Hangar 19. She parked the sedan in an open spot, left the keys in the ignition and grabbed her stuff, just as Commander Pat Connelly stepped outside and waved to get her attention.

She waved back, briefly wishing she had more time to spend catching up with her friend. He was a typical pilot, an inch under six feet, lean, with mirrored sunglasses and an ego the size of a tanker truck. He was also incredibly skilled and had been the one flying the chopper when she'd been rescued in Libya. They'd been friends ever since, staying in touch even when he'd left the SEALs and taken a promotion to work out here.

She tossed her bag on the ground and gave him a hug.

"Hey, gorgeous," he said. "You seem to have some pretty hefty connections these days. I've never had an unexpected flight request go through so fast."

"It's good to see you, Pat. You're still handsome as ever."

"And still single," he said, lifting his eyebrows up and down suggestively. "In case you wondered."

She laughed. "I didn't, but I'll keep it in mind. What have you worked out for me?"

"I got you clearance to fly out on the next Category I Red Cross flight," he said. "It's ready to leave whenever you are."

Her lips pursed as a memory crossed her mind. "I thought those flights had been suspended and the pilots didn't want to take them in."

"Most of them don't," he said. "But I will. I'm your pilot for the flight and you owe me, Peterson. Big time. These flights are a pain in the ass, and the landing strip there is maintained by angry gophers."

Peterson smiled, leaned in and kissed him on the cheek.

He grinned. "Maybe this will be a good flight, after all."

STANDING IN THE SMALL ROOM that served as his technology and communications center, Kabilan Vengai felt strong. His trip to America had been worthwhile. In spite of the complications, he had returned home with money, the new software and, most importantly, the ability to move forward with his campaign. Dilvan was already ensconced at his computer station, working on installing the software.

His second in command, Rajan, entered the room and sketched a salute. The two men briefly embraced.

"I just heard of your return," he said. "How did you find America?"

"Profitable," Vengai said with a grin. "The programmer did his job and developed the software, which Dilvan is installing now. As soon as it's up and running, we'll see how developed it truly is."

"That is excellent news," Rajan said. "You should be proud."

"I will be proud when we succeed in our aims. What news since I've been away? One of the men told me that you've taken an interest in the Daniels girl. Is that a problem?"

Rajan laughed and clapped him on the shoulder. "You know me better than that, Kabilan. She's an attractive woman. I saw no harm in taking some pleasure in her company."

Vengai nodded. "And what of the ransom?"

"It hasn't been paid yet," Rajan admitted. "Though I expect it to be."

"Perhaps it's just time to kill her and cut our losses," Vengai said.

"We would do better, I think, to put some additional pressure on her father. It may be possible that he doesn't believe in our sincerity."

"You could be right," Vengai replied. "Let's go."

They went into the main living room of the house where Daniels was sitting on the floor with the children. "You will come with us now," he said to her.

She got to her feet obediently and followed them to Rajan's office. "Sit," he said, indicating a chair. When she hesitated, one of the guards shoved her into it, and her eyes immediately went to Rajan. Vengai wondered if his second would have the strength to destroy his new toy.

"Miss Daniels," he began, "I trust you've found your...accommodations acceptable?"

"It's not the Fairmont in San Francisco," she said, "but considering the circumstances, I have no reason to complain."

Vengai laughed. "And yet, Rajan tells me that your father has yet to pay your ransom. I am not convinced he will, that it would be better to kill you and dump your body in the ocean. Rajan says that perhaps your father needs more urging to cooperate."

"I...he'll pay," she stammered. "He wouldn't just leave me here to...to die."

"We will call him," Vengai said, "and you will convince him. If he does not assure me of his intentions, then tonight you will sleep at the bottom of the bay." Vengai typed a code into his cell phone and then handed it to Daniels, leaving the call on Speaker. She tapped in the number and her father picked up immediately.

"Hello?" he said. "Who's this?"

"Daddy! Daddy, it's Heather."

"Oh, my God," he said. "Honey, are you all right?"

Vengai took the phone and punched the button for video and aimed it at Heather as he spoke.

"President Daniels, if you will accept the video feed?" he suggested.

"A moment," he said. "I never use the damn thing."

The faint sound of fumbling with the cell phone was followed by his tense voice. "I see her," he said.

"As you can see, we still have your daughter. She is

safe and has been well treated. Yet, you have not paid her ransom. Such a paltry sum for the safety of your little girl and you delay. Perhaps you do not care about her as much as she thinks you do."

"Daddy," Heather said, "they say they'll kill me if you don't pay them."

"You'll get your money," Daniels snapped. "It takes time to put together that much cash and get it moved. Most of my assets aren't liquid."

"As the former President of the United States, there is nothing that should be that difficult for you. I feel you are in need of some encouragement." Vengai nodded at one of the soldiers. He raised his rifle butt and swung toward her, but Rajan stepped forward and pushed it away. Then he backhanded Heather across the face, once, then again. The sound of his hand hitting her flesh would undoubtedly be clear, and the red bruises were in immediate evidence.

"No!" Daniels yelled. "Stop!"

"Oh, so you don't wish for her to be harmed," Vengai said.

On the video screen, Daniels's face was beet-red with anger. "You son of a bitch," he said, his voice low. "I almost had you in Washington. If you lay one more hand on her, I will never stop hunting you. Never."

"Ah, so those *were* your people in D.C. You should make better hiring decisions, President Daniels. I was in your country for quite some time, socializing, having dinners and leaving some gifts as mementos of my stay. I never got to meet your friends personally, of course. But understand this, Mr. President—I will not extend your deadline. There will be no extra time. If you do not pay, then she will die."

Daniels said nothing, just stared at the screen, which was unsatisfying. Vengai held the camera out to one of his men. "Show him this," he ordered, then grabbed Heather's hair and yanked her head backward, forcing an involuntary whimper.

"You have made grave miscalculations, Mr. President. Every day here is another day that this sweet, young skin is a temptation for my men. They are unused to being around such a beautiful young woman. So, let me assure you that if you have some noble notion of not succumbing to our demands we will take the time to find our pleasure before her death."

Vengai kept his tight hold on Heather's hair with one hand, while the other slid down to cover her breast and squeeze the nipple. She struggled against him, but he only laughed.

"Let her go, damn you! You've made your point. You'll get your money."

Vengai shoved her away, and she nearly fell out of the chair and into Rajan, who held her upright and forced her to look into the camera. The tears spilled down her face and the bruises from the blows Rajan had given her were beginning to darken.

"This is your last warning, Mr. President. If I do not have my money by the deadline, the next time you see your little girl will be a video recording of her being used by my men just before she dies." Vengai clicked End on the phone and laughed.

Rajan chuckled, too. "That should get his attention."

"Indeed," he agreed. "Take her back to the children."

"Yes, sir," he said. "Now that you've returned, I would like to move her to my quarters for...her sleeping arrangements."

The girl's eyes widened as she looked up at Rajan.

"Interesting," Vengai said. "I admit I was thinking that perhaps I would take a turn with her myself. You've been quite selfish from what I hear, Rajan, keeping her for your pleasure alone."

"She was my capture, sir," he said. "That's always been our rules."

"Of course," he said. "She is your prize, and perhaps we will get the money her father promises for her, after all. Just remember that if she escapes or is missing, you will take her fate upon your shoulders."

"Yes, sir," he said, grabbing her by the arm and yanking her to her feet. "Let's go," he snapped, pulling her out of the room.

Once he was gone, Vengai waved over the soldier Rajan had interfered with.

"As soon as we have the money, I will order Rajan to kill the girl. If he hesitates, you are to kill them both. Understood?"

"Yes, sir," the man said, saluting, then returning to his post by the door.

Vengai returned to the computer room, pleased to see that Dilvan's eyes were lit with excitement and his fingers were flying over the keys.

"Are you making progress?" Vengai asked.

"Better than progress," Dilvan said. "I've got everything installed and now it's just a matter of getting the satellites online."

"How long before you can get the program running?"

"It shouldn't be too long," Dilvan said. "But it will take a little time. As each satellite comes online, I have to run a brief communications diagnostic. It's important to get it right the first time, as some of them are linked together."

"Very good, Dilvan," he said, smiling. "Keep me informed."

RAJAN PULLED HEATHER OUT of the room and down the hallway. "Keep crying," he whispered in her ear.

She wept as he pulled her along and he wasn't certain that she would trust him after what he'd done. He'd known that it was likely that he would have to get physical with her in front of Vengai, but he hadn't realized how much it would hurt him to hit her. Still, better his hand than the butt of a rifle. That could have, and likely would have, done far more damage. He pulled her across the courtyard and into the smaller house where his quarters were, barking orders to the soldiers about being left alone as he went.

He continued his charade until he was inside his room, locking the door behind them, then pulling her into his arms while she cried.

"I am so sorry, Heather," he whispered. "If I hadn't hit you, things would have been so much worse." He pulled her toward the bed. "Come here and let me see."

He pulled her over to the bed and she sat with her face buried in her hands. Grabbing a cool, wet cloth from the bathroom, Rajan tilted her chin with his finger and pressed the rag to her cheek.

"You know I had to, Heather, or we'd both be dead. Please forgive me."

Heather jumped off the bed and moved out in front of him. Her face was tear-streaked and her eyes were red, but she was also in control of herself again.

"Okay, Rajan, enough is enough. Tell me what in the hell is going on. You're not one of these guys, I know it. If you were really one of them you would have let that guy use his gun as a club."

He sighed and waved her back down next to him.

"It's why I asked that you be allowed to stay in my quarters. I check it every day for listening devices. The truth is that I work with the Sri Lankan government. You would call me a spy. My job was to infiltrate what was left of the old KP Branch of the LTTE, find out what they were plotting and discover the most effective way to stop it."

"You're a...spy?" she asked, stunned.

"Yes," he said. "When I found out they were working on a plan to steal this software technology from the United States, my mission parameters changed and I had to stay a part of the organization until it was delivered," he said.

"That's what those guys are working on," she said.

"Yes, they've killed for it and now we have to stop it."

"So why are we sitting here?"

"Because the ties to the LTTE run deep, and I can't report until I know they have everything that they are after and how they plan to use it. Are you angry with me?"

"You beat the crap out of me, Rajan," she said. "I'm not what you'd call happy."

"I was trying to save you from worse. If they think that you're mine, none of the others will try and use you except perhaps Vengai. No one would be able to stop him if he wanted you."

"So, what's the plan?"

"Right now we must wait. Your father obviously has operatives looking for you, and I'll try and get information to my commander, though it's much harder to do when all of Vengai's technical people are here. I will wait until they are all busy with the new program. I am sorry," he said.

Rajan reached out and ran a finger along the side of her cheek and then started to move away. Heather reached out her hand and stopped him.

"I know you felt like you had to, Rajan. And I know that because of you I've been saved from so much. Thank you."

She leaned forward and kissed him. Uncertain of the advance, he gently cupped the back of her head as she leaned further into him.

"You're welcome," he said.

CHAPTER FOURTEEN

The Executioner's flight to Singapore was uneventful, and while the Changi International Airport was insanely busy, private flights like his were routed in to separate landing lanes to help control the congestion. The pilot only had to circle twice waiting for his turn to land, and once he was on the ground, he taxied to a private hangar that Bolan had arranged for along the way. He shook hands with LaLonde and thanked him for his help.

Bolan grabbed a cab at the airport and had the driver drop him several blocks away from Bashir Faizal's warehouse. He went the rest of the way on foot. The opulent buildings meant for tourists dropped behind him as he entered the warehouse district. Once, many of the buildings had been painted white, but black mold had stained them. Faizal was waiting for him when he reached the entrance.

The small man reminded Bolan of a bad adventure movie cliché—Faizal could have stood in for any sidekick known for his fast feet and scavenging ways. Cargo pants, wife-beater T-shirt with a dark brown button-down over the top, but open all of the way, white newsboy hat and a smile so wide it looked as if it might reach all the way around to the back. He reached out to shake hands, and Bolan immediately turned sideways to keep his wallet out of reach during the greeting.

"Cooper, so glad to see you made it," he said, grinning and pumping his hand enthusiastically. "I was beginning to wonder."

"You had doubts?"

"I always have doubts. That's what keeps me alive."

"You're smarter than you look," Bolan said. "What do you have for me?"

"Everything you asked for including this." Faizal pulled out an envelope with pictures and intelligence.

"Give me the highlights," Bolan said, scanning through them quickly.

"There's no light in this tunnel, Cooper. The Ocean Tigers are definitely connected to the LTTE, and they've basically driven all the other pirates out of the Bay of Bengal for the moment. There are a couple of exceptions, but give them another six months working this area and those will be gone, too."

"Charming," he said. "How many of them are there?"

"From what I've been able to figure out, they've been coming in slowly, a few at a time, joining the cause, but they're not coming on fast and strong because they know it's only a matter of time until they land on either Thailand or Sri Lankan government radar. Right now, there's enough internal problems that they aren't going to spend a lot of resources on what passes for the last straggling batch of a defunct terrorist group."

"That makes sense," Bolan said, studying the

photos. "So where are they based out of? One of these islands?"

Faizal shook his head. "That's the tricky part, my friend. No one really knows. They seem to be everywhere and nowhere in the water. They are operating with military precision to keep their raids going. The trades for hostages are happening fast and the boats they take are being either sunk or sold on the black market."

"The bay is a big place to search," Bolan said.

"Our best bet is going to be outside the Malacca Strait, probably one of the islands along the eastern edge of the Andaman Sea."

Bolan looked at a map of the region and nodded. "That makes sense to me, too. If they grabbed the girl between here and Port Blair, chances are they're working east of Port Blair, keeping it between them and Sri Lanka."

He folded up the map. "Let's go inside. I want to take a look at the equipment."

They headed into the warehouse, and Bolan's hand-held computer gave the tone for an incoming call. He saw the identification number and answered.

"Hello, Hal," he said.

"Striker, you have really pissed off the pope this time," Brognola said. "What are you doing?"

"You mean Daniels?" he asked. "He'll forgive me later. She was extra weight I don't need on an operation like this."

"Striker, he's still got a lot of pull in the White House. And a short time ago, he received a video call where he got to watch his little girl being beaten up and Vengai threatening to rape her. He's not in a forgiving mood."

"Hal, listen, I had to leave her behind. She was too emotionally attached to this thing. You got my latest secure update and even Daniels has to recognize that the mission priorities have changed. It's his daughter, we all understand that, but she takes a distant second place to letting a terrorist have control over our satellites, don't you think?"

Brognola sighed heavily. "Striker, you've got my full support. Hell, I thought it was a mistake to send her in the first place. Just…give me something, anything, new to tell him."

"I've got on-the-ground confirmation that the Ocean Tigers are connected to the LTTE. If you can make sure that word gets leaked about that to the different governments in this region, that will help turn the heat up a bit."

"I can do that," the big Fed said, "but they won't interfere until they have to. Sri Lanka is on the other side of the bay, and Thailand has its own problems internally. Do you have anything else?"

"Not at the moment, but at least we know the target now. I'll do my best to get the tech and Heather out alive. Reassure Daniels that it was necessary. If she's not back to him by now, she should be soon. I left her with Johnny."

"You've got a grudge against your younger brother?" Brognola asked.

"He'll live," Bolan grunted, ending the call just in time for it to ring again.

"Speak of the devil," he said as he answered. "Is Michelle giving you hell, Johnny?"

"I'm sure she would be if she were here, brother mine."

"What do you mean, she's not there?"

"She woke up, we had breakfast, we chatted, and then she realized what was going on and demonstrated how well the CIA trains their agents. She has a mean back spin kick."

"She beat you up?" Bolan asked.

"Yeah. Sort of. She plans on catching up with you and she's out for blood."

"I don't have time for this kind of distraction. How far behind me is she?"

"Forget about it, Mack. You focus on what you need to do with Vengai. I'll track down Michelle. As soon as I have ahold of her, I'll give you a heads-up."

"All right. Get after her and get her out of the region. She may be a badass, but she hasn't been in the field in a long time and these guys are the real deal. It's too personal for her. Stay safe, Johnny."

"I always do," he said, then hung up.

Bolan turned his attention back to Faizal, who offered him a quizzical look. "Trouble?" he asked.

"Nothing out of the ordinary," Bolan said. He hoped that Johnny would get to Peterson before she was wandering around the Bay of Bengal, looking for a fight.

Faizal had a small truck in the warehouse, in addition to the equipment he'd requested. "All right, Bashir, let's get this stuff loaded and back to the airport."

Working together, it took them very little time to

load the truck with the equipment: communications units, grenades, claymores and C-4 explosive, as well as extra ammunition for his Desert Eagle and rifles for them both.

Curious to see what Faizal had come up with, Bolan opened the small crate containing the weapons, asking, "What did you find?"

Bashir grinned. "British Enfields, the L85A2's with the SUSAT sights."

"Nice," he said. "Where'd you find those?"

"Poker game," he said shortly. "There's one there for each of us and twenty filled magazines, as well. I've heard that they're good out to 500 meters, but based on the design, I'd say closer to 400."

Bolan closed the crate and was just turning to tell Faizal it was time to go when several small pickups careened around the corner and blocked the now-open doors of the warehouse.

"Friends of yours?" Bolan asked.

Faizal popped his head out from beneath the canvas tarp covering the back of the truck, then ducked back in, disappearing in a blink. If he were to be a gambling man, then the smart money was that these were definitely *not* friends of his. Bolan held up his hands to show that they were empty when the men got out of the trucks with weapons drawn. There were six of them and they looked very, very angry.

UNTIL SHE'D FLOWN WITH Cooper from D.C. to San Diego, Peterson had never really given a great deal of thought to how slow some planes seemed to move. While Connelly was an excellent pilot and the Red

Cross flight was uneventful, from her perspective, it also seemed incredibly, irritatingly slow. The flight, with stops, took the better part of a day, and she wondered how long it had taken Cooper with his fancy, borrowed jet. When she did the mental calculation, she groaned. He would have been able to do it, even with stops for fuel, in less than twelve hours. Of course, Cooper knew that, which was yet another reason he'd ditched her.

By the time they were on the ground in Port Blair, Peterson was so tightly wound she could barely sit still. The clock in her head seemed to get louder with each passing minute. Still, she forced herself to take her time saying her goodbyes to Connelly, thanking him for the help and giving him a warm hug.

"I'll be here for a couple of days," he reminded her. "So don't be shy if you need a hand with anything, okay?"

"I won't," she said, "but honestly, I don't even know how long I'll be here. I have a job that I need to do and it will probably take me closer to Singapore."

"Well, I'll check in with you before I take off, just in case."

She hugged him again. "Thanks, Pat," she said before leaving him to his duties.

The Port Blair airport felt like she was stepping back in time. It was little more than a few simple structures, a limited staff, and minimal arrivals and departures. But with a relatively select group that traveled through the area, it was big enough to handle the basics well enough. The arrival of the Red Cross flight was big news and several people stopped to watch as the aid workers began to unload the supplies and gear they'd been waiting for.

Peterson separated herself from the group and made her way out of the airport. It wasn't far to the docks, and it felt good to stretch her legs after being cooped up in the plane for so long.

The sun was going down, and the boats were coming back into the port for the night. In spite of her exhaustion, Peterson knew that she had to try to find a captain that evening. If she waited until morning, it was likely that she would lose another day before she could make arrangements.

The first few captains refused to speak to her at all because she was a woman, but eventually the captain of the *Hermit* was willing to give her the time of day. Peterson was excited when she heard the boat was captained by an American, but her excitement dimmed when she saw him. Just under six feet, scraggly black-and-gray beard and clothes that she was certain he'd been wearing since the last decade.

"Hello, Captain. My name is Michelle Peterson and I have a proposition. Permission to come aboard?"

The captain didn't speak, but nodded, and Peterson jumped onto the deck. He turned and walked to the stern of the boat and she followed. He continued to repair an engine part that he'd been carrying in his hand, but glanced up at her expectantly.

"Sir, I need a boat to help me get to an island near here."

"This ain't Jamaica, lady, and these here islands around here ain't for sunbathing and drinking daiquiris. The men in these waters mean serious business."

"I'm not some wilting flower, Captain…"

"The name is Teach. Captain Edward Teach."

"Really? That's the name you're going with? Look, Captain…Teach, I'm not looking to cause trouble for you. In fact, I'm looking to get someone else out of trouble, but first I have to find her. Can you help me or not?"

"Can you pay?"

She nodded.

"This person you're looking for get mixed up in the Tigers' business?"

"Yeah, something like that."

"No wonder everyone's been turning you down, lady. Those Tigers, they don't just want a toll, they want the whole package. They've pretty well left the fishermen alone and we do the same in turn."

"Does that mean you're turning me down?"

He rubbed his beard and pondered the problem.

"I tell you what I'll do. I'll think on it. The fishing is bad this time of year, anyway. You meet me at the bar on the top of the hill there tonight at nine. We'll have ourselves a bite and talk about your proposal."

"Fair enough," she said.

"Just be warned. I ain't cheap."

"Fine. I'm not all that into charity, anyway. I'll be there."

PETERSON CHECKED INTO a small hotel on the island that had seen many better days, took a shower and changed clothes. What she really wanted was to sleep for about a week, but she needed to get this deal done so they could get under way in the morning. Her phone rang and she saw that it was Johnny Gray calling.

"What do you want, Johnny?" she asked, getting to the point.

"I want you to get your tail back to the States and let Cooper do his job."

"He can do his job all he wants," she snapped. "I'm going to do mine."

"Then let me come out there and help you," he said. "That way, at least someone's got your back."

"Yeah, that worked so well when I trusted Cooper. All I ended up with was getting stranded in San Diego. Listen, Johnny, I've got to do this." She paused, thinking about it, thinking about what had happened to her in Libya. "I *have* to do this."

"Explain it to me, Michelle. Why do you have to do this? You might be mad as hell at him, but Cooper is very good at his job. He'll find Heather Daniels and the tech that Vengai stole. There's nothing for you to prove here."

She knew he wouldn't stop badgering, and she couldn't talk about her reasons and the horrible events in Libya that were driving her. At one time, she could have separated it all out, would have agreed with Cooper and Borelli that the satellite software program that Vengai stole was more important than Heather Daniels. But that wasn't who she was anymore, and trying to explain it to someone like Johnny or Cooper would never work. She sighed into the phone. "I'm done talking about it, Johnny."

"God, Michelle, don't go out in those waters without some damn support."

"I'll be fine, Johnny. Good night."

Peterson hung up the phone and looked at her reflection in the full-length mirror. Stretch jeans and a sequined shirt gave just the right amount of sex appeal and the high-heel boots were the final touch. She tucked her snub-nose .38 into the top of her boot and a throwing blade into a special sheath on the inside of the jeans at the small of her back. One last fix of her lipstick and she was heading out to the bar.

She walked in and made her way across the smoke-filled room. Two prostitutes in slinky dresses stepped in front of her, and Peterson pulled out her government identification. The girls glanced at the badge and walked away. She chuckled. Her badge had no real authority outside the United States unless she was in a territory or at an embassy, but people respected it all the same.

Captain Teach was sitting at the bar sipping on a beer. He'd made an attempt at his appearance with clothes that were slightly cleaner and a little less wrinkled. The biggest plus was that he didn't reek of fish when she stood next to him. He rose and pointed to the seat beside his and waved the bartender over.

"What will you have?"

"Scotch neat," Peterson replied.

"Scotch. My kind of lady."

"Don't bet on it, Captain," she said. The bartender poured her whisky and set it in front of her on the bar. She slugged it back, feeling it warm her all the way down. "Let's get down to business. If you and I can't come to terms, then I need to find another captain before the night is over."

"I'm sure we can reach a...suitable arrangement, but why don't you tell me what it is I'm getting myself into?"

"Well, Captain..."

"Look, you can skip all the 'Captain' stuff. Just call me Teach."

"Still going to stick with the Blackbeard name, eh?" she asked.

"In this part of the world, it's as good as any," he said.

"Fine then. Teach. Just to be clear—you won't be 'teaching' me anything. I've got no interest in you other than the use of your boat."

"Well, now, I can think of another use that you might have for me."

He smiled over the rim of his glass as he raised his eyebrows in a clumsy flirtation attempt. Peterson knew better than to encourage him too much or she might find herself dumping him overboard halfway through the trip the next day.

"Look, Teach, I'm not here for a good time. I'm here to get a job done. A girl was kidnapped by the Ocean Tigers and I intend to get her back. I need you to help me find the island and stay anchored a safe distance away while I go in and get her."

"Trying to catch a tiger by its tail? Get it?"

"Yes, I get it, but what I need for you to do right now is to name your price. We can negotiate from there."

"You know what happens when a girl like you gets hold of a tiger? She gets eaten."

"The price, Teach, now, or I'll find someone else."

Teach finished his beer and took his time setting it back on the bar. He rubbed his hands together and then put one hand on the bar and the other on her thigh.

"What I want, honey, is fifty thousand dollars U.S. and you in my bunk each night we're out."

She leaned in, picked up his hand and placed it firmly back on his own leg. "How about twenty-five, and I let you keep your hand still attached at the wrist?"

He appeared to consider her words with some care, then shrugged. "Sure. I'll do it for twenty-five, but the bunk time is nonnegotiable. It's been a long time since I've seen a genuine American woman as fine as you wandering through here, except the damn missionaries, and they're so damn holy they won't even think twice before turning a man down."

"Then we're done here, Teach."

She stood and walked out the back door of the bar, then stepped into the half shadows near the wall and waited. If there was one thing that seemed universal the world over, it was the consistent presence of arrogant men who thought women needed to be taught a lesson when they crossed whatever lines were in their idiotic heads. She didn't have long to wait; Teach stumbled out almost immediately after.

"Hey!" he said as he spotted her. "You're waiting for me. Does that mean you changed your mind?"

"No. Did you?"

"No, but I thought maybe we could have a private conversation."

"I don't think so," she said.

She was prepared for the lunge, stepping sideways to grasp his arm and using his own momentum to flip him on his back. The ground behind the building was cracked concrete, and he hit it with enough force to rattle his molars. Mentally she reminded herself to look up her jujitsu instructor and thank him for the excellent training. Teach groaned and tried to roll onto his side. Peterson placed her booted heel on top of his shoulder and dug the spike into the nerve cluster there. His groan turned to angry spasms. She dug in further and then eased up the pressure until he stopped moving.

"Now, you listen to me, Teach. Tomorrow I'm going to go and find my friend. If I find you in the harbor when I get down there, you and I are going to start having problems, you got me?"

"I got it," he said.

"If so, then you've had a good day. You've learned something."

She turned on her heel and walked away. Teach didn't follow.

DECIDING THAT A FEW hours' sleep would be time better spent than trying to find a sober ship captain, Peterson waited until first light to head to the docks. In truth, she was desperate enough to consider stealing a boat, but she didn't want to attract that much attention to herself, and it wasn't out of the question that a confrontation with the authorities would eat up what little time she had to work with. If there was no one this morning, she would have to come up with a new plan.

The docks were full of the sounds of seabirds and departing fishermen, as well as the noises of crewmen doing their final preparations. Spotting a newer-looking boat sitting at the end of the docks, with the name *Mariah's Wish* stenciled on her side, Peterson headed in that direction. She walked to the end of the pier and stepped onto the deck. The boat appeared to be deserted.

She peered around the docks once more and made her decision. No one was watching her and this might be her last shot. She moved to the helm and began to look for the keys. Not finding any, she reached for the knife behind her back.

"So, you steal cars *and* boats. What would the President say about such criminal behavior?"

Peterson turned to see Johnny Gray standing behind her with a gun pointed in her direction.

"What are you going to do, shoot me?"

Johnny pulled off his sunglasses and she burst into laughter when she saw the black eye she'd given him during their last encounter. He put the handgun in a low-slung holster on his leg, then moved to sit in the seat next to her.

"No, Michelle, I wouldn't shoot you, but I'm giving some serious thought to tying you up and tossing you in the hold until I can figure out how to make you listen to reason."

She grinned. "I think you're just cranky because I kicked your ass."

"My pride's hurt more than my ass," he said. "In

any case, I've decided you need help and I need to redeem myself from getting beaten up by a girl. Cooper's already had some fun at my expense with that one. So, how about instead of me trying to stop you and you running from me, I lend you a hand?"

She considered the cocky grin on the face of the man beside her, then smiled in response. He was a hell of an improvement over Blackbeard, anyway. "All right, Johnny. What did you have in mind?"

CHAPTER FIFTEEN

As the men looking for Faizal moved slowly toward him, Bolan kept his hands in plain sight. If he was lucky, his friend would stay hidden in the truck, the men wouldn't bother to search it and they'd accept his word that Faizal wasn't around. In his experience, however, he was rarely lucky in those kinds of ways, and it was the random encounters like this one that made doing missions all the more dangerous. These men meant nothing to him, except that they were slowing him at a time when he needed to get moving.

"Any of you speak English?" he asked. "Maybe Russian?"

The closest of them stopped and said, "American, where is thief Bashir?"

Bolan shrugged. "I think he went for coffee."

"Don't move," the man snapped, raising his gun and stepping closer. In Thai, he ordered one of the others to search the truck.

The leader climbed onto the bumper and peeled back the heavy tarp, peering into the shadows. Bolan anticipated what was about to happen. The shot that killed the man startled the five remaining goons badly.

The Executioner stepped inside the reach of the man closest to him and grabbed the barrel of the rifle, yanking it out of his hands. Bolan reversed it, spinning it up into port arms, and caught the man directly beneath the chin. The stock of the weapon cracked his jaw and sent him to the floor of the warehouse.

Bolan dived toward the truck, while in the back, Faizal quickly accounted for another man, leaving three, who'd quickly taken cover behind the barrels and crates near the entrance. All three had recovered from their surprise enough to be shooting wildly into the warehouse, punching holes in the tarp and through the walls. It would only be a matter of minutes until the police arrived, even in this district, so he knew that they had to move fast.

Sliding on the floor, Bolan positioned himself under the truck, using the back tire as cover from one side of the entrance. The rifle was really no use at this range, so he drew his Desert Eagle and waited for a shot. It came a moment later when he spotted the booted foot of one man trying to peer around the entrance. Bolan fired, and when the man screamed and hopped into view, he fired a second shot, killing him instantly.

Faizal took advantage of the moment as one of the man's compatriots had started to step out to help him, and shot him in the belly. That one dropped his weapon and fell to the ground, too, clutching his bleeding abdomen and screaming.

"Where's the last one?" Bolan yelled, unable to spot him from his position beneath the truck.

"Yellow barrel at eleven!" Faizal yelled back, ducking low as the last man sought to escape.

"What a waste," Bolan muttered. He sighted on the center of the barrel and fired three quick rounds, the heavy ammunition punching through the steel barrel with no more trouble than it would have had with aluminum foil.

The man behind it screamed and jumped to his feet, and Faizal took him with a single headshot.

Bolan maneuvered himself out from beneath the truck, then popped in a fresh magazine, putting the other one aside in his rig for later reloading. Faizal climbed out of the back of the truck and walked quickly to where the wounded man lay squirming on the ground. He fired once, ending his misery.

"That one's still alive," Bolan said, pointing out the unconscious man.

"Leave him," Faizal said. "He'll live to tell his boss the story of their failure."

"Your choice," the Executioner replied. "Who are they, anyway?"

"Bad poker players," he said. "Let's get going before the police arrive."

In the distance, Bolan could hear sirens, so he jogged to the passenger side as Faizal climbed in and started the engine. He drove the truck out of the entrance on the opposite side of the building, turning into a narrow alley and then down to the main street. They turned into traffic as the police went by a block away, headed for the warehouse three minutes too late.

The drive back to the airport was quiet, and for once, even Bashir kept his peace. He wasn't a bad man, Bolan knew, but he was a con artist, and that sort of thing tended to make enemies for a man. He could only hope that they'd have no more trouble related to Faizal's other activities.

Once they arrived at the airport, Bolan directed him

to the hangar where the pilot and the plane waited, and the three men set about the task of moving the equipment from the truck into the passenger compartment of the jet. Since it wasn't furnished yet, it was just as easy to keep everything there—and accessible—as it would have been to store it in the small hold below the cabin. In less than forty-five minutes, they had the truck unloaded and parked behind the hangar and were ready to leave.

Once they were on the tarmac, the pilot radioed the tower and got clearance and runway instructions. Faizal was almost giddy riding in the fancy jet. "How long will it take us to get to the airfield in Phuket?" he asked, peering at the controls from the navigator's chair.

"Not very long," Bolan said. "We'll be up and down in less than an hour."

"That's fast," he said. "It sure beats taking a boat."

Bolan grinned. "I figure that the sooner we get you out of Singapore, the better off we'll be."

"Probably true," the small man admitted. "But I'm never boring!"

"Agreed, but on this trip, maybe you could work on that." The pilot got the signal to take off and pushed the throttle forward. They began to taxi down the runway, picking up speed. Once they were on the small island, Bolan knew that they could run into members of the Ocean Tigers at any time.

He was looking forward to it.

HEATHER DANIELS FELT as though there was a clock ticking in her head, second by second counting down how long she had left to live. If it weren't for the sudden surprise of Rajan in her life, it probably would have driven her mad. Instead, in those quiet moments when she heard those threatening ticks in her mind, it made her both angry and sad. So far, Vengai seemed content to allow her to continue to oversee the children, but she knew that he watched her constantly.

Every time she saw the sharp-eyed man examining her from beneath his hooded eyes, she wanted to run away. And as much as she wanted to be patient and wait for Rajan to finish his mission, she was beginning to realize that the technology he was after was more important than her life and that she was just as likely to become collateral damage when the two men finally faced off.

A discreet tap on the door was followed by Rajan walking into the bedroom they now shared. Daniels sat up on the bed, pulling the coarse sheet and blanket with her in an unconscious act of modesty. A part of her mind reeled at the events of her life in the past week. Kidnapped and held hostage, nearly raped, only to be saved by this mystery man who, against all odds, she was attracted to. And how, she wondered, could she be attracted to a man who could act the part of a vicious killer during the day and then be so kind to her at night?

"I have a task for you, if you're willing," Rajan asked.

"What can I do?"

"First, you can be positive. If you have faith in God, then be positive that He will protect you. If you focus on your fears, you will panic and I cannot have that happen at a time when I need you to think and act. *I will protect you, Heather.* If things start going really bad, I'll get you onto a boat and radio my superiors to have you picked up in the bay and taken to safety."

She took a deep breath and nodded. He was right. She had to let her faith be a shield. "Okay, done. What next?"

"This part, I think you will find, is more difficult. Today, I'm going to send you a signal, and when I do, I need a distraction."

"What kind of distraction?" she asked.

"Since Vengai has returned to the island, I have been unable to get away to contact my superiors. He is watching me very carefully, and I think he questions my loyalty. While he was gone, I was able to use the communications equipment in the main house, but that won't work. If I can get down to one of the boats, I will use one of the stored satellite phones to get in touch with them for instructions. Vengai is moving fast, and I think the time to act will be soon. Do you think that you can come up with something that will avoid getting you in serious trouble?"

Thinking she didn't have a clue what she could do, she agreed. At least it was something to do to try to help. "I'll come up with something."

"I knew that I could count on you. Watch for the signal," he said. Then he got to his feet and left the room.

After taking a quick minute for a field washing in lukewarm water, Daniels dressed for the day and joined the children in the main house. She was so thrilled to have something to do that she hummed while she played with them, but as the day wore on, she was having a difficult time coming up with ideas for a distraction that wouldn't get her killed. She sat next to the children at the kitchen table and watched as some drew letters while the little ones tried their best and ended up with alien-shaped monsters that vaguely resembled letters.

Still wondering what she was going to do, she saw Rajan step onto the front porch and glance inside. He held up five fingers, then disappeared. Daniels assumed that meant he would be ready in five minutes. Or maybe he needed a five-minute distraction. She didn't know for sure what he meant, only that the time for her to create something out of nothing had come.

Glancing out the back window of the house, she noticed the young couple that had become one of the more pleasant things to see on the island. He was a young soldier and she was one of the village girls who performed menial tasks such as laundry and cooking. They snuck away whenever they could, and appeared to be very much in love. Sadly, as they struggled to fix their appearance while simultaneously move back toward the front of the house, one of the guards she hated saw them and began berating the younger soldier.

The girl stepped forward, trying to defend him, and the older man lashed out with one hand, bloodying her lip. She ran off wailing, and the younger soldier, stunned, turned back to him with attempted retribution written all over his face. It was a fruitless effort, as the older guard gave him several quick blows and dropped him to his knees. Pulling a pistol, he pointed it at his head and the younger man began to babble and beg for his life.

All in all, it was a disgusting display, and Daniels wondered if she was going to witness a murder over something so purely wonderful, but eventually the older of the two relented and put his sidearm away. Taking a final drag on his cigarette, he flicked it to the ground and walked away. The younger man got to his feet, staggered and headed off to return to his post, no doubt thankful to be alive.

Daniels instantly knew what to do. Leaving the children to their letters, she grabbed a bottle of rubbing alcohol from the cupboard and slipped out the back door to where the cigarette butt was still burning brightly. She shook a few small drops of the liquid on the dried leaves and a small fire began to flare up quickly. Shaking the bottle again, she tried to create an indistinct trail. Then she returned to the house, shutting the door quietly behind herself and returning the alcohol to its place. Finally she resumed her place with the children and sat, doing her best to look as though nothing was out of the ordinary.

It wasn't long before she heard confused shouting, then someone yelling, "Fire! Fire!"

Daniels grinned as she saw the older soldier come running. The fire had moved to a small shed at the back of the house, and she had to restrain the glee that filled her as more and more soldiers came to put out the blaze.

Vengai was furious for the interruption. He was there almost instantly, barking orders and directing the chaos. She had to hand it to him, before he arrived there was a certain amount of confusion, but no one dared to contradict or question any of his orders. The fire continued for a good twenty minutes before they had the blaze completely under control and then Vengai turned his attention to the house.

He ran up the back steps and stormed into the kitchen from where she and the children were watching. The children instantly hid behind her and she shooed them out of her way, then moved to the refrigerator and took out a bottle of water. She offered it to him and he batted it away, knocking it to the floor.

"This was your doing, wasn't it?" he accused.

"What was my doing?" she asked.

"Don't play games with me. You started that fire." His eyes burned on hers and she saw tiny flecks of spittle at the corners of his mouth. A muscle twitched in his cheek.

"I didn't start the fire," she said, trying to keep her voice calm. "Why would I do that? I like this house and I would never risk the children."

Vengai paused thoughtfully and looked at the kids.

"Did any of you see anyone out there?"

"Soldiers," one little boy said.

"Which soldiers?"

"The one soldier kissed the girl, and then the other soldier came and hit her and then he was going to kill the young soldier."

"Did one of them start the fire?" Vengai asked.

"I don't know, but he's always smoking his cigarettes," the little boy said.

"I know who you're talking about. Careless. I

should kill him, but he's a good soldier." He turned back to her. "Perhaps you are not to blame, after all."

Rajan entered the front of the house and walked into the kitchen. "What happened? Did we lose anything?" he asked, out of breath.

"Where were you?" Vengai snarled at him. "I cannot afford any more interruptions!"

Rajan offered a short little half bow. "Respectfully, sir, I was where you asked me to be—waiting at the dock for the new supply shipment. They're unloading it now."

"Good." He spat, then turned on his heel and stormed away.

Rajan waited a moment, then took her hand. "Come with me for a moment," he said, pitching his voice low.

Daniels followed him out the back door, then paused long enough to have one of the other women go inside to look after the children. Together, they walked past the burned area and into the heavy foliage and trees. Rajan looked around one more time before he could speak.

"You could have gotten yourself killed for that," he said. "You took a terrible risk."

"It was the best I could come up with," she said, more relieved than she wanted to let on that she was alive. "Did it work?"

"Yes," he said. "I have new information, but we'll talk tonight when it's safer."

They could hear someone crushing through the jungle looking for them.

"Ah, hell," he said. "It's got to be Vengai, looking for us."

Daniels quickly pulled her shirt off over her head and Rajan unbuckled his pants. He wrapped her in his arms, then pushed her up against a tree, kissing her passionately. The nearby sounds of movement paused, and Rajan knew they were being watched. He continued to kiss down her neck and then Vengai showed himself.

"Rajan," he snapped, looking a bit wild-eyed, "save that for bed and when you're off duty. We've got work to do."

Vengai left the little clearing, and Rajan helped her straighten her blouse.

"Come on," he said, taking her hand once more. "We live to fight another day."

CHAPTER SIXTEEN

Bolan watched as Faizal guided the boat out into the Bay of Bengal. The sun was rising behind them, refracting on the water and turning it a fiery golden-red color that would have been blinding without sunglasses. The warm water and mild climate along with secluded beaches provided by the numerous islands brought people from all over the world. They'd just left the docks, and he'd noted the odd mixture of expensive tourist vessels, privately owned yachts and even rusted-out longboats that were miraculously still afloat and used by the poor locals. Still, it was a beautiful part of the world, and Bolan wondered again at how a place could look like a postcard on the one hand, yet represent such incredible danger on the other.

That's what the tourists in this part of the world, and many others like it, either didn't know or didn't want to know. The human dangers. Every year, in places like Africa or South America or Mexico, tourists simply vanished or their bodies were found floating in a cove or shattered in an alley. There was beauty in the world, but only a fool ignored the dangers around him or her. The Bay of Bengal was a haven for pirates, and the beautiful water caves that attracted many tourists were a perfect hideout for smugglers.

The bay was dotted with islands, some of which

were inhabited and some that weren't. While they had little hope of randomly finding the island where the Ocean Tigers were holed up, exploring some while they looked for signs of the organization was about the best bet they had. Bolan only hoped that they wouldn't run into any additional trouble from either other pirating operations or other criminal types. While Faizal was a very competent thief and a man of many talents, he wouldn't be worth very much in serious hand-to-hand combat. Oh, he could shoot a gun and didn't hesitate like many others would, but he was better at running and hiding—or shooting from the cover of the back of a truck—than he would be in a genuine combat situation.

They spent the morning with Faizal piloting them around sheer rock faces, while Bolan scanned distant vessels with high-powered binoculars for signs of organized pirate activity. From time to time, they would pull in to a sheltered cove and tie the boat up long enough to trek slightly inland, exploring the more promising islands or searching a sea cave, but the only thing they'd so far seen of interest was a group of women sunbathing naked on a secluded beach. Another beautiful sight, Bolan thought, but not one he was currently interested in exploring.

Under normal circumstances, being out on the water and exploring gorgeous islands would have been enjoyable. Now it was simply frustrating. By midafternoon, he'd had enough.

"This isn't getting us anywhere," Bolan said.

"The situation is difficult. There are many islands and the Tigers have done a good job hiding their location. No one I spoke to before you arrived knew where they based their operation out of."

"Pull into that little cove to the east," he said, pointing it out. "Let's drop anchor there."

Faizal guided the craft to the cove while Bolan pulled out a small metal briefcase. Inside, there was a satellite uplink that he could hook into his handheld computer. He plugged the device into his handheld computer and waited for the two to sync. After a minute or so, he cursed under his breath. Something wasn't right. The two devices weren't talking to each other.

"What's the problem, my friend?" Faizal asked.

"I've got no idea," he said. "Both units have power, but they aren't talking to each other for some reason. I'm not getting a live screen."

"Let me take a look," Faizal said. His fingers tapped along the keyboard, but he came to the same conclusion. Whistling under his breath, he removed a small utility tool from his belt pouch and began to unscrew the back plate of the satellite uplink.

"What are you doing?" Bolan asked.

"I'm going to fix it," he replied. "Unless you want it broken?"

"You know how do that?"

Faizal grinned. "Yes. I completed my undergraduate degree in computer science."

"I had no idea," he said, a bit amazed. "I knew you had a talent for..."

"Theft?" Faizal asked, removing the back plate entirely, then running a critical eye on the mechanisms inside.

"I was going to say 'borrowing,'" Bolan replied. "Just to give you the benefit of the doubt."

"I can do many things, my old friend. I just rarely do them all at once." Turning his attention to the connection port, he nodded. "Ah, here is the problem. One of the wires is slightly corroded and bent."

"Can you fix it?"

"Yes. It will only take a moment." Faizal retrieved a small leather bag from his equipment and opened it. Inside, a substantial variety of technology equipment was on display. He pulled out what looked to Bolan like a very small nail file, which he used to gently remove the corrosion. Then he used a miniature set of tweezers to coax the bent wire back into place. He screwed the device back together, connected them and immediately booted up the system.

"See? If only all our problems were so easy to fix, yes?"

"I have to put in my pass code before it will let you load the satellite link." He reached for it, but the little man grinned mischievously.

"No need," Faizal said. His hands flew over the keyboard and the icon appeared, blinking "Connecting…Connecting…" then, "Connected/SMFSAT1 online." He smiled once more, then handed the unit over to Bolan.

"How did you do that?" he asked.

"Ah, my friend. Does a magician reveal his secrets? Let us say that I've more recently turned my attention to 'borrowing' via the many opportunities available to a clever man on the internet, and skills such as that one come in handy."

"I guess so," Bolan said. He slipped on his earpiece and placed a call to Brognola. There was a small delay on the screen and the usual series of faint clicks as the signal traveled to the satellite and then back down to Earth before the big Fed's face appeared.

"Go ahead, Striker, we've got signal lock on a secure frequency. What's your status?"

"Hal, I need a little surveillance out here," he said. "There are so many small islands that we could spend the rest of our lives looking for these guys."

"What do you need?"

"Can you task a satellite for a flyover, say everything within twenty nautical miles of my current position, north and south?"

Bolan heard typing. "What kind of data are you looking for?"

"Infrared," Bolan decided. "At least then I can limit the search a bit."

"Aaron has a satellite online that can do it, but it's only going to be one sweep and then it will be out of range. I can also arrange for a spy drone out of India and see if we can get some hard target information, but it will take about two hours." "Aaron" was Aaron Kurtzman, Stony Man Farm's computer genius.

"Let's do that, then. We can start with the satellite images now, then work with what the drone picks up once it's available."

"Anything else?" Brognola asked.

"Nothing right now," Bolan said. "Thanks." He disconnected and then switched the icon on his handheld computer, allowing him to bring up the satellite images in real time. Faizal looked over his shoulder and sighed.

"I wish you had a larger screen," he said. "Then we could do visual overlays with the maps we already have."

Bolan removed the scroll tube from his gear and connected it, slowly unraveling the sheet until it was flat. Faizal whistled as it came online.

"See, we still have some toys the hackers don't know about," he said.

"Oh, we know…we just haven't found a way to… borrow them yet."

The satellite images began to feed in at a steady pace, and Faizal both watched the screen and consulted the maps he had at the same time. One of the islands caught Bolan's eye.

"What about that one?" the soldier asked.

"No," Faizal said, shaking his head and looking at the map. "That's a private island owned by one of Thailand's uber rich. All the hot spots are from party boats that he has coming in and out constantly."

"That would be a good cover for a pirate operation," Bolan mused. "Are you sure he's clean?"

Faizal chuckled. "I didn't say he was clean, but he's not going to work with the Ocean Tigers. He prefers to make his money the old-fashioned way—mostly drugs and prostitution—but it allowed him to get into the film industry, as well as music. He doesn't fit."

"If you say so," Bolan said, turning back to the images. Two islands in the range showed fairly large quantities in the infrared spectrum. It was impossible to tell what the heat sources were, but out here, the chances were good that it was boats and houses. There was little else to choose from.

"Those two look like good candidates," he said. "You have anything on them?"

Faizal shook his head. "Nothing. There isn't even a village name on the map."

"Then let's start with the closest one, and if that's not the place, we'll move on to the next."

"That makes sense to me," the little man said. He marked the position of the two islands on his chart, then returned it to the cubbyhole for storage, while Bolan stored the scroll screen and satellite uplink safely away.

Bolan pulled up the anchor and returned to his seat as Faizal started the boat's engines and guided them out of the cove and back into the waters along the coast. The wind was picking up a bit and the water was getting choppy. The boat skipped along, the regular thud of the waves sounding like an out-of-sync heartbeat. He reviewed the images stored on his handheld computer once more.

The first island wouldn't leave them a lot of room for stealth. The heat was concentrated in one cove and the shoreline on that side, and the other sides of the island were sheer, rocky cliffs. "Let's come in from the south," he said when they could see it in the distance. "Maybe we can find a less obvious way in."

Faizal guided the craft as directed, but there simply wasn't anywhere to anchor safely without risking the boat or themselves. If this was where the Ocean Tigers were, they'd chosen an easy place to defend.

Signaling Faizal to coast, Bolan trained his high-powered binoculars on the cove and the boats at anchor. There were no pleasure boats, but a number of heavy-duty vessels that looked as though they'd seen the better part of a decade of hard use. There was one newer boat that he was able to pull the name off—*Mermaid's Secret*. He punched the information into his handheld computer and sent it off to the Farm via secure link. With any luck at all, the ship's name would be in a database somewhere.

A few moments later his handheld computer pinged a return message. "Bingo," Bolan said, scanning the information. "That newer boat there comes back as stolen by pirates about six months ago. It was owned by a French couple and they were ransomed off, but the boat was never recovered."

"So, perhaps this is what we're looking for," Faizal ventured.

"There's only way to find out for sure," he said. "Let's back out a ways and come up with a plan of attack."

Faizal had just fired up the engines and started to turn the boat when machine-gun fire shattered the air around them. Bullets impacted the rocks on the cliff face above and shards rained down on them. Bolan turned to see three gunboats rounding the same blind corner they'd used to get a better view of the cover.

"Get us out into the open water, Bashir!" Bolan shouted as he dived for the weapons locker they'd stowed in the front of the boat.

Faizal hit the throttle so hard that the entire front end of the boat lifted into the air, nearly knocking Bolan off his feet. The pirates were firing wildly behind them, and two rounds shattered the glass of the windshield just as he dived past it and got his hands on the locker. He ripped open the hasp and pulled out the British Enfield L85A2 and slapped a full magazine into place.

The Executioner peered over the windshield and saw that the three vessels had separated a bit, trying to flank them. None of them were in better shape than the one they were using, but they were all running fine for the moment.

"Go left," he shouted, popping up fully and sighting through the SUSAT scope. The Enfield fired a standard 5.56 mm round, just like the original M-16 rifles used by the U.S. Army. He put the obelisk-shaped target on the chest of the man driving the nearest boat and fired a quick burst. From this distance, Bolan couldn't hear his scream, but he saw him flop over backward and the boat veer away from them.

"I guess stealth is out of the question at this point," he muttered, diving back down to the deck as the pirates opened fire once more.

Faizal had their craft going at full throttle, and the vessel was getting alternately hammered by waves and the insanely fast turns he was taking to try to make it harder for them to get hit.

"Why are you on the floor?" he shouted. "Shoot them, shoot them!"

"I'm a bigger target than you," Bolan snarled, jumping back to his feet. All three boats were now back in action, though the third lagged behind by quite a ways. Switching the selector switch to full automatic, he let fly at the nearest boat. The magazine held thirty rounds when it was completely loaded, and it took only a second to empty it.

His shots forced the nearest boat to veer away, giving him time to drop back down to the deck and grab a fresh magazine. He knew that they had to act fast. It was only a matter of time until the pirates either shot one or both of them, or hit the engine—or, reinforcements would arrive and make the point moot. "Turn around!" he yelled at Faizal.

The little man looked at him as though he'd lost his mind. "What?" he screamed. "Are you crazy?"

"Turn around, damn it! We need to make a run at them!"

Swearing loudly, Faizal pushed their boat in a tight circle, surprising the two nearest craft as he shoved the throttle back to full. "You *are* crazy, Cooper!"

Bolan got to his feet, a grenade in each hand. "Get us as close to the one on our right as you can!" he shouted, knowing that if the maneuver didn't get them killed, it would only be blind luck. He pulled the pin on the first grenade, and noted Faizal's wide-eyed gaze, then popped up like a jack-in-the-box and threw it straight at the pirate boat even as machine-gun fire tore through the air all around them.

CHAPTER SEVENTEEN

Vengai was pacing in his office, contemplating ways that he might be able to catch Rajan in whatever treachery he had planned before the man did serious damage to their operation. The problem was that Rajan had proved far too valuable a tool to discard lightly. Vengai knew that he had to be certain that Rajan was a traitor before he acted. Then his actions would be seen by the men as both necessary and just. It would also provide a good display of his power, thus minimizing possible future uprisings within the ranks.

He would have to promote someone, of course, but he would give them time to fight among themselves for the position. Still, he found the moniker Ocean Tigers fitting today. The heat seemed stifling and he felt as though he were locked in a cage. He could feel the sweat beading on his forehead and soaking through his pressed BDU shirt, and the muscles in his back and face were as tight as the skin of a drum. His plans were coming together, but everything seemed to be moving at a snail's pace. If he could've roared out his frustration he would have, but instead he paced and waited, waited and paced, for news from Dilvan that the software was finally online and working properly.

"I got it!" The shout coming from the computer room brought Vengai out of his reverie and his office at a fast jog. He moved down the hall as fast as decorum would allow, and the minute he entered, the ecstatic look on Dilvan's face told him everything he needed to know.

"You have it?" he asked. "It's working?"

"Yes, sir," Dilvan said. "Or it will as soon as we boot up the main program. The hard part is out of the way. Even the decryption code that Wright left behind required several different algorithms to unravel."

"Excellent work, Dilvan. How long will it take you to start up the main software sequence?"

Dilvan glanced at the screen and scratched his head. "The software will come online in increments. The first thing that it will do once installation is complete is go out and pull information from the different databases to update the information that's already built into the program itself."

"What databases does it look at?" Vengai asked. "Will it pull from Sri Lanka?"

"When the software is fully updated, it can look at almost any database that's connected to the internet, but I can modify the update parameters to have it pull from Sri Lanka as part of the first batch. That shouldn't take long, as the size of the Sri Lanka intelligence database is going to be relatively small compared to the size of the databases in the United States or Russia."

Vengai grinned and clapped the young man on the shoulder. "You're doing excellent work, Dilvan. I'm proud of you."

Dilvan beamed. "Thank you, sir. I'll get right on it." He turned back to his computer and started tapping away at the keys, inputting the update parameters to start with Sri Lanka, Thailand and Myanmar. When that sequence was complete, he'd add the closest industrialized nations, such as India, which would give him time to expand their internal database as information came in.

Vengai began to sit, but Dilvan said, "Sir, I can port the software interface directly to your computer. I know you value your privacy." He glanced at the sequence on the screen. "You should be able to access Sri Lanka Intelligence and Military in about fifteen or twenty minutes. If the system times out, it means the information is still loading."

"Thank you," he replied, then turned and went back to his office down the hall. Sitting, he waited for the interface to appear on his screen, while considering the best place to start his information gathering. As Dilvan had promised, it took only a moment for the user interface to appear with the message "Databases 1–3 downloading." As soon as the program flashed a second message, "Database 1 available," he did a search by name for known LTTE personnel. Vengai started by pulling up his predecessor's file. As he expected, the name Kumaran Pathmanathan indicated that he had been arrested and was now in custody at an undisclosed facility.

He continued to look up information about the other members and the activities of the LTTE and found himself surprised at the depth of the available intelligence. His own name, so far, hadn't even been mentioned in a footnote. He cleared the search fields, then ran a new one on his own name and watched as his picture—a very recent one—and a detailed profile appeared on the screen. The government had more information on him than he had imagined. The names of his parents, friends, associates and even the village he grew up in and other known men from the same village that could have possibly kept ties. The file was active and as he scrolled through he realized that the government knew about the Ocean Tigers and that he was the leader. There were even pictures of him at a pier in Singapore as he watched cargo being loaded onto one of his boats. The only thing that they apparently didn't know was the exact location of his island base, but there was a secondary security encryption attached to part of the data in his file.

"Dilvan," he called, raising his voice loud enough to be heard, "why can't I see this information? I thought I would be able to see all of the information."

A minute later the young technician came into his office and looked at his screen. "There are multiple layers of security clearance in the database. Wright's program automatically sets the clearance through to the local or regional equivalent of top secret, but there are layers beyond that." He tapped in a query, then added, "This appears to be a special-intelligence-level clearance. Just like in any government, they don't always want one group talking to another."

"Can you get me into it?" he asked.

Dilvan nodded. "Yes. I'll need to run the protection protocol against a safe cracker."

"A safe cracker?"

"A program that unlocks various types of encryption codes," he said.

"Do it quickly, then," Vengai said. "They are much closer to our operation than I would have ever imagined."

"I'll have to run it from my system," Dilvan said. "When that little padlock icon—" he pointed to the screen "—disappears, then the files will be accessible." He spun on his heel and returned to his office.

Vengai watched the screen intently. If Sri Lankan Intelligence was tracking them, it would only be a matter of time until they found the island. He wasn't prepared for a military action just yet. He didn't have enough men to fend off a full-scale attack, and the Thai authorities would cooperate. LTTE's reputation as a terrorist organization, however untrue it might be, would be the only excuse the world needed. Vengai knew that they were freedom fighters, but the world saw them as criminals. Perception was everything, at least until he had control over the satellites. Then perception wouldn't matter in the least and he could bring Sri Lanka to its knees.

Finally the padlock icon disappeared and he clicked on the file once more. This time it opened a secondary folder labeled "Field Operative Reports." Inside the folder were several documents. The first was labeled "Agent Profile." He clicked on it and found himself staring at an image of Rajan.

Words failed him. While he had felt as if Rajan was up to something, possibly a plan to take over the operation or to save that foolish Daniels girl, the idea that he was an operative for Sri Lankan Intelligence had never entered his mind. The man had killed people for him, kidnapped innocents and taken their ships for ransom. Was there any line he wouldn't cross? The depth of the betrayal was stunning, but it explained how he seemed to always interfere before Vengai's passionate zeal for their cause got away from him.

The only question was how much Rajan had told his superiors. What secrets had he given them already? What plans of theirs had he already sabotaged? Vengai's anger rose in his chest, as hot as any fire burned. He clicked on the most recent field reports that Rajan had submitted.

Vengai saw himself described as a methodical, paranoid dictator with narcissistic tendencies. The man speculated that it was only a matter of time until he imploded or was killed by one of his own men or an out-of-control hostage, but the element of risk in not stopping him was too great. His most recent report, filed by satellite phone, reported on the kidnapping of Heather Daniels and Rajan's intent to free her and the children on the island as soon as his primary mission was completed. He'd also added the details about the software Vengai now possessed and was awaiting his final orders in regard to its destruction or acquisition.

Furious, Vengai exercised every ounce of self-restraint he had to keep himself from picking up his monitor and throwing it across the room. As it was, he surged to his feet, kicking a wastebasket out his way and cursing up a storm.

One of the house guards poked his head inside the door. "Is there something wrong, sir?"

Taking a deep breath, he sat at his desk and held his head in his hands. The Sri Lankan government knew everything now. The only saving grace was that they were counting on Rajan to do things surgically rather than risking a full-out military encounter. The temptation to find and kill Rajan immediately in the courtyard was almost overwhelming. But that would lead to questions and the need to explain himself, at least somewhat, to his other officers. Dissension in the ranks was bad, but if they knew that he had allowed a traitor to get this close, they might turn on him entirely. No, he needed to catch Rajan in his treachery and the soldiers would rally around behind him.

The soldier, whose name he'd forgotten, politely cleared his throat. "Sir?"

He looked at the soldier, who'd at least shown sense enough to check if there was a problem and be relatively patient while waiting for a response. "What's your name?" he demanded.

"Katran, sir."

"Do you want to earn a promotion, Katran?" Vengai asked.

"Yes, sir!"

"Good. Then I want you to listen to me carefully and do as I say. Gather a handful of men that you trust to keep quiet, and take three boats. Go out into the open water and wait to hear from me."

"Shall I inform Rajan?" he asked.

Vengai shook his head. "He has other things to worry about, Katran. This doesn't concern him. You understand?"

"Yes, sir," Katran said. The soldier saluted, turned and headed out to obey his orders.

In the meantime, Vengai knew that he had to keep it together. Rajan and the girl would both die...together.

THE TEA WAS LUKEWARM, but Daniels didn't want to make a fresh cup. She sat on the sofa in the front room sipping on it absentmindedly while the children took a nap. Her thoughts were a thousand miles away, but what she really wondered was if her father planned on paying Vengai or had some other plan already in motion. It would be totally out of character for him to agree to pay that kind of money to a terrorist, but surely he would if it meant saving her life. She shook her head. No matter what he might or might not do, she couldn't rely on his help. She had to focus on what was happening right in front of her.

At that moment, Rajan stepped into the room and took a seat next to her. He presented a whole different set of problems that she'd never expected to encounter in this situation: love and desire. Even if they somehow escaped, what would happen to their blossoming relationship? It didn't seem likely that he would move to the United States, and she had no intentions of living in Sri Lanka.

"You're far away," he said. "What are you thinking?"

She sighed and set her tea on the table. "I'm thinking that we make quite a pair," she said. "And that I don't know where we go from here—if we go anywhere."

He laughed quietly and looked around to be sure they were unobserved before he spoke. "You'll get out of here, Heather, I promise. And when you tell people about me, they'll say that you have Stockholm syndrome."

"If you were my captor instead of my hero in disguise, I suppose that would be true." He ran his finger along her bruised cheek and Daniels leaned into his touch, trying to savor the moment while knowing that it would end.

"I can't tell you how bad I feel about that," he said.

"It's a vast improvement over a rifle butt to the head," she said. "No one else matters. I understand why you did it. Let's just get out of this alive. Somehow."

A little boy ran into the room, but paused when he saw Rajan sitting next to her.

"It's okay, Philippe, what do you need?" she asked. He was a cute little boy, but he never spoke, only gestured.

He grabbed her hand and pulled her along, Rajan following in their wake.

"What is it?" she asked, trying to figure out what he needed.

He held a finger to his lips, then pointed to the back window where two new soldiers had been posted behind the house. Rajan started forward, but the little boy blocked his path and waved them lower to the ground. Amazingly, a vent in the kitchen wall allowed them to hear what the soldiers were saying.

"I can't believe there's a traitor. Do you think that it could be Rajan? Is that why we were sent to guard?"

"I don't know, but I heard that little weasel Dilvan talking to Vengai and they've got the software working now and they've already brought a bunch of databases online. He says they'll have control of the satellites within hours. Once those are in play, there is nothing that will stop us."

Daniels and Rajan moved back into the house. Philippe stood motionless and stared at Rajan.

"Thank you, Philippe," Daniels said. She leaned down and kissed him gently on the forehead and he favored her with a beaming smile, then ran off to play with the other children.

"I think it's time we got off this island," Rajan said, pitching his voice low.

"I couldn't agree more," she said. "How?"

"I managed to secure a boat in one of the nearby coves, but I can't leave without that technology. I'd hoped to have orders by now, but we're out of time. I'm going to assume that I should take it, rather than just destroy it."

"Maybe it *should* be destroyed," she suggested. "Maybe no one should have it."

"I'm sorry, Heather," he said. "I...you know, I just do my job the best I can. It's not my place to make that decision, okay? Do you understand?"

She nodded. "Of course. I just think that anything that's so horrible Vengai wants it, is probably bad news. So what do we need to do next?"

"I need another distraction," he said. "A big one."

"I could start another fire," she suggested.

"I don't think that would work a second time. And we need something that will get Dilvan out of the computer systems room, too."

Daniels considered the problem for a minute, then offered up a grim little smile. "I think I know just the thing."

WHEN VENGAI LEFT THE main house to examine the newest supply acquisitions, Daniels and Rajan put their plan into action. While Rajan moved into position, she had to hope that men were the same the world over and no amount of loyalty toward Vengai could change that. Vengai had left one guard on the porch and Dilvan and another technician working away in the computer room.

Daniels walked to the front door, forcing herself not to look in the direction of the closet where Rajan was hiding. She had to have faith that he would be watching and listening carefully and that the children would stay in the backyard, playing in blissful ignorance of what was about to happen. She opened the door and the guard turned to face her.

"What do you want?" he asked. "Are you looking for Rajan?"

She smiled coyly. "I wasn't looking for Rajan. I was looking for *you*."

"Why would you be looking for me?"

Daniels shifted her weight from one foot to another and ran her finger along the cleavage exposed by her button-down shirt. She flirted with the next button and looped her finger around it, watching the guard's response. She flicked the button exposing more of her breasts.

"Some men," she said, pitching her voice to a seductive, low hum, "can get the job done, and some men…can't." She undid another button. "Can you?"

The guard licked his lips and grabbed her by the arm, pushing her back inside the house and past the closet where Rajan was hiding. She backed up and leaned against a table, pulling the guard into her arms and kissing his neck.

"Take off your clothes," the guard demanded, stepping back to give her a little room.

Daniels put her fingers on her remaining buttons and paused, eyeing his weapon. "As soon as you put your gun down," she said. "I don't know what you like, but I like a man who uses both hands on me."

"I...I..."

She finished undoing the buttons of her blouse and began to run her hands along her breasts, lifting them up, then reaching forward to pinch the nipples on each one. "Suit yourself," she said, shrugging. "If you want to sit and watch, that's fine, but I was hoping you'd participate."

The guard quickly set the rifle aside along with his gun belt. He reached forward and roughly kissed her. It took everything Daniels had not to push his hands away. He reached behind her to release her bra clasp. A part of her panicked. What was taking Rajan so long?

She knew she had to keep the guard's attention focused on her, so she did the only thing she could think of. She pulled him closer and began stroking him through his pants, using her other hand to pull his face down toward hers and running her tongue along the underside of his jaw. He groaned into her hair, and she could tell he was out of patience.

He started kissing her again, his lips rough and his tongue probing. Daniels couldn't take it anymore. Forcing back a gag, she pushed him away from her.

"So, you want to play hard to get? I can handle that." He started toward her once more, his hands outstretched, and she bit back a yelp.

Suddenly he stiffened and clutched at his back, his

arm twisting oddly as he tried once, twice, three times
to reach the source of his agony. He wheezed, sounding like a slowly deflating balloon. As he crumpled
to the floor, Rajan caught him from behind and lowered him quietly to the ground. A blade stuck out of
his body, jutting in at an angle.

"You okay?" he asked, looking up at her.

She nodded, her face pale. "It...I... Oh, God," she
stuttered. "I think I'm going to vomit."

Rajan stepped forward, taking her in his arms, then
pinching the bridge of her nose. "Take a deep breath,"
he ordered in a harsh whisper. "Three of them."

She did as she was told, and the surge of bile settled
back down.

"I'm sorry," he said. "I had to be sure his attention
was completely focused on you."

"I understand. Let's just finish what we have to do
and get out of here."

"This time it will be easier," he said. "Follow me."

She followed him down the hallway to the office.
"Just move over there," he said, pointing to the desk.
"I'll call Dilvan and there will only be one person left
to deal with."

"Don't...don't kill him," Daniels said. "Just...knock
him out or something. I don't think I could stand it."

He smiled at her and nodded. Pitching his voice in
an almost perfect mimicry of Vengai, he called out,
"Dilvan! Get in here right now!"

The young programmer's voice responded almost
immediately. "On my way, sir!"

Daniels heard the quick patter of his footsteps in
the hallway, then he stuck his head around the door

and paused in confusion when he saw her. "Sir..." he started to say, looking around just in time to catch Rajan's punch with his face. He sagged to his knees, looking up at the man with the bleary gaze of a drunk.

Surveying his work with a rather critical eye, Rajan aimed carefully, then hit the younger man once more. This time, he went out like the proverbial light. Rajan dragged his body into the small storage closet in the room, then shut the door and shoved a chair underneath the handle.

"One to go," he whispered. "Come on."

He went out the door and Daniels followed on his heels. It was a fast walk along the hallway and Rajan was on the other man before he could do more than glance up from his screen and start his sentence. "What did he want now—" His voice was cut off as Rajan wrapped an arm around his throat.

With his air supply cut off, he thrashed around, but very quickly lost consciousness. Rajan lowered him back into his chair. "That's all of them for now," he said.

"Which computer do we take?" she asked.

He scanned the room. "It's not the computer we need," he said, removing a cable from the back of one system. "It's this." He held up a portable hard drive.

"Great, can we go now?" she asked. "I'm more than ready to get out of here."

"Almost," he said, sitting at Dilvan's station. "I just need to make sure that we don't leave him anything to work with." He tapped away at the keyboard, bringing up a command prompt. He accessed the main drive and typed the command F-DISC. The system asked him if he was sure and he typed yes, then hit Enter.

"What will that do?" she asked.

"Reformat the hard drive of Dilvan's computer. It will wipe it completely." He got to his feet and slipped the hard drive into the small pack on his back. "Let's get out of here."

"I just wish we could take the children," she said. "I hate leaving them behind."

"I promise you," Rajan said, guiding her down the hallway, "when the Sri Lanka military arrives, they'll do everything they can for them."

"I pray that's true," she said.

Stepping over the dead guard, he led her to the back of the house and across the small yard. Both of them waved at the children as they walked past and into the jungle. "The cove isn't far from here," he said, holding her hand. "Once we're on the water, we're home free."

"I hope so," Daniels said, peering around the jungle. "It doesn't feel real to me yet."

"It will," he said, picking up the pace. "As soon as you're safely home."

She forced herself not to look back and tried to push her fears from her mind. Something about their plan didn't feel quite right, but she didn't have the first idea what it might be. Some detail they'd overlooked. All she could do was pray for their safe escape, but in her experience, all the prayers in the world wouldn't necessarily stop a madman.

CHAPTER EIGHTEEN

It took less than half an hour to reach the cove, even struggling through the jungle. Somehow, Rajan had managed to spirit away a boat. "It's not pretty, but the engine is sound and it's light," he said. "Get in."

She climbed aboard while he untied it from a tree then jumped in himself. He tucked his backpack safely beneath the seat and started the engine. It seemed incredibly loud to her ears. What if one of the guards heard the engine and came to investigate? Daniels suddenly felt like a sitting duck and wished they'd been able to wait until nightfall before trying to escape.

Rajan began guiding the craft out of the cove, steering slightly north and away from the main cove where all of the Ocean Tigers boats were docked. "We're almost there," he said. "If we can get out into the open water of the bay, we can make a run for it, even hide if we have to."

"Where would we—" Daniels began to ask when the first shots rang out, peppering the side of the craft.

"Son of a…" he muttered, slamming the throttle forward. "Hang on."

He yanked the wheel, pushing the boat farther into the open water of the bay itself. Behind them, three boats were giving chase, and soldiers in each one were firing rifles as fast as they could pull the triggers.

Daniels automatically ducked low as more bullets burned the air around them. "Can we outrun them?" she asked, raising her voice loud enough to be heard.

"If we don't, we're dead," he said. "I should've known this was too easy. Vengai set us up. Such a simple trap." Then he grunted as a bullet punched through the meaty part of his thigh. Blood spattered the white fiberglass of the boat as he staggered, and the wheel slipped through his hands.

The boat careened wildly, and Daniels found herself grabbing the wheel and trying to keep them going in a straight line.

"Damn, that hurts," Rajan swore through clenched teeth. He dug into the compartment on the passenger side and pulled out a first-aid kit. "Keep driving while I get this bound up."

"Which direction?" she asked, feeling the fluttery wings of panic in her chest. "What do I do?"

"We need to go east," he said. "So long as they're behind us, keep veering left, right, whatever. It's hard to shoot someone in a boat, let alone a boat that's going all over the place." He cracked open the kit and pulled out a large trauma bandage, then another.

Daniels yanked the wheel back and forth, feeling the water slamming into the underside of the rickety craft. "She won't hold together," she snapped.

"She'll have to," he said with a groan as he tightened his belt around the bandages. "It's a little late to get another one."

She risked a look behind them. The three boats giving chase were closing the gap slowly. "They're going to catch us," she said as he got to his knees, then eased back into the driver's seat.

"There's a rifle up front, in the bow storage compartment. Do you know how to use one?" he asked, pulling the wheel hard to the right and nearly knocking her off her feet.

She nodded. "My father taught me."

"Get it out," he said. "It's already loaded."

"You want me to…shoot…shoot at people."

Another barrage of fire forced her to her knees, and she crawled into the bow area.

"Now's not the time for moral problems, Heather," he snapped. "I'm going to turn us around and when I do, I want you to shoot in their direction as fast as you can. Don't worry about hitting anybody, just try to make them duck."

She pulled the rifle out of the compartment, but she'd never seen anything quite like it. "I… What the hell kind of rifle is this?" she asked, shouting to make herself heard.

"Singapore Kinetics," he yelled in reply. "Military assault rifle."

"I can shoot a .30-.30 lever-action Winchester, but not this!" she objected.

"Fine, switch with me!"

They traded places once again, and Daniels saw that the other boats were nearly on them.

"What do you want me to do?" she asked as he hobbled toward the stern.

"Turn around and run right at them. When I tell you, veer left," he shouted over the wind and the gunfire.

"When?"

"Now!" he said, pulling the rifle into his shoulder. "Turn us now!"

Daniels pulled the wheel hard to the right and for a long, excruciating moment, she wondered if the boat was going to just flip and roll like an out-of-control car on the highway. Somehow, they stayed upright and she ducked low, barely peeking through the windshield, as bullets flew in all directions.

Almost immediately, Rajan opened fire. The weapon was fully automatic, and he burned through the first magazine in fast, short bursts. "Right between them," he called, and out of the corner of her eye, she saw the driver of the boat on her left clutch at his chest in the second before he flew backward and into the water.

She kept going, pushing the boat as much as she dared, while Rajan scattered their pursuers like quail. They obviously hadn't expected them to turn around and start shooting.

"Veer left," he yelled, popping out one magazine and putting in another in a flash, then continuing to fire.

Daniels did as she was told, yanking the wheel hard left. The three boats were now scattered and trying to turn and give chase. Rajan fired through his third magazine, and when it was empty, he reloaded and tossed the rifle into the passenger seat. Then he shooed her out of the driver's seat and took the wheel.

"That will buy us a little time," he said, looking pale and in pain. "Maybe it will be enough." He yanked the wheel once again, turning them back toward the bay.

MARIAH'S WISH GLIDED smoothly over the bay, heading east by northeast. The plan they'd agreed on was simple: work north to south, beginning twenty or so miles north of Phuket. Somewhere, on one of those islands, the Ocean Tigers were holding Heather Daniels. At the helm, Johnny steered the craft confidently, glancing at the compass from time to time to adjust their course. Peterson watched him from the navigator's seat.

"Are you going to refuse to talk to me?" she asked.

"I'm not *not* talking to you. I'm just thinking about this mission and how I wish you would have listened to me back at the dock and waited for us to hook up with Cooper."

"Why, so we can sit and twiddle our thumbs until he decides it's safe enough?" She shook her head. "Heather doesn't have time for that."

"You can be pissed at him for ditching you, Michelle. I can understand that. And Cooper is a lot of things, but he's not a coward in any way, shape or form. He'll improvise when it's necessary, but he prefers a good plan of attack instead of just blundering around."

"We're not 'blundering' around!" she protested. "We're looking for Heather, and we have a general area to accomplish that."

Johnny laughed. "Five thousand square miles of ocean and islands is a bit bigger than a general area."

Before she could object, he said, "Michelle, only a fool swims in shark-infested waters with a bloody steak hanging around his neck. We're out here, exposed, with limited firepower, searching for a damn needle in a grain of sand in the Sonoran Desert!"

"You're exaggerating," she said. "We have Heather's

last-known location, and it's a safe bet that the Ocean Tigers are using at least a fairly good-size island. We don't have to check the entire ocean, just likely targets. We'll find her, probably before Cooper even gets near here."

"And our cover story is that we're a couple out on vacation?" he said. "We seem so close. I'd believe it."

"It's a simple story. Besides, if we stay away from other boats it won't be an issue."

"So, in the event that we are faced with a gunboat filled with angry pirates, your solution is that we play dumb?" He shook his head, then looked at her sternly. "You're out of your mind, Michelle. You've let this mission get personal, and you aren't thinking like a field agent. You're thinking like a normal, everyday human being, and you're trying to prove to yourself and everyone else that you're okay. That's fine, if no one's at risk, but in this case, it's likely to get Heather—and us—killed. You need to wake the hell up."

Peterson knew he was right, that it was personal, that this was an incredible risk. Pirates kidnapped or killed civilians in these waters all the time, and being a tourist was a lousy story. But the nagging urge to do *something,* anything, was like a drumbeat in the back of her head, forcing her to keep moving no matter the cost. "Just… Look, I know this is a risk, okay? But I also know that the software Vengai stole is a lot more important to Cooper and everyone else than Heather Daniels is. She's my mission."

Johnny scoffed. "You know, I get that, but what I don't think you get is that *planning* and good intelligence are at the heart of operations like this. Cooper does. Maybe you've been out of the field so long you've forgotten that, or maybe the kind of ops you did for the CIA and the NSA were fly-by-the-seat-of-your-pants missions with no time for that kind of thing. I don't know, and I don't really care. I just want you to understand one thing."

"What's that?" she asked, feeling crappy because she knew he was right.

"If you get me killed, I'm going to be really, really pissed off." He glanced at the compass again, then at the horizon. "How close are we to the last contact point?"

Peterson consulted her GPS. "Not much farther. They used a satellite phone for the call, and it took a while to unscramble, but unless they've moved her, I think it will be one of the islands up ahead."

She picked up the binoculars she'd brought along and began to scope out the nearest island. There were a number of boats in the distance and four in the open water in a diamond pattern. She sighted in on the lead boat and gasped in surprise. "Oh, my God!"

"What is it?" Johnny asked.

"Those boats out there, that's Heather."

"There's no way you could tell at this distance," he said.

"Normally I would agree with you, but these are Xomin Digital Nauticals. Image stabilization is flawless at even two thousand meters."

"Take the helm and let me see," he said, stepping away from the helm.

She took the wheel as she handed him the binoculars and slid into the captain's chair, punching the throttle. Johnny reached out and barely caught himself as he was jolted backward. The fast-moving boat skipped along the waves, with some of the larger swells leaving a big gap and the bow smashing into the water.

"What in the hell are you doing? You're going to get us killed," he shouted.

Johnny reached forward to throttle back the engine. Peterson had her Glock out of its shoulder rig and pointed at him before he could even put a hand on it. "Look, I like you, Johnny. You're here and that's something. But if you interfere with this mission I *will* shoot you," she said.

He held up his hands and nodded, looking at her as though she might be more than a little crazy, and maybe at this point she was.

"Easy," he said. "I'm not trying to interfere. I just thought it might be nice to show up in one piece. If you think it's better for us to show up as driftwood, then be my guest."

Peterson sighed. After holstering her gun, she throttled back and the boat cruised along the waves. They were getting closer, and Johnny checked through the binoculars again.

"They're taking fire," he said. "And even with us, we're going to be seriously outnumbered."

"Who's they?"

"I don't know. There's some guy on the boat with her."

DANIELS TUCKED INTO the bottom of the boat as another hail of bullets came across the bow. She sat up, glancing behind them. The three boats chasing them were making up the distance far more quickly than she'd imagined.

"They're getting a little too close for comfort," she called to Rajan, looking over at him to see beads of sweat rolling down his forehead and blood trickling from a fresh wound in his arm. He leaned on the steering wheel, trying his best to maneuver the boat.

"Sweet Jesus!" she cried, staggering toward him.

"Stay down," he snapped, his eyes focused on the water ahead.

"I'm not going to sit here and let you bleed to death!" she said, tearing a long strip from the bottom of her shirt and pressing it to the wound to try to stem the flow of blood. The bullet was still lodged in his shoulder, and Rajan winced as she applied pressure, trying to stop the flow.

She looked through the cracked windshield and saw another boat heading toward them. "Maybe we should give up," Daniels said. "You've been shot twice and now there's four of them."

He shook his head and she noticed how pale his features were. The bandage around his leg was soaked and the one on his shoulder not much better. "We can't," he said. "They're not going to let us live if we give up."

"But I don't—"

"Heather, we have to keep going. I promised I'd get you out of here."

He stretched out his hand and ran a finger down her cheek. She leaned her head into his hand and smiled. He smiled back.

She felt the passage of the bullet as it missed her face by a fraction of an inch. It registered in her mind, and she flinched. Time slowed and everything came in staggering flashes. She opened her mouth to say something when she saw the blood blossom on his shirt, soaking his chest more and more crimson with each stuttering pump of his heart.

Rajan clutched weakly at his chest, his eyes wide with surprise, then fell sideways. The wheel spun as he toppled, and the boat veered left, its weight shifting beneath her and bringing her to her knees beside him.

"Rajan!" The cry tore out of her throat as though someone else were saying it.

The jarring movement of the boat made it difficult to stand. She had to stop it. She couldn't treat his injury while the boat was still moving in wild circles. They crossed the wake from another craft and the force of it rocked her backward again. She smacked her head on the railing and slumped to the floor. Lights danced in her eyes. It was hard to think and she shook her head, trying to clear the cobwebs. Rajan needed her.

The sound of bullets striking the boat came once more, this time centered on the outboard engine. It coughed and sputtered and the boat started to slow, curving in a lazy circle. Suddenly she realized that she was staring into Rajan's vacant eyes. He was gone, and there was nothing she could do. He'd died trying to save her and she'd been…helpless. Helpless! The futility of all of her efforts, all his efforts, over the time she'd been captured swelled up and tried to swallow her into the abyss.

More shots rang out and at first she ignored them. Then it became clear that the boat she'd seen in front of them was shooting at the pirates behind her. She peeked her head up over the rail and saw the boat coming from the open sea. There was a man crouched in the bow with a very mean-looking rifle, and he was picking his targets with the precision of a sniper. A chorus of confused shouts rose from the pirates.

She didn't know who was in the other boat and she didn't care. She couldn't allow Rajan's sacrifice to be in vain. Daniels pulled herself up and jumped behind the wheel of the sputtering boat and turned it toward her potential saviors.

"THEY'RE BACKING OFF," Peterson yelled. "Keep firing."

"Right now, I'm just keeping them pinned down," Johnny replied. He raised the Ares Shrike to his shoulder once more and fired several more shots in succession. "About the best I can do bouncing around like this!"

"We just need a little time, so keep at it!"

Johnny opened up with the assault rifle once more, and Peterson wished he'd brought belts of ammunition instead of magazines. Though the weapon itself was enough to intimidate damn near anyone. It looked like something out of a science-fiction movie. She shook her head at men and their toys even as she pressed their boat closer to Heather's. She'd seen someone on the boat fall, and then the other person as the boat turned, out of control, and she silently prayed that the young woman was all right.

They were closer now and Johnny's rifle was beginning to inflict serious damage. She saw one, two, then a third man go down as she slowed their speed and they weren't bouncing as much. He dropped the magazine and grabbed another. In the distance, she noted two more boats leaving from the numerous piers on the nearby island. At the current rate, he was going to run out of ammo before they could manage to escape.

They reached Heather's boat, and the look of surprise on her face when she saw Michelle was replaced by one of desperate hope. She tried to push her own boat faster, but the engine was done in. Leaking oil burned black as it coughed and rattled.

Peterson pulled up alongside the boat and Johnny set down his rifle, reaching out a hand to Daniels.

"It's not Triple A, but we'll have to do," he said as she put one foot up on the rail.

The pirates saw what was happening and opened fire again. Daniels jumped back into her boat and crouched on the bottom. Peterson grabbed Johnny's rifle and laid down a barrage of cover fire.

"Heather! Move it right now!" she shouted.

Daniels grabbed her bag and grabbed Johnny's arm, leaping over the rail. He caught her in midair, pulling her aboard, then swinging her around and depositing her in a chair in one graceful move. "Get us out of here," he said, taking the rifle back from her.

Peterson had just throttled up the boat when the next round of bullets pierced the side of *Mariah's Wish* and one of them ricocheted into the flesh of her calf.

"Son of a bitch," she swore, reaching down to grab her leg while trying to steer the boat at the same time.

She looked up even as Johnny hit the deck. The pirates were all around them. She pulled the kerchief from around her neck and tied it around the wound in her calf. Fortunately, it was a clean exit.

"Thoughts?" she asked.

"We're outnumbered and outgunned," he said, lowering the Ares. "And they've stopped shooting. Maybe their orders changed or something, but even if we tried to run for it, we wouldn't get very far."

Peterson looked sadly at Daniels, who appeared to be phasing in and out of shock. "I'm sorry, honey," she said. "It's not much of a rescue."

"Lower your weapons!" one of the pirates shouted.

"Michelle?" Johnny asked. "What's your play?"

She looked at the pirates all around them and shook her head. "We're done for now," she admitted. "Go ahead and drop the rifle."

Johnny did, and Peterson couldn't help but notice the expression on his face. If it had been a headline on the front page of the *New York Times,* it would have read I Told You So in huge, black letters.

CHAPTER NINETEEN

Vengai stood in the center of the compound, impatiently waiting for the return of his prisoners and the hard drive they'd unexpectedly stolen, while contemplating his own foolishness. When he'd returned to the house and found the dead guard, along with Dilvan and his other technician unconscious, he'd realized how much he underestimated Rajan and the Daniels girl. He'd known they would try something, and his own willingness to allow them to entertain him had nearly cost him everything he'd worked so hard to achieve. In point of fact, his little entertainment had been quite expensive.

Between Rajan and the other prisoners, he had ten dead soldiers and two boats in serious need of repair. Still, Katran had radioed ahead and informed him that Rajan was dead, and that the others were in custody. Vengai was quite curious to learn who these unexpected guests were and what they were doing here. He'd suspected that they were agents from Sri Lanka, but Katran had told him they were American. That changed the possibilities considerably. He watched as the boats pulled up to the pier and the prisoners were unloaded. The captured boat was a very nice vessel that would be an excellent addition to his small flotilla.

The prisoners were marched into the compound,

then shoved to the ground at his feet. In addition to the Daniels girl, there were two others, a man and a woman. The Daniels girl was clutching a bag, which he yanked out of her grasp. She tried to fight him, but he backhanded her casually, forcing her into the other woman. Inside the bag was the stolen hard drive, but his sigh of relief turned to fear as he realized the outer casing was cracked.

"Get this inside to Dilvan and tell him I said I want it working again as soon as possible," he snapped, handing it to one of his soldiers, who took it and made a beeline for the house.

Vengai then turned back to his prisoners. "Who are you?" he asked.

"Please, just let them go," Daniels pleaded. "They're just tourists. They thought they were helping me."

Vengai laughed. "You must believe me to be stupid," he said. He nodded at Katran, and the soldier brought forward the rifle he'd confiscated, handing it to him.

"This is an Ares Shrike assault weapon," he continued, moving to stand in front of the man on his knees. "I might believe a *tourist* would carry a handgun, but this is the weapon of a soldier or a mercenary, isn't it?" He waited for the man to respond, and as he started to get to his feet, Vengai lashed out with his boot, kicking him in the jaw and sending him back to the ground.

The man began to laugh under his breath. "I thought you wanted to talk," he said, rubbing his jaw.

"You can talk from the ground," he snapped. "Who are you?"

"So much for island hospitality," the man replied.

"And here I was hoping for a mai tai with a little umbrella."

"I will only ask you once more," Vengai said. "Who are you?"

"Captain Kangaroo, of the good ship *Lollypop*," the man said. "No, wait! I'm Captain Ahab, but you can call me Ishmael."

Vengai charged the receiver on the Shrike and pointed it at his head. The other woman lunged forward and Katran kicked her in the face. Noticing the man's reaction, he pointed the barrel at the woman. "Perhaps you value her life more than your own," he said. "Tell me who you are or this woman dies."

The man shrugged. "You can call me Jester," he said. "We can dispense with the other formalities, since we already know who you are."

"How do you know who I am?" he snapped. "Are you a spy from the U.S. government? Did you read my name in a file?"

"Nothing like that," the man replied in mock surprise. "But I can spot a giant dickhead from a mile away."

Katran chambered a round and Vengai held up his hand, though that didn't stop him from using the butt of his rifle as a club, slamming it into Jester's back. This time, he sprawled flat, eating dirt.

"I thought you were going to kill me," Johnny said, spitting. "This is boring."

Vengai grinned. "In time, you'll wish I had. For now, I think you'll find some excitement in the entertainment I have planned for you."

He circled behind Daniels and crouched on one

knee. She tried to move away, but he grabbed a fist-
ful of hair, pulling her to him. "Your beloved protec-
tor is now dead. I think it's time that I had a taste of
the sweet honey you were offering him."

"No!" she said, struggling. "No!"

Vengai kissed the side of her neck as she continued
to try to pull away.

"You are mine to do with as I wish," he purred.
"Continue to fight me and you will not only make it
worse for yourself, but far, far worse for your friends.
I will ensure that their torture and death is far more
exquisite than anything you can imagine." He ran his
tongue along her neck once more, then got to his feet
and moved to stand in front of the other woman.

He patiently waited for her to look up at him, and
when she finally did, her eyes were filled with hatred.
"I see the hate in your eyes," he said. "I do not antici-
pate that you will be any more cooperative than your
companion."

"Then you won't be disappointed." She spit.

Vengai smiled. "I am amazed at your confidence.
If the Americans were competent at all, I would have
been captured when I was in Washington, D.C. Instead, I came and left as easily as a ghost." He
shrugged. "So, what name shall we call you?"

"We almost had you, you know," she said. "And the
two men you left behind to clean up your mess won't
be coming home."

"They were expendable," Vengai replied. "Why do
you think I left them?"

"People aren't expendable, you moron," the woman

snarled, climbing to her feet. "What is it about petty dictators that makes them believe that?"

Taken aback by her accusation, Vengai slapped her, once, then again, drawing blood from her lip. "You foolish, idiotic woman! I am not a dictator. I am the leader of a movement that will free the Tamil people from the chains of —"

"Oh, save it for your press releases, you piece of shit," she said.

This time, he hit her hard enough to knock her to the ground. Then he took a deep breath. Expending energy on her or any of them at this critical time was useless. "I believe we shall call you Bitch, as you seem to be little more than an angry dog, woman. And I'm pleased to know that you and your friend were the ones interfering with me before. When the two of you die, we'll no longer have to worry about any immediate threats from the Americans."

"I wouldn't count on it," she said. "And you can call me Bitch all you want. It's more polite than what I'd call you."

"I'm sure," he said. "Call me what you will. The two of you have failed once again. As soon as our new software is working properly, we will use it to make a statement to the world that will never be forgotten."

"You'll be a footnote in history," Johnny interrupted.

"Even in these dark times, the death of three U.S. citizens is noticed, but when those three are a President's daughter and the two people sent to save her, this will give, I think, a glimpse of our power."

He turned to Katran. "To the cages, and put the man

on the wheel. He may be more talkative once his joints start to dislocate. The Daniels girl may go to the children in the house, but double the guard."

Vengai stalked back to check on Dilvan's progress. He mentally chided himself for failing to put extra security on the computer lab. This wasn't the time for omissions. He could have everything he wanted, but stupid mistakes would only get him killed. He expected his men to be willing to die for their cause, but he had no intention of becoming a martyr.

The instant cool of the offices when Vengai walked in was calming until he noticed that the technicians weren't diligently bent over their individual computers, but instead had their chairs pushed together and were bickering loudly while pointing at the hard drive that Rajan had stolen.

"What seems to be the problem?" he asked. "Why do you not have the hard drive back online?"

Dilvan turned sheepishly to him and Vengai could see him gathering his courage to stand and answer. Already knowing he wasn't going to like what they had to say made him more short tempered. Reaching forward, he yanked Dilvan to his feet.

"Speak up, boy!"

"I…he reformatted part of my system, and when I tried to hook up the hard drive, the program didn't run properly. I believe it may have been damaged in the fight. I can see the files, but they aren't running. I…I think it's a hardware malfunction."

"Can you fix it?" he demanded, silently raging about Rajan's traitorous actions. He'd kill him again if he had the chance.

Dilvan shook his head. "No. No, sir. Not on my own. My specialty is code and programming. I don't know enough about hardware and if I try, I may make things worse."

"So, who can fix it." His tone grated.

"I know a man. He usually works out of Singapore."

Exasperated at yet another delay, Vengai released his hold on the boy. "Fine. Call whoever you need. Just get him here and get the damn thing working."

Vengai stormed out of the room and hesitated for a moment on bringing yet another person to the island, then dismissed the concern. As soon as the hard drive was fixed, he would kill the man and that would be the end of it.

THE GRENADE SPIRALED through the air to land in the bottom of the boat, its shape making it roll wildly. The pirates dropped their weapons to try to grab it, and a couple jumped overboard just as Bolan pulled the pin on the second one and tossed the bomb into the chaos, as well.

"Go!" Bolan yelled to Faizal. "Four seconds!"

The man hit the throttle, rocketing the boat forward out of blast range. The dual explosions sent debris flying through the air as the boat broke apart under the force. Mutilated bodies were tossed through the air like dolls, and the screams of the wounded were loud enough to be heard over the motors and the waves.

"Swing around," Bolan ordered. "I don't want the others thinking they can try again."

Faizal shook his head in despair, but turned the boat back toward the remaining two pirate boats as ordered. Bolan stepped to the weapons locker and considered his choices, then decided that a rifle was too target specific for the result he wanted and chose the MPS AA-12 shotgun, which was sometimes called the Sledgehammer. Virtually recoilless, the AA-12 used a 32-round ammunition drum and was fully automatic. Designed as an assault shotgun for the military, it could fire a variety of shells and was about as intimidating a weapon as he'd ever used. He selected two drums of fragmentation rounds and positioned himself low in the bow. He locked in a drum and called back over his shoulder, "Two passes, one by each boat should do it!"

Faizal pushed the throttle all the way forward, and as they closed on the first boat, Bolan opened fire. Initially, the pirates began shooting their rifles, but the AA-12 sent them scurrying for cover as he decimated boats and pirates with equal prejudice. The shotgun sounded like the sound track to a war movie all on its own. They passed the first boat, leaving it a smoking ruin of holes and bloody bodies.

"Keep moving," Bolan called, pointing to the last remaining craft. He loaded a new drum, dropping the empty one at his feet, then heard Faizal laughing.

The other boat had turned tail and was running in the opposite direction.

"Do you want to go after them?"

Bolan shook his head. "No, don't bother. They don't have any fight left in them."

"Who would after seeing that shotgun in action?" he asked, turning the boat once more and heading back toward a small island. "I've never seen anything like it."

"It's quite a weapon," Bolan admitted, returning it to the weapons locker. "Sometimes an effective display of violence works as well as anything else."

Faizal sailed into the small cove of the uninhabited island and anchored the boat. Bolan sat looking at the map as his friend moved to sit across from him. "This isn't working," he said.

"Yeah, I got that with the attacking pirates. They weren't the ones we're looking for, either. The LTTE doesn't train their people to retreat, and I'd expect them to be far more disciplined. My guess is that those guys were part of the little mercenary operation I heard about, which means another waste of time." He held up the map. "I don't see any other indication of one over the other. Since this one was a bust, it's likely to be the other one, but I think I'm going to have to do what it takes to make an aerial search happen. It's another delay, but if it's not the other island, we're going to run out of time entirely. We've only got one more shot at this, I'm thinking."

"I agree. Why don't we just stay docked here until we know our next move?" he suggested. "There's no point in traveling without a direction."

"I'll get in touch with my people and see what I can set up in terms of a flyover. Why don't you do the same in terms of updated intelligence?"

"I'm not likely to find much," Faizal said, "but I'll try."

Bolan pulled out the satellite equipment and added a splitter cable to the arrangement, then linked it to their phones. The signal wouldn't be quite as strong, so it would limit his ability to download files, but for the purposes of calling, it would suffice. He'd no sooner gotten them online than Faizal's phone began to ring.

Looking surprised, he shrugged and answered it, while Bolan started to write out a quick note to Brognola, requesting the flyover and an updated intelligence report on the Ocean Tigers. With his mind on that task, he'd ignored his companion until the man tapped him on the shoulder.

Bolan looked a question at him, and Faizal pulled a cord out of the communications box and plugged the call into the headset jack on Bolan's phone, allowing him to listen in.

"All right, Dilvan, slow down," Faizal said. "What's the problem now?"

The voice on the other end sounded young. "I have a portable hard drive that got damaged. I can see the data, but I can't access it. It doesn't look like a software problem. The casing was cracked. I can't run the program I need without it."

"You sound like it's important," Faizal replied. "And if it's running off a hard drive, it must be huge. Something new you wrote?"

"No, not me. If I wrote it, I'd have backed it up in two or three extra places. This is the only copy I've got and it's irreplaceable."

"Irreplaceable?" he asked. "What have you gotten into, Dilvan?"

"It's…uh, it's a hacking program for satellites and stuff," he finally blurted.

"What are you doing with that?" he asked sharply.

"If I've told you once, I've told you a thousand times that you don't mess around with government systems."

"And I told you that I was going to make some money while I could. The guy I'm working for is a little crazy, but he pays well."

"Money isn't everything," Faizal replied darkly. "I should know."

"Come on, Bashir," Dilvan said, "you've done plenty of jobs for the money, and I know it. Look, I know we didn't part on the best of terms, but I could really use your help. It's easy money, and I don't really know anyone else who is as good with hardware as you are," Dilvan said.

"How much?" Bashir asked.

"Twenty-five thousand," Dilvan said, "*if* you get the hard drive running again."

Faizal whistled softly. "That's a lot of dough. You've moved up to the big time, I see."

"So you'll do it?" Dilvan asked.

"Are you in Singapore now?"

"No, I'm not even close. If I were, that would make this easier. I'm on an island out in the middle of nowhere."

Bolan and Faizal exchanged a look, along with a smile.

"As it turns out, I'm traveling right now, Dilvan. If you send me the coordinates, I can give you an estimated time of arrival."

Dilvan sighed with relief. "Great," he said, gushing. "That's so great. You're a lifesaver, Bashir, literally."

"Yeah, yeah, kid. I'm wonderful. Just text me the coordinates and I'll get there as quick as I can." He paused, then added, "And try to stay safe, Dilvan. Guys that can pay twenty-five large for a hardware fix in the middle of the ocean usually play hardball if they don't get what they want."

"I can take care of myself," he replied. "See you soon."

Faizal ended the call and looked at Bolan.

"You might be the luckiest bastard I've ever met, Cooper," he said. "I think we just found the Ocean Tigers."

The phone beeped as the text message came through. He handed the phone to Bolan, who typed the coordinates into his handheld computer. As they'd expected, the map that came back was of the second island they hadn't searched yet. At least this information would save them having to wait for a flyover and even gave them an excuse to be on the island.

"Tell me about this Dilvan," Bolan said.

"I trained him," Faizal said, then shrugged. "Kind of. I got him his start in computer hacking, but he surpassed me quickly. He was a true prodigy when it came to programming and software, but he could never talk to the hardware. I tried to tell him it takes both kinds of information, but then he got dodgy about a lot of things and took off. For someone so brilliant with code he sure couldn't figure out the wiring."

"Do you trust him?" Bolan was direct about it. This wasn't the time for games.

"I don't trust anyone, Cooper, you know that. If you actually existed, I'd know everything about you before I ever worked with you. I find your lack of existence reassuring."

Sadly, Faizal's words hit home. Bolan knew that the small man was right, he truly didn't exist like other people. Maybe someday he'd be able to change that, but for now he had a job to do. "Fair enough," he said. "Humor me."

"Like I said, he got dodgy about what he was doing and who he was doing jobs for. One day about six months or so ago, he simply left and didn't come back. We've talked a couple of times since then, but nothing more serious than pleasantries."

"You don't seem upset about it," Bolan observed.

Faizal shrugged. "He didn't owe me anything. I figured he found an opportunity and ran with it. There's no honor among thieves, you know."

"Of that I have no doubt," he said. "Is there any reason for you to believe he isn't playing straight?"

He shook his head. "No. He doesn't have a reason to lie, and there's no way he knows I'm working with you. Everything between us has been below the radar...well, except for that little incident at the warehouse, but there's no connection there. My bet is that he's gotten himself into a technology jam and he needs a way out so he called me."

"All right," he said. "Let's go check it out. For once, I think we caught a break."

And then his phone rang.

CHAPTER TWENTY

Bolan saw that it was Brognola calling and immediately picked up. "Cooper here," he said. "What's going on, Hal?"

"A complication," he replied. "Both Michelle and Johnny have gone off the grid completely."

"What do you mean?" he asked. "Michelle took off and Johnny was supposed to go get her and bring her back to the States."

"I'm aware of the plan, Striker, but something's gone wrong. Johnny tracked her to Port Blair, but then...nothing. I got in touch with someone over there, and they were seen headed out into the Bay of Bengal on a charter boat. My source says that Johnny paid to rent it for three days."

"Damn it," Bolan growled. "How long since you heard from him?"

"Almost a full day," Brognola replied. "My guess is that somehow she convinced him to take her to look for Heather Daniels, and they're either still out there somewhere or they've run into trouble of some kind."

"Is he carrying a sat phone?" he asked. "Did he requisition any kind of equipment?"

"Nothing except our help getting an emergency flight to catch up with her," Brognola said. "I tried to ping the GPS based on his last check in and got nothing. So the phone is either turned off, broken or…lost."

"All right," he said. "I'll keep my eyes open for them. We've got the location narrowed down now, and we're going in undercover. You can cancel the drone flyover for now, since I'm going to be boots on the ground within an hour or so."

"Will do, Striker," Brognola said. "Stay sharp out there, and do what you can about Johnny and Michelle, but the mission priorities are unchanged. Retrieve or destroy the stolen software and rescue the Daniels girl."

"Understood," Bolan said, then disconnected the call and began putting his satellite equipment away.

"Problem?" Faizal asked.

"Nothing unusual," Bolan replied. "Just people not doing what they're told." He filled him in on Johnny and Peterson, explaining that if they were on the island, it could potentially mean extra allies…or complications.

"That's karma, my friend," Faizal said, grinning at Bolan's annoyance.

"Karma?"

"It gives and it takes away. We found the island, but now your mission is more complicated," he said simply.

"Well, then, karma sucks," Bolan replied. "Now let's get going."

USING THE COORDINATES that Dilvan provided to Faizal, along with the satellite maps, they had no trouble finding the sheltered cove where the Ocean Tigers had built the pier for their own boats, as well as those they'd stolen. As they slowed to a sedate pace, Bolan spotted the ship that Heather Daniels had originally taken from the port in Singapore. The name had been recently painted over, but it was obviously the same vessel. There were at least a dozen boats in the cove, and many were heavily armed. One ship, with the name *Mariah's Wish* painted in script on the side, was obviously out of place, and Bolan suspected that he would soon discover that both Johnny and Peterson were here, too. As prisoners.

Assuming they weren't dead.

He muttered a curse under his breath and Faizal looked up from the helm. "What's that?" he asked.

"Never mind," Bolan growled, irritated that his brother had been unable to stop Peterson from getting into this, yet somewhat impressed by her resolve.

"How do you want to play this?" Faizal asked. "I'm sure they'll search us before we're allowed anywhere near the main building. I assume you don't want to go in guns blazing."

Bolan shook his head. "No, let's see how much we can scout out first. Ideally, we'll find a way to get everyone we need to out alive, along with the technology, with a minimum amount of shooting and explosions. That sort of thing tends to get unprepared people killed."

Faizal laughed. "You surprise me, my friend. I thought you enjoyed shootings and explosions."

"When they're necessary," Bolan stressed.

"Agreed," he said. "By the way, they may not like that I've brought someone along. You look a little…"

"A little what?"

"Menacing."

"Tell them I'm your bodyguard," Bolan replied. "Trust me, they want this system up and running more than they'll be worried about me."

"I hope you're right," he said, guiding the boat to an empty piling on the dock.

The boat was met by a group of several soldiers and a young man that Bolan presumed was Dilvan. Faizal stepped out of the boat and onto the dock, but one of the guards stopped Bolan short, pointing his rifle. Bolan held up his hands to show they were empty.

"You should have come alone," Dilvan said. "Even you know that."

Faizal gestured to the bullet-riddled boat. "As you can see, I've had some security issues. This is my bodyguard, Cooper."

Bolan stood with arms crossed and glared at Dilvan.

"Making friends as usual, Bashir? He'll have to wait here."

"Then, good luck with your hard drive, Dilvan. It was nice seeing you." Faizal turned back toward the boat. "Come on, Cooper, we're leaving."

Dilvan paled. "Wait! Just wait a second, okay? He can come, but he must leave his weapons here."

Faizal turned to Bolan. "Cooper?"

Bolan nodded and removed the shoulder rig he was using for the Desert Eagle, placing it on the seat of the boat. "It better be here when I get back," he said, staring hard at the guards and then Dilvan. "It's got sentimental value."

"Your boat will be undisturbed, I assure you," Dilvan said. "You have my word."

Bolan sneered, then climbed onto the pier and allowed one of the soldiers to frisk him for weapons. Satisfied, Dilvan led the way along the pier to where a Jeep was parked. He climbed into the driver's seat, which left the front passenger seat for Faizal. Bolan and one of the soldiers climbed into the back. The others were apparently staying behind.

It wasn't a long drive to the small compound, but Bolan watched everything they passed with great care. There were two groups of younger soldiers training, perhaps a total of twenty, and older soldiers were supervising them. He guessed in all that Vengai had to have somewhere in the neighborhood of sixty, perhaps as many as eighty men. In addition, there were several small groups of women—most of them at work on cleaning-related tasks—as well as children. This wasn't just a military compound, but a small community.

They pulled into the middle of the camp, parking the Jeep, and Bolan spotted the cages. Made of bamboo, and barely large enough to hold an average-size man, they left no room to sit and no protection from the elements. Vengai had perhaps a half dozen of them, but only two were currently occupied. One held his brother, Johnny, whose hands were tied to the top of the cage over his head; the other held Peterson. Both cages were flanked by guards and a quick glance told him that while they'd been roughed up a bit, neither was seriously injured. He breathed a silent sigh of relief and turned their situation out of his mind. There would be a chance to deal with it later.

They walked into the main house, and Bolan was pleased to see Heather Daniels sitting with a small group of children. Her face showed a few bruises, but otherwise she, too, didn't appear to have suffered overmuch. She ignored the men passing through, and they walked along a short hallway to a small computer room. Bolan stood back and played bodyguard while Faizal and Dilvan sat at the computer stations and began examining the hard drive. The one terrorist who'd accompanied them asked Dilvan if he was needed and the young man shook his head negatively, barely bothering to look up from his work. The man shrugged and went back down the hall. A moment later Bolan heard the front door open and close again. To the best of his knowledge, there were no other guards inside the house itself. When it appeared that both Faizal and Dilvan were completely engrossed in their work, he slipped away from the door and moved down the hallway to where Daniels was still sitting with the children.

He moved closer to her, then spoke in a low voice. "Ms. Daniels, a moment, please."

She turned, her eyes wide at his apparent knowledge of who she was. She got quickly to her feet and moved to stand next to him. "Who are you?" she asked, her voice barely a whisper.

"Matt Cooper," he said. "Your father sent me."

She looked confused. "I thought...Michelle?"

"It's a long story," he said. "If we all live through this, maybe you'll get to hear it."

"If…" she said, her voice trailing off. "Will you be able to rescue all of us?" she asked.

"I'm going to try, but I need you to do something for me. As soon as you can, I need you to get word to Michelle and Johnny that I'm here and to watch for my signal."

"Will you be rescuing the children, as well?" Daniels asked, her eyes cutting to the little ones playing happily on the floor.

"We'll save anyone we can, but I'll be honest in that you and what Vengai stole are my priorities. Right now, I have to get back. Look for my signal, and tell the others, okay?"

"I will," she promised.

Knowing that would have to suffice, Bolan slipped back along the hallway to the computer room. Dilvan looked up and nodded, but then went back to work. Faizal looked over at Bolan, who nodded.

They'd discussed options on the way in, and the Executioner had decided that trying to steal the software wouldn't work. Besides, something like that was better off destroyed, anyway. Bashir turned back to the keys and began typing the virus code that would begin disabling the program, ultimately causing it to unravel and fail.

"What is that?" Dilvan asked, looking up from his work and peering at Faizal's screen.

"Nothing you need to worry about," he said.

"I worry about everything," he replied, watching as his one-time mentor typed rapid-fire on the keys.

Faizal hesitated for the briefest of seconds, then typed in the final commands.

"Hey!" Dilvan yelled. "That's a virus code!" He reached out and hit a button on his desk and immediately an alarm began to sound. Then without another word, he began to type furiously on his keyboard.

"We'll have guards on us any second," Faizal said, typing without looking up. "You've got to buy me some time."

Bolan didn't bother replying as the guard from the front of the house came charging down the hallway. He lifted his gun and Bolan held up his empty hands, and he slowed, with a confused look on his face. As soon as he was in reach, Bolan stepped in, engaging an arm bar to immobilize his weapon hand.

The guard started to struggle, all too aware of his mistake, but it was too late. Bolan drove a knifehand into his throat, crushing his larynx into a bloody mess. The soldier swayed, reaching for his throat and retching in a desperate attempt to find oxygen. The Executioner lashed out with a boot, knocking him to the floor.

Bolan grabbed his handgun from the floor and turned in time to see Faizal take a right hook to the jaw from Dilvan. "You bastard," he yelled, coming after him. "You'll ruin *everything*."

The guards from outside came charging into the house and down the hallway. Shots rang out as they fired blindly at Bolan's shadow and he ducked back into the room, slamming the door shut. Dilvan and Faizal were still battling.

Dilvan stumbled backward, knocking a computer monitor to the floor with a crash, and Bolan took aim with the 9 mm pistol he'd taken from the first guard.

Just as he fired, Faizal jumped forward, pushing the younger man out of the way. Bolan's round took him in the shoulder, spinning him around and dropping him to the floor.

"Bashir!"

Bolan ran over to his compatriot and tried to stem the flow of blood. The guards were hammering on the door, and he knew he only had a few seconds and was running out of options.

"Why the hell did you do that?" he asked Faizal, who was struggling to stay conscious.

"The little bastard beat me on the keyboard," he said, groaning. "The code isn't complete. The system is still up. We need him to tell us what he did."

Bolan looked up in time to see Dilvan throw open the door. He rolled to his feet, but was too slow. The bullet from the close-range 9 mm gun tore through the air. He felt the impact, knew he'd been hit, and then the cold darkness took him.

WHEN THE FIRST SHOT sounded, Daniels paused and wondered if it had been her imagination. She got to her feet, peering down the hallway, and saw the body of one of Vengai's soldiers on the ground. Wondering if that was Cooper's signal, and deciding it probably wasn't, she urged the children into the kitchen, then watched as other soldiers burst through the front door.

They ran down the hallway, shouting, and then several fired additional shots, just as Vengai came through the front door, as well, following behind them. He glared at her as he passed, but she ignored him.

Giving him a few seconds, she decided to creep down the hall to find out what was happening.

She'd only reached the back of the crowd when the door to the computer room opened. On the other side, she could see Cooper, but before she'd even thought to warn him, one of the guards fired. Cooper hit the floor with an audible thud. She stared in stunned silence at the prone form of her would-be rescuer. She was a nurse. Daniels knew she should try to help, yet watching him fall had a devastating impact on her mind.

Her last hope of rescue was gone. There was nothing—no one—left to save her, let alone Michelle, Johnny or the children. They were all going to die because her father would never pay a terrorist money. It would violate everything he believed in.

Vengai looked at the controlled chaos, then turned and grabbed Daniels by the arm, yanking her back toward the main room and barking orders as he went. She could feel his fingers digging deep into the muscles of her arm. Both Cooper and the other man were unceremoniously dragged through the house and out the door. Vengai pulled Daniels along in his wake, yanking her to her feet when she stumbled on the steps.

Cooper was unconscious and was tossed into the bed of a truck. The technician was groaning and trying to pull away, but one of the soldiers kicked him in the head. The man's groans were silenced and he, too, was lifted into the air and tossed into the back as though he were a bale of hay.

"Let me help them," she said, turning to Vengai. "They're hurt."

"It would be a waste of your time," he said, "and a waste of supplies."

"So you're just going to let them suffer?" she asked, unable to keep the outrage from turning into a cry. "What kind of a monster are you?"

"I am not a monster!" he yelled, slapping her across the face while keeping a firm grip on her arm. "I am the man who will bring back the LTTE to its former glory and restore the honor of the Tamil people."

Daniels spit blood, wiping the corner of her mouth. "You are a pig without honor," she said. "Letting men suffer because it pleases you."

Vengai took a deep, calming breath. "Then you will be pleased to know that they will not suffer for very long.

"Get in," he snapped, shoving her into a Jeep that was parked behind the truck. As soon as he got into the driver's seat, he honked, and the two vehicles headed down the rutted dirt path to where the boats were docked.

Fighting back tears, Daniels knew that Vengai had something horrible planned for those two men. People were dying because of her, for her, and there was nothing she could do to stop it. If Rajan hadn't gotten involved with her, he would still be alive and probably have gotten out with the technology that was so threatening, but her presence stopped that. It was because of her that he was dead, because of her that her father's Secret Service agent was now captured. It was because of her that their last hope of rescue was about to die.

They arrived at the pier and the bodies were dragged onto the boat Bolan and Faizal had arrived on.

Katran briefly questioned the decision to destroy such a nice prize, but Vengai said that keeping it might make them even more of a target. A boat on the bottom of the ocean, however, was much harder to spot.

Daniels tried to stay in the Jeep, but her captor wanted her to see what was about to happen. He pulled her from her seat and shoved her in the direction of the pier where the boat was being prepared. Both of the men lay in the bottom of the boat, bleeding from their wounds. One side of Cooper's face was awash in blood, while the other man's eye was nearly swollen shut just from the kick the guard had given him. "Just let them go," she said. "It's not like they're in any condition to come back."

"You'd like that, wouldn't you?" Vengai asked. "But no mercy was shown to my people, and I will show none to anyone else." He handed her a metal box that had several blinking lights and a handful of visible wires. Staring at it, she felt her heart rate increase, and beads of sweat pearled on her forehead. "Put that in the boat," he ordered.

She shook her head, trying to hand it back to him.

"You want to live?" he asked.

"Yes, yes," she said, nodding.

"Then put that on the boat with your friends!"

"I can't do that. Please, don't make me do that," Daniels begged.

"If you refuse, I will have you bound and placed in the boat with them...along with the children. Now no more games! Put the device in the boat, or should I have Katran bring the children down to the pier?"

"No, no! I'll do it!" Daniels stepped onto the boat, her heart racing. The shame of helping these terrorists, even if she was being forced, was almost more than she could bear. She placed the device next to Cooper, and bent to make it look as if she was looking at his head wound. Behind her, Vengai was giving instructions to his men, telling them to take the boat out into the bay and blow it up. From his position, she didn't think he could see her.

At a glance, Cooper's head wound appeared superficial. A graze near his temple. His breathing was steady and even. She saw the fillet knife beneath the seat and used it to cut his bonds, cleanly slicing through the ropes that bound him.

"What are you doing?" Vengai shouted.

Taking a calculated risk, Daniels kicked Cooper in the leg as hard as she could. "And that's for leaving me here to die, you bastard!" she screamed.

The soldiers on the pier laughed uproariously, and even Vengai joined in. "You are angry at your rescuer?" he called, mocking her. "So much for heroes."

At her feet, Cooper's eyes began to flutter open. She knelt once more and whispered, "Don't move or make a sound and perhaps you'll find a way to live."

"Enough of that!" Vengai said. "Come here right now."

She climbed out of the boat and stepped onto the dock. "I guess you're right," she said. "There are no heroes."

"Now we will watch as the boat is launched and

towed out into the bay. When I tell you, you will detonate the device with this." He held out a second box with a switch on the top.

"Me?" she squeaked. "I did what you asked. Now you want me to be a...a...murderer, too?"

"Just think of how angry you are at them for their failure," he said. "Besides, it is either that, or I will add you and the children to the cargo."

"You already know my answer," she said, taking the detonator. "I just want you to know that sooner or later, someone will take you down. If not these men, then someone else. If not someone human, then God himself. There is justice in the world."

Vengai grinned at her. "In this world, *I* am justice. Now shut your mouth and do as I say."

Daniels watched as the boat was pulled away from the pier. The small craft helplessly bobbed along the water behind the bigger boat until they were about a couple of hundred yards off shore. She watched the boat carefully, but couldn't see any sign that Cooper had woken and realized the peril of the situation. She held the detonator in her hand and Vengai walked up behind her, pressing his body along her back. She tried to move forward, but he grabbed her arms and held her in place, obscenely rubbing his crotch against her rear.

"Tonight, you will come to me in my room," he whispered. "You will do all the things for me that you did for that traitor Rajan as I celebrate my victory."

Again she tried to move away, but he dug his fingers deeply into her arms. He was strong, and it felt like iron pincers were latched on to her. She could feel the bruising beginning and wanted to cry out, but wouldn't give him the satisfaction.

"You *will* come to me, Miss Daniels, or I will take one of the other women and you will be made to watch. You will come to me willingly or all those on the island that you care about will suffer the consequences and then I'll take you anyway."

He shoved her forward and Daniels fell to her knees.

"Now press the button," he said.

She fought with all her strength, but it was no use. Tears spilled out of her eyes. It was all over. She had no hope left, nothing to plead or to beg for. Vengai was implacable, and he was going to win. She looked up at the boat out in the water and held up the detonator. Barely able to see through her tears, she held it in her shaking hands, then took a deep breath and pressed the button.

The signal happened in a millisecond, but for Daniels her whole life moved in front of her. All of the victories and defeats seemed little compared to this moment. She was a murderer and nothing could ever change that. God would never forgive her.

The explosion shattered the still air, echoing across the shoreline with the force of a sonic boom. The soldiers cheered and clapped, and Vengai smiled as he pulled her to her feet.

"See? That wasn't so difficult at all, was it?"

Daniels tried to slap him, but he stopped her easily, then shoved her toward Katran. "Take this killer back to Rajan's room," he said. "She'll want to clean up before tonight."

CHAPTER TWENTY-ONE

Bolan felt the boat begin to drift and heard the sound of the other boat moving away. He knew that Vengai would detonate the device at any moment. Swiping blood from his eyes, he tried to ignore the headache pounding in his ears, each heartbeat feeling like a gong going off in his brain. He rolled onto his stomach, grabbed Faizal by the belt, and started dragging him toward the bow. Staying as close to the floor as possible, he passed by the helm, grabbing his Desert Eagle rig from beneath the seat.

Behind him, he heard the high-pitched whine of the explosive unit receiving a signal. He reached the front of the bow in the same millisecond that the bomb detonated. The force of the explosion felt like a giant hand picking him up and throwing him forward. He hit the water so hard that he lost his grip on Faizal, and barely managed to keep a grip on his Desert Eagle. The water churned and swirled, and Bolan kicked for the surface.

Knowing that he had to move quickly or risk being spotted from shore, he peered around for his friend. Faizal was floating facedown in the water nearby and Bolan swam to him, grabbing him by the shoulder and turning him over. A piece of fiberglass from the boat explosion was embedded in his throat. Faizal was dead before he even got wet.

"Damn it," he grumbled, reluctantly letting go of his friend. It would be right to see to it that he got an honorable burial, but this wasn't the time or place for that. The best he could do was to let him go, and hope that the tides treated him with kindness. Now he was truly on his own. Johnny and Peterson were both imprisoned, and the former President's daughter was still in the hands of Vengai, as was the software.

Bolan scanned the debris floating in the water and saw that the weapons locker was bobbing in the waves, feeling a flash of gratitude that Faizal had thought to get one that would float. He swam to it and began making his way toward shore, out of sight of the cove where the pirates docked their boats.

It would take precious time, but by then it would be dark. Vengai believed him dead and didn't even have the sense to empty his pockets, let alone to check over their boat. That arrogance would prove his undoing. Bolan fully intended to get back to the compound, rescue Johnny, Peterson and Daniels, and kill the man responsible.

It took the better part of two hours to reach a rocky shoreline that was out of sight. As soon as he was on land, Bolan dragged the weapons locker ashore, and stretched out to try to catch the last bit of the sun. He needed the warmth and the rest before he made his move. A half hour later, he got to his feet and opened the locker.

Inside, he found the Sledgehammer, along with extra ammo drums. He also removed a handful of extra magazines for the Desert Eagle, which he broke down, dried and reassembled to assure himself that it was in good working order despite the soaking. Bolan double-checked his handheld computer, but the water had seeped in and ruined it.

He debated on a few other weapons, but settled on a set of throwing blades, as well as a good combat blade. Finally he selected one of the extra British Enfield assault rifles, slinging it on his back for later use. He didn't take any grenades. At this point, the killing would have to be fast, up close and personal, which was how he preferred it, anyway, given the circumstances.

Leaving the rest of the weapons in the locker, he stowed it out of sight and began making his way up the cliff face, one slippery handhold at a time. Several times, he nearly fell as the loose shale crumbled beneath his grip, but he eventually reached the top, paused for a quick breath, then continued overland.

The island wasn't particularly large, and he didn't know what kind of security Vengai might have in place, so he was forced to take his time and move with caution. Even if the situation hadn't demanded it, the terrain would. Palm trees intermingled with other species and fat, heavy vines made easy movement almost impossible. He didn't want to get into a firefight at this point, let alone set off some kind of perimeter alarm. It didn't seem likely that the Ocean Tigers leader would invest in that kind of technology, but then again, he'd had the foresight to hire Tim Wright to develop satellite hacking software.

It was full dark now, and that slowed his progress even more. Pressing a button on his combat watch, Bolan glanced at the illuminated hands and calculated that it had been almost five hours since the explosion, and that he was about two hundred yards outside the main compound.

He almost didn't see the sentry, probably wouldn't have, except that he'd stopped to light a cigarette. Bolan tracked the man through the heavy foliage, the glowing ember from the cigarette winking in and out of visibility as he walked his post. Easing forward, the Executioner positioned himself behind a large palm and waited.

The man never knew what hit him. As he passed by, Bolan slipped behind him, covering the man's mouth tightly with his left hand, while driving the combat knife deeply into his back, puncturing the lung. He twisted the blade, hard, and severed the man's spinal cord. He shuddered once, twice, then died as Bolan lowered him to the ground. He had no way of knowing how often the guards rotated in and out, nor where, so he left the body where it was. Besides, in this dark, with no moon, someone would have to step on him to find him.

Bolan continued moving toward the compound, reaching the tree line behind the main house without encountering any other roving guards, though he suspected that there were at least a couple more wandering around. He peered into the open yard behind the main house.

Two guards were posted by the back door and the main compound itself was lit by a number of lights. The path around the house was well lit, and from his current location it was the only way to get to where Johnny and Peterson had been imprisoned in their cages. Bolan scanned the grounds carefully, then moved parallel to the house. The hum of a generator hinted that perhaps all the power came from a small building on the edge of the grounds. It was easy to see the wires from the perimeter lights running to an exterior box on the wall of the building.

Bolan reached the rear of the metal building without any difficulty and he could hear the low hum of a generator inside. The problem was that there was only one entrance—at the front and facing the guards. It seemed unlikely that he could get inside without being spotted. He paused, watching the guards and considering his options.

Easing around the side of the building, Bolan reached the box that the power lines ran into and found it open. Keeping one eye on the guards, he eased the front panel open, and then pulled the lever that shut down the power. Immediately, the compound went dark, and shouts of confusion came from inside the house, as well as in other locations.

He pulled back immediately, even as one of the guards yelled, "Hold your positions! The generator just went out again."

Bolan knelt at the side of the building, waiting for the guard to come investigate. He had to work by sound and sense as his eyesight was useless. The switch from the bright lights to the pitch-dark made him effectively blind. He listened carefully, knowing that he would have only one chance to accomplish his task. The guard's footsteps crunched on some gravel near the front of the shack, then he opened the door.

Bolan moved silently around the building, slipping

in behind him. The guard had a flashlight aimed at the generator and was peering at it in an attempt to figure out what was wrong. He started to turn when he felt the razor-sharp edge of Bolan's combat knife press up against his neck and his strong hand cover his mouth.

"Not a sound," Bolan said. "Nod if you understand."

The guard nodded.

"Take your weapon off your shoulder and lower it to the ground," he ordered. The guard complied, and Bolan slid it away into the darkness. "Now call out for the other guard. If you try to warn him in any way, you'll be dead before the words leave your lips."

He released his grip over the man's mouth. "Call for him. Now!"

The soldier called out a name and added that he needed help.

"Good," Bolan said, then cut his throat in one swift slice. It was cruel, but he couldn't afford mercy in his current situation. He lowered the man's body to the ground, leaving his flashlight aimed at the generator, then stepped to one side.

He had only to wait a moment for the other guard to arrive.

"Bala?" he said, stepping into the shack. "What is it?"

Bolan took him from behind, as well, driving the blade into the side of the man's neck and puncturing his larynx to ensure his silence. When he was dead, the Executioner moved to the generator. It was a simple enough setup and he quickly disabled it by cutting the lines that allowed it to feed power to the main box. Stepping over the dead guards, he slipped back outside.

Inside the main house, he could see candlelight, and he knew that it would only be a matter of a couple of minutes until the area was swarming with guards. Not long after that, they'd send someone to try to repair the generator, which wouldn't take that long for even a somewhat skilled mechanic. For now, they seemed to be holding their positions, shouting out to one another occasionally to try to determine what was going on. He moved down the path, staying as silent as a ghost and using the deep shadows of the main house to try to reach the prisoner cages he'd seen on his way in the first time.

He reached the area where the cages were located. He moved in closer, hearing the sounds of the guards shouting back and forth now, trying to determine what was happening. "Johnny?" he whispered.

"Cooper," his brother replied. "I figured as much."

"What's your condition?" he asked, moving to the front of the cage and going to work on the lock.

"Not as bad as it could be," Johnny quipped. "At least I'm not dead."

"What about Michelle?" he asked, silently cursing that the lock was old and rusted.

"She was… They took her for a while," he said. "After they put you and Bashir on the boat. Down to the main barracks building. She was unconscious when they brought her back. She has been ever since."

Bolan sighed. "Damn it," he said. "Did you see how bad?"

"She's naked in that cage," Johnny said quietly. "It was bad."

Still struggling with the lock, Bolan cursed again. Twisting hard, the hasp finally gave way, and he pulled the door open. It screeched like a barn owl and the compound went silent, then more shouts erupted. "Perfect," he said, stepping into the cage and cutting through the bonds that were holding Johnny's arms over his head.

His brother groaned quietly as the pressure relented, swinging his arms back and forth.

"We have to go now," Bolan said. "Are you functional?"

"Give me a weapon and I'll show you just how functional I am," he said.

Bolan handed him the extra rifle. "I'd hoped that Michelle would be okay to help, but we'll have to manage it on our own."

"Bashir?"

"Dead in the explosion," he replied. "I tried to get him clear, but no luck."

Johnny worked the action on the rifle, and Bolan handed him three extra magazines, which he tucked into the waistband of his jeans. "What's the plan?"

"We'll start at the docks," Bolan said, "and work our way back to the main house. I don't want anyone coming in behind us."

"Standard two by two?" Johnny asked.

"Yeah, I'm out first," he said. "Oh, and Johnny?"

"Yeah?"

"We take them all. This ends now," he said.

"Lead the way," Johnny replied, then followed him into the darkness.

IT TOOK LESS THAN TEN minutes for them to work their way down to the docks. By then, most of the soldiers had moved up toward the main house, forming a loose perimeter. They slipped between crates of supplies until they reached the dock farthest from the main road to the compound. In all, Bolan had counted six men along the docks.

"I'd like to do this quietly, if we can," he told Johnny.

His brother nodded, screwing a sound suppressor into place on the Enfield rifle while Bolan sighted along the docks through a night-vision optic. "Start at the far end of the dock," he said, "and work back toward our position."

"Got it," he said.

"First target is located at the far end of the dock, eleven o'clock," he said. "Got him?"

"Acquired," Johnny said.

"On my mark," Bolan said, scanning to make sure none of the other guards was moving toward them or the first man. "Mark."

Johnny squeezed the trigger and the silenced rifle uttered a muted *phhft* sound. Through the optic, Bolan saw the man stagger, clutch at his chest, then topple backward into the water. The guard closest to him moved to investigate the splash, and even from his position, he could hear the echo of him calling out a name.

"Take him," Bolan said. "Moving into position at two o'clock."

Johnny fired again, this time scoring a head shot. The weapon was a tiny bit louder. Each time he fired, it would get louder still. Above them, the main house suddenly flared into light and a siren began to sound. As the compound came to life, Bolan scanned the activity. He could see some people moving into position and knew that their secret was out.

"They found the guards and restarted the generator," Bolan said. "So much for trying it the sneaky way."

"Move out?" Johnny asked.

Bolan looked through the optic again, shutting off the night-vision component, which would be useless as the lights along the path began to brighten. "Take the next two," he said. "Quickly."

Johnny peered through the scope, squeezing the trigger twice, then a third time, when his second shot was a little high. The two guards closest to them heard the sound of the last shot.

"We're made," Bolan said. "Time to get personal."

Johnny folded the stock, and adjusted the weapon so he could use it as more of a traditional assault rifle. "Whenever you're ready," he said.

"Now," Bolan said, rising to his feet from behind the stack of crates they'd been using for cover. He pulled his Desert Eagle and fired twice, taking the nearest man with the heavy .44-caliber slugs in the chest. The report of the pistol brought a sharp contrast to the muffled shots from the rifle. It was like the starting bell at the Kentucky Derby, men running into different positions, some running for their lives, and Bolan and Johnny moving in for the kill.

Johnny put a 3-round burst into a second man.

"Let's go," Bolan said, jogging along the pier and

using the crates once again as coverage, with Johnny close behind. "We'll hit the main path and work our way to the house."

By the time they reached the end of the pier, more soldiers were coming down the path. "Don't stop," Bolan said, firing as he moved into a cover position behind a tree.

Johnny hit the ground, rolled behind a steel barrel and came up firing. The soldiers returned fire, and Bolan knew the fight was on for sure. By his count, nine of Vengai's men were down. He estimated that there had to be at least twenty more on the island, maybe as many as thirty.

He sighted and fired several more times, mostly to keep the soldiers pinned down, moving to a place near Johnny. "We've got to hold off," he said. "Draw as many of them as possible down here."

"You want more of them?" Johnny asked, his voice unbelieving. "Why not take them a few at a time?"

"The more we take out down here, the fewer Vengai will have at the main house," Bolan explained. "I'm going to move again. Cover me."

Johnny popped up from behind the barrel on full-auto, using suppression fire to keep the soldiers down. Closer to the main path now, Bolan used a concrete barricade for cover as shots started heading their way. He risked a glance over the barricade and saw that more and more of Vengai's guards were streaming down the path toward them. He loaded the Sledgehammer with a fresh drum and gave them a full five count before he popped up and began to open fire.

The closest three soldiers died screaming before the

others even knew what hit them, and when Johnny saw his brother making his move, he switched to sniper mode and began picking them off one by one. The frangible rounds rapidly turned the path into a bloody mess, but Bolan had to give Vengai's guards credit. They didn't run, but did their best to hold their ground against the horrible onslaught.

With the closest guards out of the way, Bolan and Johnny began to move forward, the sand creating a slow march. The sound of the shotgun echoed over the small island. Turning to his left, the Executioner fired and dropped two more, and Johnny took a third with a head shot. It was clear that Vengai's guards were unnerved by the direct assault as they fired wildly. They seemed to be in more danger from a ricochet than a direct hit.

"Go right," Bolan called to Johnny, who took cover behind a large palm tree.

Bolan took a knee behind a cluster of rocks and scanned the area. By his count there were still at least a dozen soldiers between him and the main house. With the power back on and time running out, Vengai wouldn't wait to kill Heather or to activate the software. They needed to get up to that house as fast as possible.

"Options?" Johnny yelled.

"I think we just have to push through them," Bolan said. "We're running out of time."

"Push through them? Really?"

"It's our only choice, really," he said. He loaded the Sledgehammer with the last drum and chambered the first shell. "Ready?"

"Not really, but you're not giving me a lot of options!"

There was a cluster of five or six of Vengai's soldiers that had taken shelter on the far side of a parked pickup. The rest of them had taken cover at various points in the compound yard. Bolan thought that the truck was probably their best bet. Johnny was staring at him, waiting for some kind of signal. Bolan held up five fingers and pointed at the truck, and his brother nodded.

For his plan to work Bolan knew that they'd need the truck, so he slung the Sledgehammer and switched to the British Enfield. From their current positions it would be easy to stay relatively sheltered while picking off the guards using the vehicle for cover. There had been a brief lull in the firing as Vengai's defenders waited for them to make their next move. Now was the time.

"On my mark!" he called. "Try to keep the vehicle intact if you can."

"Let's just do this thing!"

"Three...two..." he yelled, putting the obelisk in the SUSAT sight on the front of a boot he could see sticking out from behind the front passenger tire. "Now!" He squeezed off the shot and saw the man's foot explode. He screamed and jumped to his feet, exposing himself, and Bolan put another round in his heart.

Everyone started shooting at the same time, and the night was filled with the echoes of various types of guns going off. In a way, Bolan was thankful that the Ocean Tigers had focused their efforts on piracy instead of weapons smuggling. They weren't armed with the latest and greatest, which made a big difference in this kind of fight. He adjusted his point of aim and when one of them popped up over the bed of the truck to take a shot, he put a round in the man's throat.

Johnny was wreaking havoc of his own as he shot one man who'd been hiding beneath the truck itself. A 3-round burst in a contained space like that did a lot of damage and the soldier flopped and rolled trying to get away but it was a futile effort and he died, scrabbling at the ground in agony.

A voice from the direction of the house roared over the din, "Flank them, you idiots!" and Bolan recognized it as Vengai himself. He immediately switched focus and spotted him through the sight. He aimed center mass, but just as he pulled the trigger, a bullet from elsewhere hit the rocks he was using for cover and sprayed stone chips into his face. His shot went wild, driving Vengai back into the house.

"Damn it," he cursed, glancing left and spotting the shooter. He used his left hand to pick up the Desert Eagle and squeezed off three rounds, hitting the mark twice and killing the man who'd ruined his chance to end one of the main threats here once and for all. Setting the powerful handgun down, he resumed his work on the guards using the pickup.

Johnny had taken down another man creeping around the tailgate. That one was trying to crawl away, but his brother finished him with a second shot. Bolan focused on the hood, waiting until one of the men

risked leaning over the top to fire. His first shot was a
bit high, but sufficed to force the soldier out of cover,
allowing Bolan to take him with his second shot. The
bullet hit him just above the eyes, blowing the back of
his skull off and killing him instantly.

The last of Vengai's men using the truck as cover
decided to make a run for it, sprinting left toward the
house. Johnny fired once, taking him in the back and
dropping him to the ground.

"Move up!" Bolan yelled, grabbing up his weapons
and sprinting for the truck. Automatic weapons fire
dug up the ground around him and he made his move.
Out of the corner of his eye, he saw Johnny break from
cover and join him in his mad sprint for the vehicle.
Bolan reached it first, yanking open the driver's door
and diving inside. Johnny took a running leap into the
bed of the truck.

"Stay down!" Bolan yelled, slamming the door shut.
By a stroke of luck, the keys were in the ignition and
he started the engine, which roared to life. Bullets
ricocheted off the body and starred the glass, but as
Bolan had guessed, Vengai had modified this vehicle
with some basic protections. It had looked too new for
just an island Jeep to get back and forth.

Bolan shifted into Reverse, spinning the wheel hard
and backing down the rutted path away from the main
house. Bullets sprayed the grille of the pickup, and
he could hear Johnny cursing in the back as he was
bounced around by the movement of the truck. The
main house was on stilts that were perhaps three or

four feet high; the truck was much taller than that, and Bolan aimed for the front steps.

He involuntarily winced as the soldiers concentrated their fire on the windshield in the front of the truck, but so far the armored panels and bulletproof glass kept him safe. He kept the gas pedal pushed to the floor, and they were ten yards from the house when he saw the guard step out from behind the corner of the house with the shoulder-mounted rocket.

Bolan had a split second to see the fiery trail of the rocket and to yell "Incoming!" before it smashed into the front of the vehicle. The explosion was a gigantic ball of fire, the missile penetrating the armor plating of the truck and shattering the engine. The smell of burning gasoline and oil filled the cab, but the momentum was too much and the truck smashed into the front steps of the house. The wood broke like dry kindling under the force of the impact and the porch crumbled.

They finally shuddered to a stop with the nose of the truck inside the main room, and both Bolan and Johnny bailed out of the burning vehicle immediately, trying to find cover. The place was strangely empty. Vengai's soldiers began closing in on the house, but they had a good position now, and Bolan knew it was time to split up.

"Johnny, here," he said, tossing him the Sledgehammer shotgun. "Use this to take out as many as you can. I'm going to check the rest of the house to find Vengai and Heather."

"You got it," his brother said, taking a position near

the truck that afforded a view of everything approaching the wreckage. Two men broke from cover and the Sledgehammer boomed, dropping their bloody bodies to the turf. "Wow...I love this gun," he said, grinning. "I've got this. Go!"

CHAPTER TWENTY-TWO

Bolan turned away, confident that the front of the house was covered, and moved past the front room and into a short hallway. To his left was a kitchen, and there were more rooms farther down the hall. He'd just decided to move down the hall when a brief flicker of light caught his eye, and he turned to see the blade of a machete coming for his head.

He threw himself backward and to the side, trying to avoid it, and was partially successful as it tore through the sleeve of his shirt and traced a deep, bloody furrow into his arm. Cursing, he kept moving, but went in the unexpected direction. He dived forward into his attacker, slamming an elbow underneath his chin and catching him off guard. The man stumbled back into the kitchen area, nearly losing his footing on the tile floor.

Bolan could see that this wasn't one of Vengai's regulars. He wore insignia of some kind on his collar. He didn't want to kill him immediately—the man might have information that was useful. "So, you must be one of Vengai's senior lapdogs, right?" he asked, drawing the combat blade from its sheath. He held it in a reverse grip, ready to counter, thrust or throw as necessary.

"I am Katran," he said, spitting blood from where

Bolan's earlier blow had caused him to bite his tongue. "And I will kill you for my leader." He moved closer and Bolan slid sideways, buying time.

The machete had substantial reach on him, and this was no small, poorly trained recruit, but a well-muscled soldier who had been trained to fight hand-to-hand. Katran lunged at him, swinging the machete in a vicious arc that would have taken Bolan's head from his shoulders if he'd been holding still. As it was, he ducked low, reversed his own blade and stepped inside the man's guard. He counterthrust with the edge, slicing upward, and opened a six-inch-long gash in the man's leg. Almost immediately, the blood began to flow.

Katran grunted in pain, but then made the mistake of looking down at the wound.

"Artery wound," Bolan said softly. "You're going to bleed out in a matter of seconds unless you tie that off."

Ignoring his injury, the big man yelled in anger and rushed him, bringing the machete up high over his head. "Die!"

Once more, Bolan stepped sideways, rotated and swept Katran's legs out from beneath him. The man went down with a grunt, the machete flying from his grip. Completing the turn, Bolan lashed out and drove a booted foot into the gash on his leg. Katran screamed, involuntarily reaching for the wound.

"Time's running out," Bolan said. "There's still time to stop the pain."

Groaning, the man relaxed, his arms flopping weakly to his sides. The kitchen floor looked like an abattoir, with bright streaks of crimson blood everywhere. Some of it belonged to Bolan, and he glanced at the wound on his arm. It could've been worse, but it had sliced deeply enough that he'd need stitches fairly soon.

He kept his boot pressed down on the wound in Katran's leg. "Where's Vengai?"

"The last I saw him, he was down the hall in the computer room," he said, his voice drawn with pain. "Bind me up, man."

"And the girl?" he inquired.

"Same place." He writhed on the floor, but sat up quickly with a small pistol in his hand.

Bolan had drawn the Desert Eagle already, and he pumped two quick rounds into Katran's chest. "That should take care of the pain," he stated.

Johnny's voice sounded from the living room. "You okay back there?"

"Perfect," Bolan said. "What's your status?"

"I think he's running out of men," Johnny called back. "Looks like there's only three or four left out there, and they're not rushing toward the place."

"Stay put. I'm going to finish this," he called as he holstered the Desert Eagle.

He bent and cut a long strip off the bottom of Katran's shirt, using it as a makeshift bandage for his arm. He hissed as he pulled it down tightly with his teeth. Stitches were definitely going to be needed at some point. For now, he'd worry about taking care of Vengai.

Bolan slipped his blade back into its sheath, then stepped into the hallway once more. He moved down it cautiously, not wanting another surprise like the man in the kitchen had been. The first door on his right was closed and he paused briefly, listening. There was no sound on the other side and he pulled his Desert Eagle, then reared back and kicked the door inward.

It opened onto an empty office space. The desk was cluttered with papers and a computer system that had been smashed. At a guess, this was Vengai's office and he'd destroyed it when he realized that his compound was under assault. Bolan left the room as it was and returned to the hallway.

Another door revealed only a small bathroom. That left one final door at the end of the hall, and he moved to it quickly. Like the others, this door was shut. From the front of the house, the Sledgehammer fired twice, and Bolan wondered if Johnny was putting a permanent end to Vengai's men.

He paused only long enough to listen at the door briefly, then kicked it inside. Two computer stations were set up in this room, and a young man who looked the part of computer nerd more than soldier was dead on the floor. His throat had been cut. On the far side of the room, there was an open window. Vengai and Heather Daniels were nowhere to be seen.

Swearing to himself, he entered the room and looked at the computer screens. Both appeared to be running some kind of software sequence. The interface was pretty rudimentary, but even he could tell that it was running a countdown sequence of some kind.

He looked at the various fields, and saw that three of them were for satellite stations that he was already familiar with—Department of Defense units that could send and receive coded signals from authorized bases and high-ranking military personnel, as well as from Air Force One and the Office of the President of the United States.

The question was what the satellites had been ordered to do. He saw a toggle labeled Command Interface and clicked on it. A secondary window opened on the screen and Bolan felt his blood run cold.

Vengai had ordered a self-detonate sequence to the nuclear weapons in their bays on U.S. soil. Knowing he was about to be captured, he'd simply lashed out at who he perceived to be his tormentors. The clock was counting down and showed less than thirty minutes.

"Son of a bitch," Bolan said, scanning the screen for some way to shut it down. This was technology, however, that was beyond him. If he'd still had his handheld computer, maybe he could call Brognola and work something out, but that was gone and there wasn't a phone in sight. "Damn it!" he swore, jumping to his feet.

He ran back along the hallway, hitting the main room and nearly slipping on an area rug. "Johnny, we're in it deep," he said. "We've got to get Michelle up and functioning."

"What are you talking about?" his brother asked, getting to his feet from where he'd been kneeling and using a hole in the wall to take out targets.

"Vengai and Heather are gone," Bolan said. "But he left us a present. He's set the software to detonate our own nukes back in the States. I don't know how to stop it."

"And she does?" he asked, his face paling.

"I guess we better hope so," he replied. "How many are left out there?"

"Not very many," he said. "I saw two making a run for the docks a couple of minutes ago, but that's about it. I think the rest are either dead or hiding. Pirates don't make very good soldiers."

"Good," Bolan said. "Let's go get Michelle."

They climbed over the front end of the truck and out onto what remained of the patio, jumping the couple of feet down to the ground. Bolan had no idea what they'd do if Peterson couldn't or wasn't up to stopping the detonation sequence.

NONE OF VENGAI'S PIRATES bothered them as they ran for the cages where they'd left Peterson. The distant sound of a couple boats leaving could be heard, and Bolan assumed that most of them were taking off for safer territory. There couldn't have been more than a handful remaining, as between himself and Johnny, the compound was littered with bodies. It looked like a battlefield, and for all practical purposes, that's what it was.

They reached the cage where Peterson was located and saw that she was sitting upright, with her arms curled around her knees. Her eyes, even in the odd light of the lamps, were wide, frightened and empty.

"Michelle?" he said, kneeling to her level. "It's Matt and Johnny. We're going to get you out of there."

She shook her head in the negative, and he turned to Johnny. "Get the lock open, would you?" he asked, tossing him the autopick he carried.

Johnny went to work on the lock, talking in a soothing voice the whole time. "Hang in there, Michelle. This will only take a minute."

Bolan could see the marks on her fully nude body where the men had ravaged her. Bruises on the backs of her legs, scratches on her arms. He silently thanked God the light wasn't better and he couldn't see even more. "Michelle, I know you've been hurt, but I need you to snap out of it. We're in trouble."

"Leave…leave…leave me alone," she stuttered, her teeth chattering in fear and reaction. "Don't touch me."

The lock on the cage door popped open and Johnny stepped back. "We're not going to touch you, Michelle. No one will hurt you."

Bolan moved to stand in front of the door, holding out his hand. "Come on out, Michelle," he said, keeping his voice low and soft. "Give me your hand."

She shook her head once more and tried to scoot away from him. If she hadn't already had her back pressed against the back of the cage, he suspected she would have crawled away.

"She's been through the ringer, Cooper," Johnny said. "What are we going to do?"

"I'm not sure yet," Bolan admitted. He knelt by the cage opening. "Michelle, I know you're scared, but…" His voice trailed off as he tried to think of what might reach her. "But the mission, your mission, isn't complete. You have to think about Heather."

He saw her eyes glint at the mention of the girl's name. "That's right," he said. "We still haven't rescued Heather and we never will, unless you can help us."

"Heather?" she asked, her voice filled with curiosity. "You haven't found her?"

"Give me your shirt, Johnny," Bolan said. When his brother handed it to him, he passed it to Michelle, setting it on the floor of the cage close to her feet.

"You might feel a little better if you put that on," he suggested.

She snatched it up as though it was food and she was starving, and yanked it over her head. It was long enough to cover her to midthigh and at least afford her a little modesty.

"Michelle," Bolan said, "Vengai took Heather before we could get to him."

"Then...then you have to go after her!" she said, her voice fierce. "You *have* to."

Bolan shook his head. "I can't," he said. "Not without your help. I know that you've been through a lot, but you're stronger than this. Stronger than them, and Heather needs you. Do you think you can come out of there and lend us a hand?"

She thought about it for long seconds—seconds they didn't have, he knew, but he also knew that pushing her would be useless and might even set them back.

"What do you say, Michelle? Help us so I can help Heather?"

Finally she nodded and moved toward the edge of the cage. Once there, she stopped and scanned the compound yard. "Are they dead?" she asked. "All of them?"

Johnny peered around the yard with an exaggerated motion. "If any are still alive, they aren't here to say so," he replied. "We got most of them. The rest ran off."

"What about Katran?" she seethed. "Is that… Is he dead?"

Bolan nodded. "I killed him myself," he told her. "In the kitchen of the main house."

"I tried to kill him," she said, her eyes far away. "I tried to kill them all when they took…took me…" She turned to Johnny. "You couldn't stop them, could you?"

"No," he said, his voice filled with sadness. "I'm sorry."

She looked around at the carnage once more. "I just wish I could have killed them myself. They…they—"

"Michelle," Bolan said, interrupting her before she could get started. "I know they did horrible things. I'm sorry for that. But if we're going to stop Vengai from doing even more horrible things, and find Heather, I need you in the here and now." He looked at her, his eyes boring into hers. "Can you do that?"

She nodded and got slowly to her feet with his help. He did his best to ignore the wounds on her face, the blood seeping down her legs. The bastards had raped her savagely, and the fact that she could function at all was a testament to her strength of character. "Let's go over to the house," he said. "I'll show you what's going on."

Johnny took up a position on one side of her, and Bolan took the other. Together, they guided her around the worst of the carnage—the Sledgehammer loaded with frangible rounds was not kind to the human body—then over the debris of the truck and into the main house. They stopped in the front room.

"May I have some water, please?" she asked, looking at the wreckage.

"Good idea," Johnny said. "This man wouldn't even slow down long enough for me to get a drink."

"Check the kitchen," Bolan suggested, "but do it quickly."

Johnny ran into the kitchen and came back a short moment later with three bottles of water. He handed each of them one, keeping one for himself, and the three of them drank deeply. In combat, it seemed there was little time for something as simple as a drink, let alone a meal, which none of them had had for over a day—and likely wouldn't be able to for quite some time yet. Bolan gulped down the water, then tossed the bottle aside.

Once Peterson had finished, some of the color had returned to her face and she didn't look quite so fearful. "Better?" Bolan asked.

"At least I'm not thirsty," she said. Her voice was still a bare whisper. "Now what?"

"Now we go to the computer room and you save the world," he said.

Startled, she looked at him askance. "What's...what do you mean?"

"Come on," he said, taking her by the elbow gently. "I'll show you."

The three of them made their way along the hallway, pausing only long enough for Peterson to stop and stare hatefully at Katran's dead form on the kitchen floor. "Did he...did he suffer?" she asked.

"He paid his dues," Bolan lied, thinking that short of a month or two with some really talented torturers, there was nothing that would put to paid for what he'd done to her. "Come on."

They continued along the hall to the computer room and he guided her to the station. "Take a look," he said. "It's running the software that Vengai had developed."

She stared at the screen for several seconds, then looked at him. "Is it okay if I…"

"Do whatever you've got to do," he said. "I'm no programmer."

She gingerly sat in one of the computer chairs and tapped a couple of keys, bringing up two new, smaller windows on the screen. "He used the software to hack into the satellites, then backfed the launch data right out of the DOD servers. Was this his plan all along?"

"I don't think so," Bolan said. "I think he just got vindictive when he realized that his base was under attack and that there was no way that he was going to escape."

She glanced at the body on the floor. "He even killed his tech geek."

"Probably so no one would know how to stop it," Johnny said. "It's a pretty standard bad-guy move. But he didn't realize that we still had an ace in the hole. I think he expected his men to slow us down more than they did."

"The question is whether or not *you* can stop it," Bolan said. "As you can see, the countdown is well under way."

She looked at the screen again and shook her head. "I don't know," she admitted. "I'm not familiar with the software, and it's not like there's a manual. This shouldn't even be possible."

"Well, I can't stop it and Johnny here can't stop it, so that leaves you," he said.

"What if I can't?" she cried. "I'm…God, I'm useless! If I'd only listened to you to begin with, none of this would've happened!"

"What are you talking about?" Bolan asked.

"I'd be safe in San Diego, and you would've stormed in here, killed everyone and rescued Heather. Vengai would be dead. Rajan would be safe."

"Who the hell is Rajan?" he asked.

"I wish I knew," Johnny said. He quickly filled Bolan in on how they'd met up with Daniels and Rajan trying to make their escape. "Seriously tough," he added. "And he almost pulled it off."

"Well, then he wasn't civilian, that's for sure. My guess is Sri Lankan Intelligence or some kind of military. We had intelligence that said that they might have someone on the inside."

"Either way," Peterson said, "he would've known how to stop this. I don't. All I'm good for is getting people killed, or getting myself tortured and raped." The sound that escaped her mouth then was somewhere between a sob and a laugh.

Bolan considered the situation. With every minute that passed, Vengai was closer to escaping with Daniels and the nukes were closer to detonation. He needed Peterson to be who she truly was, and not this sad, broken product of circumstance. "Stand up," he barked. "Right now."

Her eyes widened. "Wha…what?"

"Stand up!" he repeated. "On your feet."

She slowly got out of the chair. There was fear in

her eyes, yes, but something else, too. "Now, it's possible you're right. My plan might have worked. But it didn't. Maybe you didn't see Bashir and me get blown up out there on the water, but my plan got him killed and myself nearly blown up. Sometimes plans work, sometimes they don't. That's field ops, and I'd think someone with your experience would know that."

"Yeah, but I—"

"Shut it," he said. "No excuses and no bullshit. When you've got your head on straight, you're a good operative. You've been through hell and I'm sorry for that. Right now, you're in no condition to go chasing after Vengai and Heather, and I've never been in a position to figure out this kind of software. We've got a choice. We can sit here and wait for the end of the world, or we can do what field operatives do and adjust based on the circumstances."

"They gang-raped me, you son of a bitch!" she yelled. "In every single way they could!" Then she slapped him.

"Good," he said, his cheek stinging from the slap. "Now at least I know you're alive. So, are you going to give up and wait to die or help out?"

Her shoulders suddenly sagged and she scrubbed her face with her hands. "You shouldn't have left me behind to begin with," she said quietly.

Bolan was silent for a moment, then nodded. "You're right. I shouldn't have. I apologize. I don't like it when missions get personal. It gets in the way."

"Sometimes," she said, sitting in the chair, "that can be a good thing. Just ask Johnny here."

"Me?" he asked. "Why ask me?"

"Because you didn't let me go alone," she said. "And that was a personal decision."

"Well, I expected it to be more fun than it's been so far. Not my idea of a vacation."

"Can you stop it?" Bolan asked, pointing on the clock counting down on the screen.

She shrugged. "I can try, as long as you go after Vengai and get Heather back safely."

"I'll try my best," he said. "Johnny, you'll stay here and watch over Michelle. See if you can find a sat phone and get hold of Hal. If this all comes apart, we may need to make some other adjustments in the plans."

"Nuclear armageddon calls for 'adjustments,' Cooper?" he asked. "My God, you're a master of understatement."

"Just look for the phone," he said, "and keep her safe while she figures out how to stop it. I'll be back as quick as I can."

He slung the Enfield over his shoulder and reloaded the Desert Eagle. He wanted to follow Vengai's route as accurately as possible, so he climbed through the window the man had gone out of, spotting the tracks of his boots, along with a second, smaller set of prints next to them.

They led into the jungle, away from the compound, and Bolan followed, knowing that somewhere out there was the man responsible for everything—and that the Executioner was just the man to make him pay for his crimes.

CHAPTER TWENTY-THREE

The night air felt stifling, and no wind blew off the Bay of Bengal at all to cool the small island. The smells of the jungle were of thick, dark dirt, odd flowery smells like walking past a perfume store, and a mold that came with the dampness and high humidity. It was a perfect night for sitting on a porch, drinking something cold and watching the waves roll in. But with a barely visible trail and a hostage, it was a terrible night for a hunt. Still, that was the job and knowing that Johnny and Peterson would do their best to stop the software from launching the missiles, Bolan could focus on the task at hand.

He spotted a barely visible footpath leading through the trees and began to follow it. The island wasn't flat by any means, but he did know for certain that there were no other coves or good places to land a boat. He and Faizal had checked before they'd come in the first time. That meant that somewhere on this island, Vengai had gone to ground and taken Daniels with him. It was just a question of finding them.

The path, which was little more than a less overgrown area no wider than a person, wound back and forth, picking its way through the heavy trees and hanging vines. Several times, Bolan thought he'd lost it entirely, only to find it on the other side of a boulder or a cluster of palms. It generally led upward, and he found himself moving faster, supremely aware of time passing.

The only logical reason for Vengai to have taken Daniels with him was to use her as a final bargaining piece. Her ransom alone, if paid, would allow him to set up shop somewhere new and start over. Not that President Daniels would ever pay it, and even if he would, Bolan had no intention whatsoever of letting Vengai live long enough to collect it, let alone spend it on something. Ahead of him, the trail widened a bit and the trees thinned enough for him to see the sky overhead. It was a clear night, though moonless, and the stars were breathtakingly beautiful.

Realizing that he had to have come close to reaching the peak, he slowed, searching as much with his other senses as he did with his eyes. In fact, he closed his eyes, knowing they provided little help in this situation and instead, tried to listen. From this distance, the sound of the waves was faint enough to be ignored, but there was another sound—close by—that he struggled for a moment to place.

It was the sound of bats feeding in the night. The high, chittering cry of their flights echoed in a nearby cave. He slowly turned in a circle, trying to pinpoint a direction, found it and moved slowly toward the east. He glanced at his watch, noting that the countdown on the computer had less than ten minutes to go, and Bolan hoped that Peterson had found some way to stop it before it was too late.

If she didn't, stopping Vengai or rescuing Daniels would be the least of his concerns. Millions would die and the world would be changed forever. He moved several more feet, paused to listen, then moved again. The cave was well hidden behind a series of trees and fat, hanging vines. There was no light coming from the inside and he had no idea what—or who—might be in there, aside from the bats.

He eased his way forward, ready to move in a split second in any direction, every muscle prepared for a fight. Ahead of him, the entrance loomed: pitch-black and filled with bats. He paused once more, looking carefully at the ground and spotting the same tracks that led from the house. Vengai and Daniels were somewhere inside.

There was nowhere left for them to go.

PETERSON WORKED FURIOUSLY at the keys, then pounded them once in frustration. "Johnny," she said, "we *really* need that phone."

He didn't question her, a fact for which she was quite thankful, then she considered the problem in front of her. There was no obvious way to shut down the system and she didn't know how the software communicated with the satellites themselves. If she pulled the plug, that would be useless—the commands had already been given, and she could see that on the screen as numerous attempts at overrides from both military and intelligence centers in the United States failed again and again.

From the other side of the hallway, she could hear Johnny cursing as he tore apart the office they'd passed. Suddenly she heard him yell "Aha!" then the sound of his feet running along the hallway. He swerved into the room clutching a phone in his hand.

"I think I've got one," he said, pushing the power button. "All we need is...a signal!"

He tossed the phone in her direction and she caught it. Now the only question was who to call. Everyone she knew would already be swamped trying to figure it out and worse still, the phone only had one bar of charge left on it.

"Who do we call?" she asked.

"What do you mean, who do we call?" he said, his voice exasperated. "You don't have any friends who might be able to help out?"

She shook her head. "Even if I could get through, they've got to be in full panic mode right now. By the time I explained everything, it would be too late."

He pointed at the countdown on the screen. "It's about to be too late either way," he said. "Give me the phone."

She tossed it back to him and watched as he quickly dialed. "Come on, Hal," he said. "This isn't the time to be taking a lunch break!"

After a moment of silence he said, "Hal! Johnny here!" There was another brief pause, then he said, "Hold on, let me put you on speaker."

He pressed a button and Brognola's voice came on the line. "What the hell is going on over there?" he was saying. "Every nuke in the country is about to go off! Where's Striker?"

"Hal, this is Michelle," she said. "Striker isn't here. He went after Vengai and Heather and left me to try to tackle the software."

There was a heavy sigh on the other end of the line, then, "So what's the problem? Shut it off before this turns into a war."

"That's just it, sir," she said. "I don't know how. I've already tried everything I could think of. We were hoping that you might have someone there who could help. None of the standard overrides are working and I'm out of ideas, so we're looking for some fresh ones."

"Stand by," Brognola said, not even bothering to put them on hold as he slammed the receiver down and yelled for "Aaron" at the top of his lungs.

A new voice came on the line. "Okay," he growled. "I don't want to confuse anyone. Do you know where the keyboard is?"

"I'm not a programmer," Peterson snarled into the phone, "but I know my way around a system. Just tell me what to do."

"Fine, fine," he said. "I didn't mean to offend. I need you to open a port, so I can see your screen." He rattled off an internet protocol address, which she typed into a fresh browser window. The page loaded, asking for a user name and password, which he also provided.

She typed them in and the screen flickered once, and he said, "All right. Now I can see what you see."

"Why can't I see you?" she asked.

"Because your webcam is not turned on," he said. "And it won't be. Just listen and do what I tell you."

"Go ahead," she said.

"A moment," he said. "I need to read the screens."

She watched as he manipulated the windows on her screen, scanning each one quickly. Peterson watched how quick and efficient each stroke was and tried to follow the screen executions like a play being performed and the end was just in sight.

"The way this software works is by using a constantly shifting communications code," he said. "This is why it was able to hack into the satellites and the databases, then in turn, lock us out of them. It automatically changes the necessary security protocols, while simultaneously running the commands it's been given."

"Great. How do we stop it?" she asked. "Considering there is—" she looked at the countdown timer "—just under ten minutes left."

The line went silent for a moment, then he said, "I'm…unsure. If you enter in a new set of commands, that may work or it may not. Let's try that first." Aaron Kurtzman had her bring up a command prompt that connected to just one of the satellites, then gave her the instructions to have it run a self-diagnostic.

She sent the command and a moment later a message popped up that said: "Command not recognized. Retry?"

"Damn it," Kurtzman cursed. "So it just bounces everything back."

"Got any other ideas?" Johnny asked. "I'd hate to think we're going to let this guy blow up the whole country."

"Just one," he said, "but there's risk."

"What risk?" Brognola asked.

"If my idea works, the satellites will go offline for perhaps as long as an hour. In addition, we will lose some data," he said.

"Let's hear it," Peterson encouraged. "Since we're out of options and damn near out of time."

"I think the problem is, we've been giving it commands," Kurtzman said, "which the software is programmed to ignore once it's running. But that doesn't mean we can't task the satellites with something else to do."

"Like what?" she asked.

"Data overload," he said. "We'll task them with uploading a copy of the internet and backing up the intelligence databases. The satellites can only receive a finite amount of data. They're probably already close to their limit now. Attempting to upload that much all at once should cause them to automatically shut down and reboot."

"But we'll be dark for an hour, right?" Brognola said.

"In most cases, yes," Kurtzman replied. "Some a little less, some more, depending on where they are in their orbit cycle. Not every satellite is linked to this system, but—"

"The President needs to sign off on this," Brognola said.

"Can you get an answer in less than ten minutes?" Peterson asked.

There was a pregnant pause as the big Fed considered it. "No. He's not that fast a decision maker."

"Then it's your call," she said.

There was only the briefest of hesitations, then Brognola said, "Walk her through it, Aaron, and let's pray that this works."

"Bring up an isolated, new command prompt,"

Kurtzman told her, "and have it pull the satellite identification information directly from the other program."

Peterson did as he told her, watching as the system
filled in the appropriate fields. "Done," she said.

"Now you're going to have all the satellites log in to
the various intelligence databases," he said. "The software already knows how to hack in, so you shouldn't
need a password."

She typed the commands, doing her best not to look
at the countdown timer, which read six minutes and
some odd seconds. "I'm in," she said.

"Good. Now type the 'Copy All' command," he
said.

Peterson typed it and waited for a second, then the
screen showed "Working." "They're requesting the
data," she said.

"Halfway there," Kurtzman said. "Now for the next
part. Repeat everything we just did, except this time,
direct the satellites to the following internet protocol
address." He rattled off a set of numbers.

"What site is that?" she asked, typing them in.

"It's a back door to the Google cache," he said. "I
built it myself."

"Okay, now what?" she asked.

"On the command line where it says 'Enter Command,' type 'Copy all and compare to current page,'"
he said. "Then hit Enter."

She typed the information on the screen, and was
reaching for the enter key when everything happened
at once. Peterson somehow heard the shot in the nano-
second before it passed through the back of her head,

somehow saw it smash into the screen in front of her, then the world went a strange purple-gray color.

She swayed and heard Brognola's voice saying, "Michelle? Michelle, what was that?"

She knew she was supposed to be doing something. Something important. Everything slowed down and she heard Johnny's voice roar with anger, and the sound of more gunfire. She felt blood running down her face, but there was no pain.

For the first time since she'd been captured all those years ago in Libya, she wasn't afraid, and no part of her—physical or mental or spiritual—hurt in the least. She had something important to do, but she decided that this time someone else would have to do it. Right now, more than anything, she needed to sleep.

So she allowed herself to slump forward in her chair, dropping her bloodied and broken skull onto the keyboard with a soft thump.

Then the darkness rushed in and she smiled as she fell into oblivion.

BOLAN CRAWLED to the cave entrance, not wanting to silhouette his own body against the light of the sky. From inside, it would be easy to spot a man-shaped shadow, even in the dim light available. He reached the entrance without a problem, then paused once more to listen. The only sounds he could discern were the flapping wings and chittering sounds of the bats as they roosted on the ceiling above. The smell of guano and bat urine was almost overwhelming.

Bolan took a position behind a large boulder, then got to his knees and took out the night optic he'd used before on the docks. He eased himself over the top of the boulder and peered into the cave. There was very little light here to make use of, even for the optic, but he noted that on one side of the cave, there was a faint flicker of light, almost a reflection of some kind.

He carefully looked around the cave again and saw no other signs of life, so he got to his feet and began working his way as quietly as possible toward where the tiny bit of light was visible. When he reached it, he saw that it was a hole leading downward.

Obviously man-made, there were rungs set into one side and, about ten feet down, the hole was filled with water. Waterproof lamps lit the way down the ladder. Even in broad daylight, it would be easy to overlook. Still, he reflected, it had to lead somewhere, and he lowered himself into the hole, using the rungs as he would on any other ladder.

The problem, he realized, was that he didn't know how long he'd have to hold his breath to get to wherever he was going. When he was up to his neck, he looked down once more, and estimated that the lamps continued for another fifteen to twenty feet, though the water made it difficult to judge distance. He took a deep breath and began to lever his way down.

Releasing tiny bubbles of carbon dioxide, he forced himself down the rungs, using leverage against the opposite wall of the hole and the rungs themselves to keep himself from floating back to the top. Bolan's estimate proved accurate as it was about twenty feet lower that the rungs ended and he saw a short tunnel open up to the north.

Underwater lamps lit the way here, as well, and he

pushed himself into the tunnel. His lungs burned with the effort and the pressure, but he'd suffered worse. This was a man-made escape route or hidden lair, so it wouldn't be impossible to traverse. He pushed himself along a bit faster, saw the tunnel open up ahead, and finally broke through to the other side and surfaced along the wall in an underground cave.

Under ordinary circumstances, the view would have been breathtaking. Water reflected from the lights on the walls, bringing to life a cave filled with quartz and corals of every color and description. Bolan didn't doubt that during the day, light from the surface had to reflect down here, rendering the lamps unnecessary and the cave itself a vision few human eyes had ever seen.

He floated quietly, scanning the shore, where he saw Vengai and Daniels seated near a fire. A large pack lay on the ground between them. Both of them held cups of steaming coffee in their hands, no doubt trying to warm up after swimming in the cold waters of the cave. Neither spoke, though Vengai's eyes rarely drifted far from her. His focus now was on saving his own life and starting over, and he had confidence that no one would find them here.

The problem, Bolan saw, was that it would be virtually impossible to get close to the rocky shore ledge without being seen. It appeared that he had few options except for direct confrontation. It would have been much easier to simply shoot him from a distance, but he'd left the rifle at the top of the tunnel. He swam closer, moving at a sedate pace, and when he was near enough to see that Vengai held a gun at his side, he stopped.

"Kabilan Vengai," he called, raising his voice slightly.

The man leaped to his feet, the gun in one hand, the coffee spilled and forgotten on the ground. "Show yourself!" he said, pointing the gun at Daniels. "Show yourself or I'll kill the girl right now!"

"Relax," Bolan said, swimming closer. He felt the water start to shallow out and began to walk toward them, holding his hands open and visible. Ocean water streamed from his clothes. "I'm not going to make any sudden moves."

"Throw down your weapon!" Vengai demanded, gesturing at the Desert Eagle. "Over by me, if you please."

Bolan nodded, easing it out of its holster with two fingers, then gently tossing it to land at Vengai's feet. "There. You can relax now. I'm not armed."

"How did you find this place?" he demanded. "How many more men are with you?"

"I'm all that's left," he lied. "I had a team of five, but none of the others made it."

Vengai eyed him skeptically. "I do not believe you," he said. He pointed to an unlit lamp on the wall. "Katran would have signaled if the all clear had been given."

"I suppose he might have, if I hadn't killed him in the kitchen," Bolan admitted. "It's not a foolproof system you've got there." He took a step closer, then another.

"Don't move any closer!" he yelled. "Who are you?"

"Matt Cooper," he said.

"I already know you are American. What agency do you work for?"

"I'm freelance," Bolan said. "Mercenary work, hostage rescue, that kind of thing. The girl's father hired me. If I'd have known what a difficult job it was going to be, I'd have charged more."

Daniels sputtered in outrage. "My father *paid* you to come get me, but he wouldn't pay to get me back?"

"Relax, sister," Bolan said. "Even if he had paid, Vengai here would have killed you anyway."

"Stop talking to her and answer my questions," Vengai demanded. "How many of my men are left?"

Bolan shrugged, taking another step closer and moving slightly sideways. He wanted to get between Vengai and Daniels, if he could manage it. "I don't really know. I wasn't exactly doing a head count when I ran for it."

"How did you find this place?" he demanded.

"Came across your tracks at the back of the house and decided to follow them," he said. "A lucky break, I guess." He watched Vengai carefully now. Soon he would try to kill either Bolan or Daniels or both. He was far too suspicious to believe that any of his men were alive; if he'd thought there was a chance of success, he wouldn't have ordered the nukes to detonate.

"You are a liar," he snapped. "Stop moving!"

Bolan stopped once more, still holding up his hands. He was perhaps ten feet from Vengai, maybe fifteen from Daniels, and still hadn't positioned himself quite right. "It's true," he said. "I am a liar."

"What is the truth?" the man asked. "What has happened to my men? To the software?"

"All your men are dead," he said flatly. "And we shut down the software. You lose, Vengai. Your plan has failed, the world is safe from you, and here in another minute or two, it won't be any concern of yours, anyway."

"That cannot be!" he screamed. "The software... the program I put in cannot be stopped."

"I wouldn't know," Bolan admitted. "One of our tech people seemed to be on top of it before I left. I'm sure by now it's been handled."

Vengai gestured with his handgun. "Get on your knees, American," he snarled. "Do it now."

Bolan took another step closer, then dropped to his knees. Vengai closed the distance between them, pointing the weapon at his head.

"You're the worst kind of coward," Bolan said, looking up at him. "Leaving your men to fight your battles—and die—for you, while you cower down here like a rat. It doesn't matter if you kill me. By now, there are SEAL teams in the water of the bay and the topside is covered. You're going to die, Kabilan Vengai, and I can't tell you how much satisfaction that brings me."

Vengai smirked down at him, then turned to his hostage. "You see, Ms. Daniels? All they do is talk and talk. And tell lies. Your ransom would never have been delivered. Your friends are all dead. You belong to me now, and the question is only whether you want to live or die."

She stared up at him from her place near the fire. "I have an answer for you," she said, her quiet voice echoing in the cave.

"Yes?" he said. "What is it?"

"Go fuck yourself," she said.

His eyes widened in outrage, and that was when Bolan made his move. Leaping forward, he swept his left arm up underneath Vengai's, shoving the gun to one side. It fired, the bullet screaming by his ear. At the same time, Bolan's right hand pulled the combat knife free of its sheath, and he drove the point of it deep into his adversary's abdomen, then ripped it upward, spilling his intestines over the quartz floor.

A huge gout of blood came from Vengai's mouth and whatever words he might have said were lost. The gun fell from his nerveless fingers and he tried to stagger away, but Bolan held him tightly, leaning close enough to whisper in his ear.

"You heard the lady," he whispered, then pushed harder on the knife, driving it into the man's heart. He gave one final twist, then shoved him away. Kabilan Vengai hit the floor with a potato-sack thud, then spasmed once and finally lay still. Bolan couldn't think of anyone who deserved it more.

He took a deep breath and turned to Daniels. "Are you all right?" he asked her.

She looked at the body of her captor for several long seconds, then her eyes met his. "I've never been better," she said, getting to her feet. "Can I go home now?"

Bolan offered her a grin. "I think we can arrange that," he replied. "But first let's get back up to the real world and see if there's anything left of it."

"What do you mean?" she asked. "I thought you said that one of your techs took care of the software."

"I lied," he said with a shrug. "I'm not exactly a mercenary, either."

"Who are you, then?" she asked. "I was sure you'd died in that explosion, yet here you are, so who are you, really?"

"You already know who I am," he said, leading her toward the far end of the ledge. "Matt Cooper."

"I know your name," she said. "I want to know who you are."

"I'm the man they call when the job is one no one else can or wants to do," he said. "No more questions for now. I want to get back to the others."

She nodded in agreement and followed him into the cold water. Together they swam for the tunnel and the cave above. The whole way, Bolan wondered what they'd find when they got back, if Peterson had somehow found a way to stop the nukes from detonating and if Johnny had kept her safe.

He hoped so. After everything she'd been through, she deserved the chance to be successful, to come out a hero in Daniels's eyes and in the eyes of President Daniels. In time, maybe she'd even find her way back to real field work again, a fully healed woman, doing what she loved and did best.

CHAPTER TWENTY-FOUR

The hike back to the main compound took less time than it had getting to the cave. Bolan knew the way and expected no trouble along the way. Daniels said little, stopping only once to tie her shoe and ask about Peterson. He explained that he'd left her with Johnny back at the main house to work on the software.

Still, it was almost two hours after he'd killed Vengai when they reached the compound and crossed the empty yard behind the house. She averted her eyes when she saw the bodies, and Bolan briefly wondered what she'd do when they went out the front. He guessed she'd have to live with it. After all, the killing had been done at least in part in her name.

He opened the back door, which led into the kitchen and found Johnny leaning against the counter. He'd brewed a pot of coffee and from the look on his face, not everything had gone well in his absence.

"Matt," Johnny said. "Coffee?"

"Sure," he said cautiously. "Pour for all of us. We could use it."

"Where's Michelle?" Daniels asked, looking around curiously. "You said she was here with Johnny."

"She was," Bolan said. "Is she still back in the computer room?"

Johnny handed him a cup of coffee and another to

Daniels. He hesitated before answering, then finally said, "Yeah, she is."

Daniels started to move that way, but Bolan caught her by the arm. "Hang on a moment," he said, turning his attention back to Johnny.

"What happened?" he asked.

"She didn't make it," his brother said, grief filling his voice. "I'm sorry, Matt. It's my fault."

"What do you mean, she didn't make it?" Bolan demanded.

"One of the soldiers was hiding out in Vengai's office closet. I didn't see him and he came up behind us. When he saw what she was doing, he shot Michelle before I could stop him. I'm..." His eyes went to Daniels's face, searching it for some sign of forgiveness. "I'm so sorry, Heather. I take responsibility for her death."

Bolan felt his own shoulders sag with the weight of the news. Peterson had deserved better. She should've gotten a chance at a real life. Instead all she'd had was years of mental and physical torture, and she'd died not even knowing if Heather was safe. He took a deep breath. It wasn't Johnny's fault. Neither one of them had searched the office. He said as much, and his brother nodded his thanks.

Daniels sadly agreed. "Thank you for trying," she said. "I cannot imagine what she went through with Vengai's men. Perhaps now she is finally at peace."

"And the nukes?" he asked, fearing the worst.

"You wouldn't believe it if I told you," Johnny said.

"Try me," Bolan replied.

"She was typing in the final commands. We linked

with Hal and Aaron via sat phone and they were walking her through it. The guy came in, fired and killed her. At the same time, the bullet took out her screen. I had no idea what was going on for sure. I turned to take him out, finished him, and when I turned back, all I could hear was Hal and Aaron yelling with joy from the phone."

"Joy?" Daniels asked. "What do you mean?"

"When Michelle died, she fell forward and, well, her head hit the keyboard, including the enter key, and the command went through. The satellites went offline about two minutes before detonation. I know it's not funny that she's gone, but she really did save the world with her last breath."

Bolan chuckled to himself and even Daniels offered a weak smile.

"So, we've got a phone that works?" he asked.

Johnny nodded and pulled it out of his pocket. "Battery is almost dead, so don't talk long."

"I just need to let Hal know to send a boat or a chopper for us. It's a long swim back to Phuket," Bolan said. Then he turned to Daniels and offered the phone to her. "But first, I think this young lady should call home and tell her father she's okay."

She took the phone and then smiled. "I imagine he'll want to ground me for at least a year," she said. "Maybe longer."

"Can you blame him?" Johnny asked.

"Not really," she said. "But my missionary days are over, anyway. It's time for me to go home."

"Me, too," Johnny said. "What about you, Matt?"

Mack Bolan, the Executioner, nodded. He'd head

back to Stony Man for a day or two's rest. Then most likely he'd head out on another mission—there was always one on the horizon.

* * * * *

AleX Archer
MAGIC LANTERN

A world steeped in magic…and a deadly curse.

In London, archaeologist Annja Creed is pulled toward the mysterious origin of an old-fashioned projector once used by eighteenth-century illusionists. As she delves into its history, a dark past begins to emerge. And someone wants to harness the power of this cursed artifact…risking everything for the treasures it promises.

Available May wherever books are sold.